Then We'll Be Safe

Jes Hart Stone

Published by Crystal Lake Publishing
Where Stories Come Alive!

Crystal Lake Publishing
www.CrystalLakePub.com

WELCOME
TO ANOTHER

CRYSTAL LAKE PUBLISHING
CREATION

Dedicated to

Chris Carlson and the sound of one hand clapping.

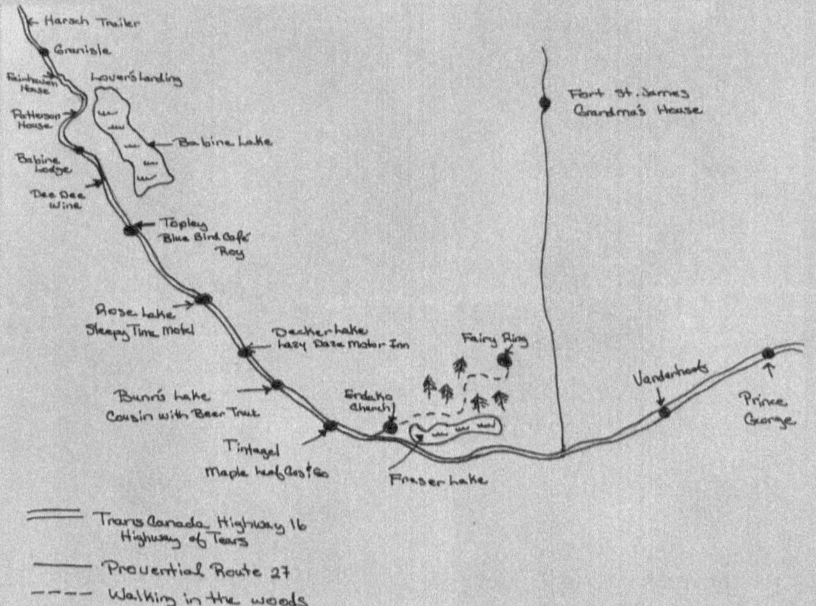
Harack Trailer
Granisle
Rainbow House
Lover's landing
Patterson House
Babine Lake
Babine Lodge
Dee Dee Wine
Topley
Blue Bird Café
Roy
Rose Lake
Sleepy Time Motel
Decker Lake
Lazy Daze Motor Inn
Fairy Ring
Fort St. James
Grandma's House
Bunns Lake
Cousin with Beer Trout
Endako Church
Vanderhoof
Prince George
Tintagel
Maple Leaf Costco
Fraser Lake
Trans Canada Highway 16
Highway of Tears
Provential Route 27
Walking in the woods

A lie cannot live.

--Martin Luther King, Jr.

Chapter One

BRITISH COLUMBIA, JUNE 1974

The neighbor used loppers to prune the branches on his old black walnut tree. Crystal Lynn Harsch used loppers to prune the fingers on Clive Reid's right hand.

Balancing the loppers on the tips of the blades, she leaned over him and stared at his face—his skin blotchy and bloated, mouth open and slack, a thin line of bubbling drool dribbling down his chin.

Clive sprawled across the battered recliner wearing only one dirty gym sock and his tighty whities, which were not tight, not white. His stomach flopped over the pulled and frayed elastic band, barely holding the underpants in place—underpants worn thin and gray except for the ochre stain at the crotch.

Empty Molson cans, fast-food bags, and pizza boxes littered the floor. His works—needle, spoon, rubber tubing—and an overflowing ashtray cluttered the TV tray table. Capsules and tablets from Clive's collection of prescription pain meds spilled from plastic bottles. The air stank of stale beer, cigarette smoke, and Clive's vinegary body odor. Crystal wanted to hurt him, wanted him to suffer, but she guessed the ludes riding the skaggy horse through his veins would block any pain.

Jesus, what does my mother see in this loser?

Clive's right hand dangled over the chair's arm. Too bad for Clive—his fat, nicotine-stained fingers hung limp like the limbs on the dead branches of her neighbor's tree.

Crystal had studied the neighbor pruning his tree. She'd observed how he opened the lopper blades as far as they would go, noticed how he positioned a branch midway between the tips and hinge, and watched as he clapped the blades together in one quick chop. One clean cut.

The neighbor's loppers were shiny and new, but the tool Crystal found in her mother's garden shed was old, the blades pitted and rusty, the hinge stiff. She'd poured cooking oil on the hinge and let it sit overnight. She didn't clean the blades.

Crystal used the old loppers to practice chopping limbs from the neighbor's clipping pile. She'd practiced at night when no one noticed, practiced until she could chop a fat branch with one clean cut. And then, she waited.

She didn't have to wait long. On this early summer evening, Clive slumped in a drugged-out stupor in the living room. Her mother crashed into a boozy blackout in the bedroom. Straightening, Crystal lifted the loppers with both hands. She took a moment to scan the room—if her plan worked, she would never see this place, this man, or her mother again.

The room her mother called 'the parlor' held several bags of weeks-old garbage that didn't make it to the dump, and four pieces of furniture—Clive's recliner, the tray table, a sofa, and in the corner, a rocking chair—or what had been a rocking chair.

The rocker's dark green top coat had chipped away, exposing three layers of paint below—white, peach, powder blue. Once, when Crystal's mother was sober, she said she used to rock in that chair with Crystal on her lap. "I used to read you stories from a book called *The Children's Garden of Verses*," her mother had said. "And I sang you lullabies."

Crystal couldn't remember her mother holding her or even touching her unless it was to lob a punch or a slap at Crystal's face. Still, sometimes, when her mother passed out or left the house to go down to the truck stop to "make some spending money," Crystal would rock in the chair, listen to the wood creak, and pretend she remembered stories and lullabies. That was before Clive moved in.

The first time he came home with her mother, Clive plunked into the rocker with all his bulk and all his fat and splintered the chair into pieces. Clive and her mother laughed so hard that snot flew from his nose, and her mother said she pissed herself.

Crystal ran from the house that night and hid in the garden shed. Alone, in the dark, surrounded by the looming shadows of rusting tools, cans of oil and paint, discarded furniture, and a box of broken dishes, she cried until she fell asleep.

Her mother didn't repair the rocker—she didn't even throw the pieces out—she left them on the floor where they fell.

Crystal inhaled a long, deep breath and exhaled slow, steady. She pressed her lips into a tight, hard line.

Just do it—just get it over with. If he comes to, run like hell.

Another long breath in. She lifted the loppers, opened them wide, and edged the blades between Clive's first and middle fingers. She slid the blades forward until the first finger, above the second joint, lay midway between the blade tips and the oiled hinge. She looked at Clive's face.

Maybe him being such a loser is bad enough.

She glanced back at the rocking chair and clapped the blades down hard. One clean cut.

Clive's finger dropped to the floor—a dull thump. He stirred, snorted, lifted his head, and made a sound. Maybe he tried to yell or swear. What came out was, "Wa, wa, waaa." He dropped his head back against the chair and snorted again.

Crystal stared at the stump where his finger had been. Blood pulsed out. Rhythmic spurts splashed the floor. She reopened the lopper blades and slid them over Clive's middle finger, again above the second joint, midway on the blades between the tips and the hinge, and clamped down hard. A second clean cut.

Clive's middle finger landed next to the first. Blood from the two stumps spurted and splattered the severed digits.

This time, Clive's body jerked. His mouth gaped, and a low groan gurgled up. His eyes pulled open, unfocused and sticky with goo. Crystal smiled and waved at him.

"Wa, wa, waaa," he said. The sound came from contorted lips.

Crystal dropped the loppers. She grabbed a crumpled fast-food bag and picked up one of Clive's fingers—warm and squishy, oozing blood. She dropped it into the bag.

Clive's body twitched, his head smacked against the back of the chair, his hand still dangled over the chair's arm, blood still spurting—splatting to the floor. "Wa, wa, waaa..." His voice trailed off. His eyes drifted shut.

Crystal snatched up the second finger and dropped it into the bag. Fat and bloody, it slid down the side of the paper through grains of salt. Clive's finger slid through salt and blood like a fry sliding through ketchup. She rolled the bag closed, dropped it into her knapsack, and then, for a few seconds, she watched blood from the stumps splat, splat, splat to the floor.

Chapter Two

Like cards in a tarot reading, Polaroid photos fanned between Majorca Fairhaven and Rhonda Patterson. Sitting cross-legged, the girls bent over the glossy images, their heads two inches apart. The late afternoon sun cast a warm glow through lace-curtained windows. It splashed pale light on pink roses climbing wallpaper, on a mound of pink throw pillows, on the row of Rhonda's well-loved stuffed animals crowded on a white wooden shelf. Rhonda's room—warm, dry, clean. Safe.

Majorca traced a heart on the white chenille bedspread and placed a photo at its center. "This one is my favorite," she said.

The two girls, best friends, eyed the photo—a ruddy-faced boy grinned back. His blue eyes crinkling at their corners, his blonde hair cut military short. Todd Furlow scoffed at the long-haired hippie types who wandered the halls of the high school, slow and stoned. At six feet two, star pitcher in the spring and captain of the hockey team when the snow fell, Todd was the pride of Granisle and the heart-throb of almost every teenage girl in town.

Rhonda selected another photo and placed it over the first. "I like this one best."

Todd balanced on blades—full gear—stick in one gloved hand, trophy held high in the other. His grin could light the rink.

Majorca grasped the heavy class ring dangling from a gold chain around her neck. Raising the ring, she gave it a quick kiss and then slipped it under the collar of her blouse. Stretching toward the photos, she selected two more.

Officially, the girls studied. Officially, they memorized French, English liter-ature, and Canadian history. With only a week until graduation and final exams starting the next day, students across Granisle poured over their books. But Rhonda's textbooks sat stacked on her desk next to the plate of cookies and the two glasses of milk her mother had brought up an hour earlier. Books and treats remained untouched. Majorca's unopened yellow book bag flopped where she'd dropped it on Rhonda's pink shag rug.

"Todd is the most handsome boy ever, and you are the luckiest girl in the whole world," Rhonda said. She selected another photo. "My dad says that next week, the bank board is voting on who's gonna get the business scholarship. I'm not supposed to know this, but Todd is in the lineup." She dropped the photo into the traced heart with the others.

"Everybody knows that, silly." Majorca gave Rhonda's arm a light jab. "But does your dad know who's gonna get the scholarship?"

Rhonda shook her head. "If he does, he can't say. But he did tell me that the boy with the highest points in grades, sports, community service, and integrity will win."

Majorca stretched and gathered the photos into a stack. Sliding off the bed, she grabbed her book bag and tossed it on the bed. Then she slipped the Po-laroids into the bag's front pocket. "Todd has all that going for him—there's no way he won't win the scholarship. His grades are great, everybody likes him, and he's the best boyfriend ever."

"But wait a minute." Rhonda scrunched her forehead into worried lines. "That scholarship pays for full tuition and housing at the college in Vancouver. That's a whole day away by bus, so there's no way you'll ever get to see him. He'll find another girl for sure. He'll find some big city girl and forget all about Granisle, and he'll even forget about you."

Although they could hear Rhonda's mother working in the kitchen down-stairs, and Rhonda's bedroom door was closed, Majorca leaned in close and whispered, "I'm not worried about that. Can you keep a secret?"

Rhonda gasped and clapped her hand over her mouth, her eyes wide. She pulled her hand back, and then, like Majorca, she whispered. "You went all the way?"

Majorca swatted Rhonda's leg. "No, you jerk. Don't be ridiculous. You know we're waiting. Todd is old-fashioned—he would never try anything like that. I mean a *real* secret."

Rhonda pursed her lips, zipped them shut with two fingers, and tossed the imaginary key over her shoulder.

"The weekend after graduation, Todd and I are going on a road trip to those hot springs down south. He's renting a little cabin for us, and he promised me that he has something super special in store for me—a big surprise." She pulled the ring from under her blouse and, gliding it back and forth on the chain, she added, "I'm positive I'll be trading in this class ring for a big ol' hunking diamond."

Rhonda squealed. "Seriously?"

Majorca nodded.

"But what about your folks? They would never let you go overnight with a boy."

"I thought about that. But I'll figure something out. Maybe I'll tell them I'm spending the night with you."

"But what if they call my folks to check?"

"Why would they do that? We've had, like, what? A bazillion sleepovers? They won't check. They trust me." She ran one finger over the four initials she'd embroidered on the bag's pocket—TF + MF. "Besides, the thing is, my folks love Todd like a son. I know he'll get that scholarship, and by the time he goes to college in the fall, we'll be married. The school has special housing for married students. I already checked."

Rhonda rolled off the bed and grabbed a floppy bear from the shelf. Squeezing the stuffed toy to her chest, she sighed. "I'm so jealous. You really are the luckiest girl in the world, and you have the perfect life all lined up and—"

Mrs. Patterson knocked once, pushed the door open, and poked her head in. "Girls, it's almost time for supper. Rhonda, I need you to chop veggies for the salad. Majorca, do you want to stay? We're having pot roast and new potatoes."

Majorca grabbed her book bag. "Thanks, Mrs. Patterson. But I should go home. Mum's making her prize-winning lasagna tonight. I can't miss that."

"Do you want Mr. Patterson to give you a ride?"

"No thanks. I'm sick of being stuck inside all winter. I'll walk."

Rhonda's mother frowned. "I don't know, Honey. It's getting pretty chilly. Did you bring a coat?"

Majorca shook her head.

"Don't worry, Mom. She can borrow my windbreaker." Rhonda tossed the bear on the bed and grabbed a light blue coat from the back of a chair. "Remember to bring it to school tomorrow."

Nodding, Majorca slipped into the jacket and slung the yellow bag over her shoulder.

Mrs. Patterson gave Majorca a quick hug. "Alright, then. You better hurry on home before it gets too dark. And see if you can wrangle that lasagna recipe from your mother for me. Lord knows I've tried hard enough."

Rhonda waited until her mother's footsteps on the stairs faded before she turned to Majorca. "Wow—two weeks from now, you'll be engaged. And...oh! Can I be the Maid of Honor?"

Majorca gave her a squeeze. "Who else? You big goof."

Rhonda pulled back. "I'm gonna miss you, Majorca. You'll be away, in the big city, married to a handsome college student, and I'll be counting coins in my dad's bank. Probably for my whole life. It doesn't seem fair."

"Hey, look on the bright side. You have a job lined up. I'll have to find a job—read the classifieds, fill out those application things, and go to interviews. After all that, I'll probably end up with a horrible job, like slinging hash in some little dive while Todd is in class."

"Maybe, but I'd rather have a guy like Todd than a job in a stuffy old bank. And the worst part is, my dad will be my boss." She scrunched her nose and shuddered. "Gross."

Outside the front door, the two friends stood close. Shrubs and flower beds flanking the Patterson's porch perfumed the air—daffodils, tulips, and Indian plum. Down the street, someone eager for summer grilled steaks on a barbecue. A tricycle bell trilled. A dog barked.

Majorca looped her arm around Rhonda's shoulders. "Don't worry, Ron. You're going to find a great guy, and pretty soon, it will be the four of us. Todd and me and you and the new guy, and we'll live right down the street from each other—maybe next door—and we'll have parties and progressive dinners, and when we have babies, they'll grow up best friends. Like us. It's all going to be perfect."

One more hug before Majorca stepped from the porch. With a quick turn and wave to Rhonda, she headed out on what should have been a twenty-minute walk home.

Chapter Three

CRYSTAL'S MOTHER LAY SPREAD-EAGLED across the bed, arms and legs wide, mouth open, snoring. The top four buttons of her blouse were undone, her flabby breasts spilled out. No bra. Her cotton skirt bunched at her waist. No underpants.

Crystal bit her lip. She tugged the skirt over her mother's thick thighs. She turned. Hesitated. Then turned back and pulled the sheet over her mother's breasts.

A brown strap hung between the box springs and mattress—her mother's handbag. Crystal yanked the strap. Her mother groaned and smacked her lips. Crystal waited a beat, then pulled again, freeing the tattered bag. Her mother moaned, rolled over, faced the wall, and farted.

"Jesus, Mom. Really?"

Shuffling through the bag, Crystal took a twenty, two fives, and her mother's Bic lighter. She stashed the cash and lighter in her knapsack, tossed the purse, and bent to retrieve a half-empty bottle of vodka. She found the bottle's cap nesting in a pile of dust under the bed. Crystal grabbed a carton of cigarettes from the closet shelf and slipped the smokes and liquor into her pack.

For years, she and her mother had shared the double bed. Despite her mother's snoring, farting, and flailing in drug and booze-fueled nightmares, Crystal pretended that snug against her mother, she was safe.

When Clive moved in, her mother liberated a hide-a-bed from the back of a dump truck. She rolled the folding contraption down the middle of their street and up their driveway. Then she and Clive wrestled the bed through the trailer's front door and into the living room. "This is where you sleep now," she'd told Crystal.

Stains soaked the thin mattress, and metal poked through the stuffing, but Crystal used her mother's kitchen knife to cut cardboard panels and placed them over the springs.

They only had one set of sheets, so Crystal's mother gave her a dollar and sent her to the thrift store behind the Catholic church. When Crystal told the volunteer woman what she needed and why, the lady shook her head and crossed herself, but she loaded a bag with sheets, pillowcases, blankets, and two pillows. Pawing through a box, she found a crocheted throw. Though frayed and worn, tiny pink flowers and green leaves danced across the throw's lavender yarn. "They're used, of course," she'd said. "But they're clean." She handed the bag of linens to Crystal.

Crystal hugged the bag.

The lady said, "You poor, poor child."

But Crystal didn't care. Crystal felt rich.

Clive lived with them for three years until he hurt somebody and ended up in prison for four years. Her mother had railed against the cops, the court system, and even Clive's victim, but Crystal had breathed a sigh of relief.

Without Clive around, her mother spent more time in the bedroom, drinking and passing out. Without Clive around, Crystal could sleep through the night.

The day before Crystal's sixteenth birthday, Clive was released and moved back in. That's when Crystal rolled her bed out the door, across the patchy dirt of their lawn, and into the garden shed. She froze in winter, broiled in summer, and had to sneak into the house to use the bathroom, but she had the thrift store blankets, the lavender throw, and water from the neighbor's hose. And, she had a room of her own.

Most of the time, Clive was too stoned to walk across the yard to the garden shed, so most of the time, he left her alone.

Blinking, Crystal shook away the memories of her mother and Clive. Today was the end of all that. She rifled through the top drawer of her mother's dresser.

She sloshed through ragged underwear, foil-wrapped condoms, and coupons her mother tore from newspapers but never used. She dug until she found the locket—smooth and round, the size of a fifty-cent piece. She slipped it into the front pocket of her jacket and then, for the last time, she looked at the lump on the bed. Backing out of the room, Crystal whispered, "Bye-bye, Mom."

Chapter Four

Happy. Majorca strolled down the road, enjoying the cool evening air and the replaying of her friend's words.

"Todd is the most handsome boy ever, and you are the luckiest girl in the world."

Rhonda is right—I am the luckiest girl in the world. And someday, very soon, we'll pick edible flowers from our gardens for big summer salads while our husbands, Todd and the new guy, nurse cans of Labatts, burn steaks on the grill, and tell stupid dad jokes. And our babies (a girl for me, a boy for Rhonda) will play together in their cribs on the lawn. And—

Majorca smacked her foot against a tree root and stumbled. Catching herself, she glanced around. Lost in her future fantasy, she'd veered off the main road and wandered onto the path in the provincial park leading to Babine Lake. She'd walked halfway to the water—a mistake that would make her late for dinner if she didn't retrace her steps. She started to turn back toward the road, but hesitated. Cut deep by glaciers, the pristine lake was a special place.

It will only take me fifteen extra minutes to loop around the north side.

In the early twilight, a scattering of stars winked in the violet sky. Fir and pine scented the air.

Mum will understand.

As kids, Majorca and Rhonda caught tadpoles and tiny turtles in the shallow water at the lake's southern shore. Later, when they learned to swim, they joined dozens of other kids in diving from the mid-lake raft, tossing water balloons, and playing endless games of kickball on the lake's sandy south shore.

Now, at seventeen, when she thought of the lake, Majorca felt a tingling in her belly, a buzzing that started high and wound down—a buzzing that both embarrassed and excited her.

The north side of the lake lacked a beach but featured a hill that rolled in a gentle slope toward the water—the hill had a name, Lover's Landing. On Saturday nights, anyone strolling down the path could count at least a half-dozen cars parked in a row, all pointing toward the lake's calm water.

From behind the cars' steamy windows came the songs on the top ten chart and, sometimes, a giggle or a gasp. Everyone at school knew the dangers of getting caught by a cop on night patrol or a nosy parent walking a dog. Cops gave lectures and warnings to move along. Parents told other parents, which meant lectures and groundings. But the exhilaration of breaking the rules—plus that tingly feeling...

Majorca tingled thinking about Lover's Landing. She and Todd had spent many Saturday evenings fogging the windows of Todd's pride and joy—his fire engine red Pontiac Trans Am. Sometimes, they steamed the windows so much that Todd flung the front doors open, letting their breathy passion escape into the forest surrounding the lake.

Once, Majorca told Rhonda that Todd's kisses were like what the song said—sweeter than wine. At least, she imagined they were. She'd never tasted wine, or any alcohol for that matter, but she'd tasted plenty of Todd's kisses. Despite what she'd told Rhonda about Todd being old-fashioned, Majorca knew he wanted more. Of course, he did. He was a red-blooded Canadian boy. And she could accept his hand under her blouse, and once, even under her bra, on the left side. Although they'd discussed the importance of waiting until marriage, she was pretty sure Todd would be content with not waiting, because he'd say things like, "You're such a good girl. But someday, some lucky guy is gonna make a woman outta you."

Thinking of those kisses, Todd's hand under her bra, and the foggy windows in his car made her pause. What if she passed a car with kids inside—would she look? What if she knew them? That might be awkward. Kids would tease her the next day, call her a peeping Tom, or worse.

A cool breeze sent gooseflesh over her arms. Glad she borrowed Rhonda's jacket, she pulled it tighter.

Tonight is a school night. Nobody ever parks at Lover's Landing on a school night. Besides, with final exams only three days away, everyone will be home, hitting the books. I should be hitting the books, too.

Head down, she hurried along the path, so engrossed in not stumbling again that she almost missed the lone car parked on the grassy slope. Music wafting from the vehicle caught her attention and drew her to a stop. She recognized the song and the vocalist right off. Marvin Gaye crooned, 'Let's get it on...' The same song Todd always played when they were fogging the windows of his Trans Am. He liked it so much that he figured out how to get the tape deck to play on repeat, three times in a row. Over and over and over, Marvin Gaye's low, sexy tones filled the car's warm interior.

From the path, Majorca could only see the car's shadow, but between the breathy lyrics, she heard a high-pitched giggle and what sounded like a groan. She wavered. It wasn't any of her business, but she was curious.

School night.

She checked her watch. Her mother would be pulling the lasagna out of the oven about now, her dad would be washing up, scrubbing the grease from under his fingernails. She should be home, helping to set the table.

But this would be juicy gossip to share with Rhonda and the girls on the cheerleading squad if, of course, the girl in the car wasn't on the cheerleading squad. Or, maybe if she was, that would be even juicier.

Just a quick peek.

The couple would be so busy making out that they wouldn't hear her, wouldn't even notice her. Stepping from the path, she trotted over soft, wet grass toward the dark shadow until she saw it. Even in the dim light, the Trans Am's bright red paint glowed. Todd's Trans Am—both front doors open. The music stopped. The silhouette of an arm reached up to the dashboard, to the tape deck. Todd's arm. Todd's tape deck. Marvin Gaye began again to urge, 'Let's get it on."

Majorca screamed.

A girl tumbled from the Pontiac's front seat and landed in the wet grass. The car's interior light cast a circle around her. She wore only white socks, white tennis shoes, her cheerleading skirt, and a lacy white bra. Auburn hair, messy and tangled, fell loose around her bare shoulders. A ring of red smeared her lips.

Todd slid out of the car, tucking his shirt into his pants and buckling his belt. "What the hell is the matter with you?" He glared at Majorca and reached down to help the redhead stand.

Majorca ran to him and pushed him aside. Then, with tears streaming down her cheeks, she slapped the other girl across the face. "Candy Jensen, you slut! I...I... thought we were friends." She grabbed a handful of Candy's hair and yanked.

Candy screeched and swatted at Majorca's hand. Majorca twisted Candy's hair and pulled back for another slap.

Candy lashed out. Pointed nails slashed Majorca's face. Wrenching out of Majorca's grasp, Candy stumbled backward.

Majorca touched her cheek, then looked at her fingers. Blood. "You bitch," she screamed. She tried to grab Candy, but the other girl was already running, slipping, and sliding in the wet grass, up the slope, away from the Trans Am, away from Majorca and Todd.

Todd stared as Candy disappeared into the stand of trees circling the lake. He turned to Majorca. "You stupid cow, now look what you did," he said.

Majorca spun around to face him. "Todd, I don't... I don't understand. How could you? We're going steady."

"What are you talking about? We're not going steady."

"But you gave me your class ring. You said we're going to the hot springs and that you had a special surprise for me. I thought that—"

"You're such a stupid little bitch. I gave you that ring so you'd put out. I figured if we went to the hot springs, we'd get drunk, and you would. But you're such a cold fish, you never will. I'm through with you." Todd glanced toward the trees, ducked back into the car, and grabbed his varsity jacket. "Candy, wait up, babes. I'm coming." He took off running up the hill.

Majorca leaned against the car and sobbed. Tears mixed with blood—blood mixed with snot. Staring at the now-empty hill, she swiped the back of her hand across her face and took a long, shuddering breath. "I hate you, Todd Furlow. I hate you."

Reaching into the Trans Am, she released the safety brake and rammed the stick shift into neutral. She knew she shouldn't do that, not without the clutch engaged. Her father had explained that doing that could hurt a car. But did that even matter now? She slammed the door closed, and then, in a move she and her friends had done many times to jump-start their cars, she laid one hand against the door, gripped the window frame, and pushed. The vehicle remained stationary, but Majorca leaned into the task and pushed harder. Todd's car rolled slow at first, then faster and faster until it picked up speed and rolled, on its own, down the slope into the lake. Majorca ran behind it, and when the front tires reached the water, she pressed her hands against the trunk and gave a final shove. The red Pontiac rolled into Lake Babine with Marvin Gaye still crooning until the front of the car dipped into the lake's deep water. Todd's Trans Am seemed to gasp as water rushed into the open doors and windows.

Majorca stood panting by the water's edge as the car disappeared into a swirl—a cloud of tiny bubbles bursting at the surface. She thought she heard something—something like a cry—but the gurgling water drowned out all other sounds.

For a moment, satisfaction filled Majorca.

Serves him right. He won't be making out with anybody in that car for a long time.

One moment. Then, the image of her father, working nights and weekends in his auto shop—working for free to fix Todd's damaged car—blocked any feelings of triumph.

"I'm gonna be in so much trouble." She wheeled around and looked toward the woods. Darkness descended over the lake, the slope, and the path. Todd and Candy had vanished.

Todd would be with her by now. Maybe he was hugging her, telling her everything was fine. Maybe he was holding her face between his hands, staring into her tear-filled eyes, stroking her hair. Maybe she was leaning against a tree, Todd's strong body pressing against hers. Maybe...

"Nooo!" Sobbing, Majorca scrambled up the slope to the path and ran toward the main road, toward home.

Chapter Five

Backing out of her mother's bedroom, Crystal pulled the door shut and glanced at Clive. The pool of blood under his right hand spread, and his breathing shallowed.

"Oh no, you don't, you fucker. You're not gonna bleed out on me. You're not takin' the easy way out."

She stood in front of Clive, biting her lip. Then, with a snap of her fingers, she turned and ran from the house across the scrubby yard. Long shadows from the neighbor's walnut tree stretched across the street, painting a dark path to the garden shed.

She'd spent long hours making the drafty outbuilding her own. She'd dragged cans of oil and paint, boxes of broken and discarded kitchenware, and bundles of rags to the pile next to the trailer, the pile slated for the city dump—the pile that never moved. She'd swept away mouse droppings and wood shavings and built a shelf for her school materials and the library books she borrowed every week. Setting up the shed had been a labor of love, but tonight, revenge fueled her work.

Moving fast, Crystal crammed a sweatshirt into her knapsack. She reached for the most recent library book and stopped.

Leave it? No. At least, maybe someday, I can return it.

She fished two tampons from a jar on the window ledge and stashed them and the library book into her pack. Rummaging through a box of tools, she grabbed a pair of pruning shears and cut a length of twine from a spool, then added the shears and twine to her small bundle. Finally, she looked at the wall next to her bed.

The certificate she'd earned in grade ten hung thumb-tacked to the rough wood. Inside a gold border fancy letters spelled her name, Crystal Lynn Harsch. Under her name, neatly printed words read, ALL GRADES #1 READER OF THE YEAR 1972. The principal, librarian, and her grade ten teacher had signed the certificate, and the principal had presented it to her during the final assembly of the year.

When Crystal got home that afternoon, she showed the certificate to Clive and her mother.

"Well now, ain't that fancy," her mother had said before lapsing into a coughing fit.

"Very fancy," Clive snickered. "And I bet it's gonna impress them old boys down at the truck stop. Bet they pay extra for a little sugar from a gal with a fancy paper like that." He had tried to snatch the certificate from Crystal, but she clutched it close and ran out of the house. The sound of Clive's laughter and her mother's coughing rang in her ears.

Leaning over the bed, Crystal pulled the thumbtacks from the wall, rolled the certificate into a tight tube, and slipped it down the side of her knapsack. Only one more thing to do.

Leaving her pack on the shed's stoop, she dashed across the yard to the rusting car sitting on concrete blocks behind the trailer—one of Clive's many half-started projects. The door squealed when she pulled it open. Crystal froze. She waited for someone to yell, 'Git the hell away from that car,' but the street was silent and still. Except for the porch light on her mother's trailer, darkness cloaked the yard.

She climbed up a concrete block, reached into the back seat, and grabbed the can of gasoline Clive had stashed there. Stolen gasoline siphoned from a neighbor's car. Fearing more creaking would give her away, Crystal left the car door open and ran back across the yard. Slipping her knapsack over her shoulders, she stepped inside the shed.

The gas can had rusted shut. Crystal pulled a hammer from the box of tools and beat on the the can until enough rust flaked off for her to twist the cap free. She splashed gasoline on everything—on the tools, the shelf, her bed. When she'd emptied the can, she lifted a sodden corner of material and used her mother's Bic to light the lavender throw. Tossing the flaming fabric onto her bed, she bolted from the building.

Wedged between two large shrubs in her neighbor's hedge, Crystal watched. Her heart pounded, and her breathing almost stopped when the old, dry wood of the shed caught fire, and flames licked at the glass in the building's only window. She jumped when the window exploded. Shattered glass sprayed across the yard. Flames lit the small space, and for one moment, Crystal saw her room bright and glowing.

The neighborhood dogs sounded the first alarm, and then, one by one, front doors flew open, porch lights snapped on, and neighbors rushed from their homes.

"Call the fire department!"

"Call the police!"

Screams of sirens split the night as flames stretched scaly arms toward the sky. Firemen in orange gear dragged heavy hoses from trucks and shot streams of water at the collapsing shed. A policeman banged on the trailer's front door. When no one answered, another policeman smashed his shoulder against the door, and the two rushed in.

Crystal grinned. "There, you bastard—no getting away now."

She watched for a few more minutes, then located her neighbor. He stood on the curb with a group of onlookers, his back to her. Crystal edged out of the hedge and slipped away into the cool blue shadows of the night.

Chapter Six

Thumb up, hip out, Crystal smacked her Double Bubble and assumed the classic expression of eighteen and bored. The pose was for practice—no drivers on the road now.

They're all home with their little vanilla families passing salads and spaghetti.
Crystal's stomach rumbled.
Probably have to walk all the way.

Adjusting her knapsack, she dropped her hand to her side and started the long walk into Granisle. Forested on both sides, the two-lane road was dark except for the faint light of the waning moon flickering through foliage to the blacktop. Her boots made a thumping sound on the road. The boots were military surplus and two sizes too big, but the man at the store said she could have them for only two dollars. He even tossed in a pair of olive-drab wool socks to take up the slack. Some of the kids at school teased her about her boots, but Crystal didn't care—the boots kept her feet warm and dry, and that mattered. The thump of her boots and the hoot of an owl were the only sounds until she heard another sound—a sound that didn't belong. She stopped and listened.

Somebody crying. Big, noisy, slobbery sobs. Crystal followed the sound to a lumpy shadow slumped at the side of the road.

"Hey. You're that prom queen, right?" She tapped her toe against an embroidered book bag.

Majorca sniffled, gulped, and swiped the sleeve of her windbreaker across her eyes and nose.

"No. I'm...I'm just..." She hiccupped.

"Just what?"

"Just an attendant. My boyfriend is...he's..." Tears gushed again. She covered her face with her hands and wept. Her body shook with each sob.

"Jesus," Crystal said, "get a grip."

Majorca pulled her hands from her face. A stream of clear snot ran from her nose.

"Ewww, gross," Crystal looked away, then, with a sideways glance, she watched as Majorca pulled a fast-food napkin from the windbreaker's pocket and blew. When she crumpled the napkin and stuffed it back into the jacket pocket, Crystal turned to face her again.

"So, what's got your panties in such a twist, girlie? Shouldn't you be home, passing green beans or something?"

Majorca gulped for air. "I...I..."

"You what?"

"I was walking home, and I saw my boyfriend's car down by the lake, and he was...he was..." Her eyes squeezed tight, her mouth formed a small 'o', and she let out a low wail.

"Stop it. I mean it. Stop it!" Crystal bent down and punched Majorca on the shoulder.

Majorca snapped her head up and stared at Crystal. "You...you hit me."

"It was a tap. But if you don't stop that blubbering, I'm gonna knock you silly. Or, maybe I'll walk away and leave you alone. And you don't look like a chick who's good on her own. Especially at night. Especially on a dark road this far from town."

Majorca rubbed her arm and sniffled, but she didn't cry.

"So what?" Crystal said. "You find your squeeze givin' it to some other girl, right?"

Majorca nodded.

Crystal chuckled. "Ha. Guessed it. Men are pigs." She reached down, offered her hand, and helped Majorca to her feet.

"So, like, what did you do?" Crystal said.

"I... I yelled at them."

"That's all? You shoulda punched that bitch."

"And I pulled her hair, and I slapped her."

Crystal nodded. "Good start."

"But Todd and I are going steady. We are, that is, we were, going to get married. We had the perfect life, and Candy is on the cheerleading squad, and I thought we were friends, and now my life is ruined and..." Majorca's face scrunched again, turned deep red, and her mouth worked toward that same small 'o'. Crystal took a step toward Majorca and leaned in close, three inches from her face. "You start wailing again, and I'm warning you...I'll punch your lights out."

Majorca stopped cold and gaped at Crystal.

"That's better. So, did you kick her or bite her? Please tell me you bit her."

Majorca shook her head. "No. She ran into the woods, and she didn't have her blouse on. Todd ran after her. I was so mad...so mad... and I, I..." Her voice caught.

"Don't push me." Crystal pulled her arm back and clenched her fist.

Majorca stepped aside, out of Crystal's range. "I was so furious because he ruined my life, and I wanted to ruin his, so I pushed his car into the lake, and it went under."

Crystal's eyes widened, and she lowered her arm. "No shit. That is totally cool. Maybe I was wrong about you, girlie."

"No, it's not cool." Majorca picked up her book bag. "I'm in tons of trouble. They're gonna pull that car out, and my dad, he's a mechanic, he's gonna have to fix it. For free, and I'll be grounded. Probably for life." She slung the book bag over her shoulder and started walking.

"Wait."

"I can't. I'm late for dinner, and I already told you, I'm in serious trouble, I have to go."

Crystal trotted ahead, turned, and walked backward, facing Majorca. "You know, you really shouldn't go home."

Majorca kept walking, head down, shoulders stooped. "Don't be stupid. Of course, I have to go home."

"Sure, of course, you have to go home. Duh. But not right away." Crystal continued to walk backward, keeping an even pace with Majorca.

"What are you talking about?"

Crystal stopped walking. Majorca bumped into her.

"Do the math. As soon as lover boy finds out you trashed his car, he's gonna pitch a fit. Right?"

"But—"

"He's gonna go straight to your house and pitch an even bigger fit—probably at your old man. Do I have that right?"

Majorca nodded.

"And you're gonna catch holy hell."

Majorca dropped her book bag and flopped on the ground next to it. Whimpering, she lowered her head to her hands. Her shoulders shook.

Crystal knelt beside her, touched one finger to Majorca's arm. "What's your name?"

"Majorca. Majorca Fairhaven."

"Majorca Fairhaven, I'm Crystal Lynn Harsch, and I have a plan. Why don't you come with me? I'm going to my gran's house for dinner. I'm gonna spend the night there, have breakfast with her in the morning, and come back home. You should come with me."

Majorca looked up. "Why?"

"You know, 'cause she's a good person, really nice to me. And I don't get to see her much, so I thought—"

"No. I mean, why should *I* go with *you*?"

"Because, don't you see? If you go home now, it's gonna be a shit show for sure. But if you come with me for the night, when you get back home tomorrow, all the yelling and stuff will be over. Everybody will be calmer. You can act all sweet and nice, and you know, everything will be cool."

She sat next to Majorca, slipped out of the straps, and fished around in her knapsack.

Majorca stared at the ground, absently picking at grass, pulling up blades, and dropping them.

Crystal pulled the carton of smokes from her pack, selected a package, extracted a cigarette, and dug again until she found her mother's lighter. "Flick my Bic, baby," she said. Lighting the cigarette, she blew a steady stream of smoke toward Majorca's head.

Majorca fanned it away.

"Look," Crystal said. "My gran is really nice. She cooks these amazing stews, and she roasts chickens, and makes pies, and bread, and cookies. Actually, her cookies aren't very good, but her bread is to die for." Crystal took another long drag, this time blowing the smoke in the opposite direction. "She keeps a bottle of whiskey under the sink. She says it's for medicinal purposes. If you get a bad cold or the flu, she mixes honey, lemon juice, and whiskey in tea, and she wraps you in quilts. You sweat like a pig, and the next day, you're fine. All better. She calls it The Irish Cure."

Majorca squinted at Crystal. "And what do your grandma's pies and whiskey have to do with me? I'm in so much trouble they might ground me forever. They might not even let me graduate."

"Stop being such a drama queen." Crystal stubbed the cigarette out and flicked the butt onto the road. "So, you dumped a car into the lake. Actually, when you think about it, that's pretty funny. Hysterical even. Besides, it's only a stupid car—it's not like you killed somebody." She stood and dusted off the back of her jeans. "Like I said, think about it. One night at my gran's. She loves to feed people, so she'll be happy. You'll get a good rest and you'll feel better. Your folks will have time to calm down, and by lunch time tomorrow, you can apologize to lover boy, and get on with your sweet life." Crystal slipped her arms into her knapsack and gave a little hop to settle the pack.

Majorca glanced up at her. "So what do you get out of it?"

Crystal shrugged. "I gotta walk into town and catch the late bus. It would be nice to have someone to talk to. If that is, you don't start crying about your jerk boyfriend again."

Majorca stood, sighed, and picked up her book bag. "Where does your grandma live?"

"That's the girl! I figured you'd come around. Vanderhoof. Not too far by bus."

"But what about my parents? They'll be worried."

"You can call 'em from the bus station. Tell 'em you're gonna spend the night with a friend. I bet girlies like you have slumber parties all the time."

"Sometimes—"

"Thought so. You guys probably spin records and practice kissing, so you'll get it right with boys."

"Well, I—"

"Never mind. It's getting cold. Let's go."

They'd walked five minutes when high beams turned the night to noon. The car slowed, rolled forward, and stopped. The driver snapped on the overhead light, leaned across the bench seat, and cranked the window down. A cloud of cigarette smoke swirled out.

"What are you girls doing on this road? You shouldn't be out here after dark."

Crystal leaned down and rested her arms on the passenger door.

"We're cool," she said. "Me and my friend are going to my gran's house for the weekend 'cause my mom has the flu, and she doesn't want me to catch it. 'Specially so close to graduation. So, we're gonna study for finals at my gran's."

The driver frowned. "Where does your grandma live?"

"Vanderhoof. We're taking the bus."

The car's big engine rumbled. A glowing cigarette butt sped past Crystal's arm and landed in the dirt by Majorca's feet.

"That's a long way, it's gonna take you hours by bus," the driver said. "Tell you what. You girls hop in and I'll get you into town. Save a little time for you anyways."

"Shotgun!" Crystal grabbed for the passenger's door handle.

Majorca grasped her arm. "We shouldn't take rides from strangers," she whispered.

Crystal halted and looked at her. "Why not?"

"Hitchhiking is dangerous. We learned that in Social Studies."

Crystal swatted Majorca's hand away. "That's bullshit," she said. "Get in."

Chapter Seven

DROOL SLOBBERED DOWN THE dog's jowls and slopped onto the yellowed linoleum floor. Beads of water clung to his gray mussel. Going for the last drop, he pushed the aluminum pan in circles around the small kitchen in the housing unit assigned to Constable Zoey Simard, the newest member of the Granisle RCMP.

Grinning, Zoey shook her head and plopped onto the room's only chair. She pulled her running shoes off, let them clunk to the floor, and then dropped her socks next to them. "Buster, we talked about this. You are the messiest dog in Canada. Please try to be a little more civilized."

The aging German Shepherd looked up, gave her a goofy dog grin, twirled his tail, and returned to pushing the pan.

Zoey stood, pulled her sweaty t-shirt over her head, and let it fall to the floor by her shoes and socks. Shimmying out of her running shorts, she dumped them on the pile and then, wearing only her bra and underpants, she wove around Buster to the refrigerator for a beer. Using a moose-head-shaped opener, Zoey popped the bottle cap and sent it whirling across the room. She caught the cap mid-flight and tossed it into a bowl on the counter. It clinked against the others in her collection. "Come on, Buster. Hang with me for a beer, then I'll shower and fix you some dinner."

Zoey allowed herself two beers a day—one after her workout and another in the evening while she watched shows on the portable black and white television she'd lugged from Vancouver.

She hadn't watched television in Vancouver—no time. Her initial posting after graduating from training had been in the city with two other female constables. As members of the first class of women allowed to join the RCMP, they'd formed a close bond. They'd spent their off hours exploring the city's shops and pubs, and because Vancouver was open and progressive, they'd even become buddies with several of the young male recruits. But this second assignment, to the backwoods town of Granisle, was a different experience entirely. At least so far.

"Look, Miss, um, Constable Simard," her boss, Sergeant Roger Gagnon, explained on day one, "The thing is, we've never had a gal on the force before, so it might take the men some getting used to. But we made a unit especially for you, so don't you worry." He'd stopped short of adding, 'Your pretty little head.'

Zoey hadn't been surprised. She and the other female recruits knew that carving out new territory would be challenging. Everything about joining Canada's elite police force had been taxing—from training to placements, from the general public's attitudes, to the attitudes of the males on the force, especially the older, more seasoned males. Like the other women in her graduating class, Zoey expected and accepted these challenges. But she hadn't expected to feel so lonely.

Slipping into baggy stretch pants and a sloppy sweatshirt, she grabbed the beer and flopped down on her worn sofa. Buster jumped up beside her. Scratching him behind his ears, she said, "Don't know what I'd do without you, buddy." The dog thumped his tail against the sofa, lowered his head to Zoey's lap, and stared up at her, his brown eyes soft and searching.

Halfway through the beer, a crash against her door made her jump. Buster went into a barking fit. "What the—"

Zoey leaped from the sofa and pulled the door open with a whoosh. Two small children, twins, tumbled into her living room. One girl, one boy. One giggling, one crying. Buster trotted up to them, tail twirling.

"Gosh, Zoe. I'm so sorry. They're out of control today."

Zoey swept past the children and into the hallway, where a young woman struggled under a load of groceries. Zoey grabbed the bags from her. "Let me help," she said.

The woman gave Zoey a weary and relieved smile, then swiveled around. "Timmy. Tammy. Leave Buster alone. Come here, right now."

Ignoring their mother, the twins continued to play with Buster, tugging on his tail and kissing his snout. The big old dog stretched out on the floor, still and patient.

"They're no problem, Rebecca. I think Buster enjoys the attention. Let's get these groceries into your place. Any more in the car?"

Zoey placed her police radio on her neighbor's kitchen table while Rebecca settled the twins with biscuits and sippy cups of lemonade. Rebecca's apartment, like hers, provided the bare minimum the government saw fit to house public servants, like a new RCMP recruit and a patrol constable's wife—a newly widowed mother.

A collection of drawings hung on the walls. While some sported frames, the majority were stuck to the wall with thumbtacks. Most were pencil sketches of the twins, but a few showed a handsome young man in an RCMP uniform smiling at the artist. Zoey guessed he was Rebecca's late husband.

"They sure are a handful." Rebecca eased into a chair and pushed a biscuit box across the table toward Zoey.

"They're cute kids." Zoey looked up at a drawing of the twins. "Did you do that?"

Rebecca glanced at the wall of art and sighed. "Yes, guilty as charged. I wanted to attend art school but you know...babies."

"I've always admired creative people," Zoey said, "I can't—" The squawk of her radio cut her off. She grabbed the radio and pressed the receiver.

"Constable Simard. I know you're off duty, but the sergeant thought this might be one for you."

"Roger that. Address?"

The scratchy voice spelled out a street name and house number. "How soon can you get there?"

Zoey glanced at her watch. "Fifteen. Max."

"I hope it's something interesting," Rebecca said. "I sure could use some non-toddler-related news. But either way, stop over when you get back. I splurged a little today—picked up a bottle of wine. I'll provide the grape, you provide the juice." A running joke between the two of them.

Zoey nodded and gave her a quick wink before hurrying to her apartment to change into her uniform.

Chapter Eight

Two firefighters rolled a heavy hose onto the truck while two others ran a ribbon of yellow police tape around what had been a small building now reduced to a pile of smoldering lumber and ash. A rank smell permeated the air as a light drizzle began.

Zoey parked her VW Beetle across the street behind a banged-up Ford Mustang. On duty, RCMP constables rode in department-issued patrol cars, but on this short notice, their personal vehicles came into play. She breathed a sigh of relief when she saw the plastic hula girl fixed to the Mustang's dash. Danny O'Brien, a year older and hired only six months before her, put as much faith in the plastic doll as others attached to their ivory virgins or carved wooden saviors. He fixed it to the dash of every vehicle he drove. A bit ironic, given his Irish upbringing and regular attendance at the local Catholic church.

Although Sergeant Gagnon had created a unit especially for her, the Unit on Crimes Against Women and Children, he'd decided that Zoey would need a supervisor. The task had fallen to Danny, the second-to-newest hire.

Scanning the scene, she saw him standing with two other constables in front of a weather-beaten single-wide trailer. The trailer's broken door hung limp from one hinge, and a thin shaft of light spilled out onto two rusting metal steps. Zoey approached the men.

Danny nodded to her, then looked down at a clipboard. The other two constables ignored her.

"So," Danny said, "looks like somebody chopped off the first two fingers on the fellow's right hand."

"Do we know the weapon?" Zoey asked.Guy Hendricks, the most senior of the constables, grinned and held up a black plastic garbage bag. He reached into the bag with a gloved hand and withdrew a set of long-handled loppers. Heavy-duty loppers, the kind used for whacking thick tree limbs. "Got 'em with these," he said. "Clean cuts, through and through, but lots of blood." Grinning wider, he lowered the loppers back into the bag.

Zoey swallowed and looked away for a second before focusing on Danny. He whistled low and muttered in his soft brogue, "Holy Mother of the Lord, that had to hurt."

"Nope," Hendricks said, "not according to the EMTs. They said the old boy was flyin' so high he wouldn't have noticed if they'd chopped his dong off."

Danny coughed. "Language, Sir."

Hendricks ignored the comment and continued. "There was a woman in the bedroom, passed out, drunk as an old squaw. We couldn't get anything out of either of them. Like I said, flyin' high."

"Where are they now?" Zoey said.

"On their way to Mercy. Lead EMT said they won't be able to talk or focus until morning."

Danny scanned the scene. "What about that?" He pointed across the yard to the pile of smoldering wood.

Sneering, Hendricks glanced at Zoey. "Ah, that's why Sergeant Gagnon called you in. You and our new lady recruit. Seems this little backyard fire has something to do with females and kids, so it's her assignment."

Zoey straightened and pressed her lips into a tight line. Narrowing her eyes, she looked directly at Hendricks.

He turned his back to her and pointed to the shed's remains. "According to the neighbors, a young girl, a teenager maybe, was living in that shed. At least what used to be a shed."

"Any—" Danny started.

Hendricks interrupted. "According to our boys with the hoses, the fire burned fast and hot. They guess gasoline. A few bits of metal, but no signs of a body. No bones or teeth."

"Do you believe the man and woman in the house are related to the girl who lived in the shed?" Zoey tried her best to keep her tone even.

Hendricks smirked. "Don't know. But I guess you two, being responsible for ladies and little kids, you'll figure it out." With that, he ambled across the yard to chat with two firefighters loading the last sets of equipment onto their truck."Ignore him," Danny said. "He's got the manners of a doped-up raccoon."

Hiding a faint smile, Zoey turned and surveyed the yard. Old car, tireless, on blocks—one door open. A smoking pile of rubble with what looked like the remnants of several garden tools, a rake, a shovel, maybe a hoe.

"Let's go look inside the trailer," Zoey said. "And after that, I'd like to chat with the neighbors. Maybe Hendricks missed something. "

Danny glanced at Hendricks, nodded, and followed Zoey to the narrow trailer.

The radio call came before they had time to enter. "The rest of this and the neighbors will have to wait," Danny said. He clipped his radio back on his belt. "Turns out we've got a couple of hysterical teenagers down by the lake. Sounds like their car went for an evening swim."

Zoey shook her head. "Two calls in one day. The sergeant might have to assign more constables to the Unit on Crimes Against Women and Children. Race you?"

Chapter Nine

Cocooned in the back seat of Dee Dee Wine's turquoise Newport, Majorca sniffled and held back hiccups. She wasn't part of, and didn't want anything to do with, the cheerful chatter between Crystal and their driver.

A voice on the radio belted out, "Bennie…Bennie…Bennie and the Jets."

"I'm sure liken this new music." Dee Dee tapped the pointed tip of her nail on the steering wheel in time to Elton John. "All we ever get from the café jukebox is country and western. Old country and western. My boss don't want nothin' modern in his café. Say, you got a favorite band?" Majorca curled tighter and gulped a sob.

I don't care if Crystal has a favorite band. And who cares about some stupid old café jukebox? I don't care about anything. My life is ruined, and I don't have anything to live for.

Dee Dee smacked her gum and tilted the rearview mirror toward the back seat. Majorca's reflection, a slumping shadow, curled against the side door. "Say, what's wrong with your friend?" she said.

"Boy troubles." Crystal leaned toward the dash and turned the radio up.

Dee Dee laughed with the raspy, throaty cackle of a heavy smoker. "Had me some of them, for sure."

"So listen, I got a boy story you won't believe," Crystal said.

Majorca tuned her out. Tuned them both out. They didn't matter. Nothing mattered anymore.

I was the luckiest girl in the world. With the best boyfriend in the world. And he dumped me and called me a stupid cow and a cold fish, and now I'm in the backseat of a stranger's car on the way to another stranger's grandma's house. My life is over.

Her sob, this time, audible.

"Ha! That's rich!" Dee Dee's laughter, followed by another hacking spell, cut into Majorca's misery.

Crystal swiveled around and bent over the passenger's seat. "Hey, you still alive back there?"

"Leave me alone."

"Suit yourself." Crystal flipped back around and cranked the radio even louder. She and Dee Dee harmonized with B. J. Thomas. "I—I—I—am hooked on a feeling..."

Majorca scootched tighter against the door, and pressing her forehead on the window's cool glass, she stared at the scenery along the highway. She touched the heavy ring on the chain around her neck. Wrapping her fingers around the ring, she closed her eyes and remembered the day he gave it to her.

They'd walked to a flowered meadow at the farthest end of the lake, a private clearing, a special place for the two of them. They'd spread out a blanket, and she'd unloaded a basket. She'd made a picnic lunch—fried chicken, potato salad, and rhubarb pie. They shared a large bottle of Coca-Cola.

After lunch, they stretched out on the blanket and kissed. All that sunlight warming their skin, the scent of meadow grasses, the hum of bees, and Todd slowly, lovingly, unbuttoning her blouse. She'd stopped him at three buttons. She smiled at the memory.

"Todd, we need to be serious before... you know..."

She remembered the look on his face, almost pain. She took it for the pain of love. And she knew she wasn't wrong because he'd pulled his class ring off and handed it to her right then and there.

"See, Baby? See how serious I am? We're serious. You and me, babes."

She remembered the weight of the ring as she slipped it on her thumb, too big for any of her fingers. Then, she let Todd unbutton the rest of her blouse, even let him slide two fingers under her bra, even over one nipple. Only for a minute.

Todd didn't mean any of that. He was confused—Candy tricked him—he was probably embarrassed. He'll apologize to me, and he'll work with Dad on the car, and everything will—

"You've got to be kidding me!" Dee Dee shrieked from the front seat. That's so funny, I might—"

Snapping from her memories, Majorca slid the ring back under her blouse, clunky gold against her skin.

"Here we are, ladies. The Blue Bird Café and Grill." Dee Dee pulled into a spot behind the café and cut the engine. The old car rumbled a moment before shutting down.

Majorca uncurled and leaned forward. She tapped Crystal's shoulder. "I thought we were going into town to catch the bus to your grandma's house."

"We are. But Dee Dee works here, and she's gonna give us some pie and coffee before we head out."

Dee Dee sloshed through her handbag. Pulling out a lipstick case and compact, she smeared a bright pink streak across her lips. Patting her hair, she smiled at Crystal. "You girls got a long stretch ahead, so a little treat and some hot joe will get you going right." She made a kissing motion at the compact's mirror. "Good as it's gonna get. Come on, girls, it's show time."

Fluorescent lighting bounced from red vinyl-covered booths and slipped across black and white checkered Formica table tops. At the counter, six stools waited for customers. Behind the counter, an open window gave a glimpse of the cook lowering stainless baskets of frozen fries into bubbling grease. He twisted the knob on a timer and then turned to grab an order from the ticket wheel. Above the window, mounted high for easy viewing, a large television played commercials, the weather, and local news. The picture, black and white. The sound, muted.

Crystal bounced into a booth and grabbed a laminated menu. "Man, I am starving."

Majorca pushed her book bag onto the bench opposite Crystal and slid in. "I thought we were having dinner at your grandma's house. If we eat now, we won't be hungry when we get there."

"I know. I'm just looking," Crystal said. "But pie sounds great, and it won't ruin our appetites. I'm going for the chocolate cream."

Majorca looked across the café to the glass cabinet housing slices of pie, cake, and one plate of brownies. "Order the cherry for me," she said. She slipped from the booth.

"Where ya goin'?"

"I'm going to call my folks and tell them I'm spending the night at Rhonda's house." Standing beside the booth, she wavered, bit her lower lip, and twisted a strand of hair.

Crystal pointed to a photo of fries smothered in brown gravy, topped with cheese curds. "I could eat a bucket of those about now."

Majorca didn't move.

Crystal glanced sideways at her. "So go already. Go call your folks."

"But I never—" "Oh, please. Don't tell me you never lied to your parents."

"Not really. Little things, maybe. But never anything like this."

Crystal lowered the menu and turned to face Majorca. "You're doing the right thing," she said.

Majorca's brows furrowed. "I hope you're right."

Turning her attention back to the menu, Crystal nodded. "Trust me," she said. "This is best. For everybody."

Chapter Ten

CRIME SCENE TAPE CORDONED off the area from the shoreline to the three RCMP patrol cars, then looped around a Mercy Hospital ambulance and stretched down the grassy slope to the bumper of a hulking orange tow truck. Halogen lights illuminated the scene brighter than high noon on Canada Day, while a bank of portable generators growled at a gaggle of news reporters and curious citizens.

Zoey lifted the tape, ducked under it, and held it for Danny. "You won the race, but it looks like we're both late to the party." She gestured to a uniformed constable approaching them. The constable's face had a flat, ashen pallor in the harsh artificial light. He glanced at Zoey, then focused on Danny.

"Jason Dickson, Prince George. I was on my way to visit my in-laws up here when I heard the call. Happened to be the first on the scene, but obviously, this is your case." He removed his hat and scratched his head. Replacing the hat, he added, "Don't have much for you. Only that it seems those two were playing a little touch-feely when, somehow, their car ended up in the lake. Gonna be hard to explain that one to the parents." Snickering, he aimed his thumb over his shoulder toward the ambulance where a teenage girl, wrapped in a blanket, sat on the vehicle's tailgate.

"Thanks," Danny said. "We'll take it from here."

Dickson touched his finger to the brim of his hat.

"By the way," Danny said, "this is her call. I'm along for the ride."

Dickson scanned Zoey from her hat down, pausing at her breasts before letting his eyes glide over her frame. "What the—"

Zoey stepped forward and extended her hand. "Constable Zoey Simard. Unit on Crimes Against Women and Children."

Ignoring her outstretched hand, Dickson mumbled, "Heard something about that. Couldn't believe it was true."

Pressing her lips into a thin line, Zoey watched Dickson wander back to his car.

"He's a jerk," Danny said. "Ignore him."

Zoey glanced at Danny and raised an eyebrow. "Ignore who?"

With a quick grin and a wink, Danny pointed to the lake. "Check it out."

Two divers in full scuba gear were talking with a heavy-set man wearing oil-splattered jeans and a dirty t-shirt. A faded company logo stretched across his chest—Blimpton's Towing and Recovery. He chewed the end of an unlit cigar and pointed toward the crane's outstretched arm and then to the lake. The divers nodded, donned their flippers, and slapped across the sand to the water's edge. One diver waded in, slipped under the surface, and disappeared. The other stood scanning the lake's dark face. After squinting at the pulley on the crane's arm, he followed his colleague into the murky depths.

"I'm gonna go have a chat with those kids, Danny. You wanna check out what's happening down there?"

Danny nodded and began picking his way over the slippery grass to the lake.

Zoey walked past the assembled reporters and looky-loos. None of the reporters called out to her for bits of information the way they had as Danny passed them.

A rotating dome light on the ambulance roof splashed an eerie combination of blood red and military blue over the scene. Red and blue, red and blue. Shielding her eyes, Zoey approached one of the uniformed constables standing by the emergency vehicle. She remembered meeting him on her first day because, unlike most of his colleagues, he hadn't reacted to the newest recruit one way or the other. He simply shook her hand.

"Constable Carlton, what can you tell me?"

"Not much. The sergeant said this one is yours because, you know, kids."

"Yes. Kids."

"I tried to talk to them," Carlton said, "but all we got from the girl was that her cousin is gonna be really, really mad. Beyond that, she was pretty much hysterical."

Zoey looked at the two teenagers. Though wrapped in the blanket, the girl trembled—her eyes vacant, her face mottled from tears and streaked with mascara. A tall, blonde boy stood next to the tailgate. He wore wrinkled khakis, a white polo shirt, and a varsity jacket. His eyes darted from the patrol cars to the tow truck and back.

"She looks completely bewildered or overwhelmed, but she doesn't look hysterical to me," Zoey said.

"That's because the paramedics gave her an injection—something to calm her down. I think she's a little loopy now."

"Do you think the car belongs to her cousin?"

Carlton shrugged. "Probably not. I think it belongs to the boy, but he's not talking until he gets a solicitor. Says he knows his rights and he's gonna lawyer up."

"Anything else?"

"No. Like I said, Sergeant Gagnon says this is your call, so I didn't push it."

"Thanks. I'll take it from here."

Without another word, Constable Carlton headed to the row of police vehicles.

Zoey walked to the back of the ambulance and smiled at Todd. "I'm Constable Zoey Simard, and I'm assigned to help local youth. Like you. So, maybe we can start with your name?"

Todd crossed his arms over his chest and glared at Zoey. She shrugged and turned to the girl.

Keeping her voice soft, she said, "You look cold. Do you want another blanket?" The girl's empty eyes chilled Zoey, but she continued to speak in the tone she used to coax Buster from under the bed when he played his game of catch me if you can. "How about something hot to drink? I think the paramedics can heat water for a cup of tea."

Candy tipped forward. The blanket slipped back, exposing her pale white shoulders and lacy bra. She wailed, a long, sharp cry. "I'm in sooo much trouble. My cousin is gonna be so mad at me. She trusted me."

"Shut up, Candy." Todd glared at her. "I told you we're not in trouble. It wasn't our fault. Shut up."

Candy's shoulders sagged and her eyes glazed over again.

Zoey pulled the blanket around Candy and then turned to Todd. Her voice dropped lower.

"You don't have to say anything to me if you don't want to. That's your right. You can wait for a lawyer if you want. But it's my responsibility to help you, and I can do a better job if I know what's going on. Of course, if you don't want any help, you can do this alone. Your call." Zoey waited a beat before turning away and starting toward the lake.

"Wait."

Zoey paused, then returned to the ambulance.

Todd licked his lips and ran his fingers over his buzz cut. "We didn't do anything," he said. "We were sitting in my car—you know—talking, and my girlfriend, my ex-girlfriend, she came running down the hill yelling at us."

Glancing at Candy sitting on the ambulance tailgate in her rumpled cheer-leader skirt, with her white bra peeking out from under the blanket, Zoey raised an eyebrow.

Todd smirked. "Yeah, well... you know."

"Go on," Zoey said. "You were in your car. Talking."

Guy Hendricks wandered over and stood next to Zoey. Todd continued. "Like I said, my ex-girlfriend came running down the hill yelling stupid stuff. I don't even know what she was on about. Anyway, she..." He glanced at Candy. "She freaked out, and got out of the car, and started running into the woods. So, I had to follow her."

"Guessing you wanted to return her missing blouse?" Hendricks asked.

Todd looked down and kicked at the dirt.

Zoey shot Hendricks a look but continued. "Then what happened?"

"I ran after her, you know, so I could calm her down.

"Exactly how long did it take for you to calm her down?" Guy asked.

Todd looked over at Hendricks and grinned. "I didn't rush things, if you know what I mean."

Hendricks returned the grin.

Zoey bit the inside of her lip, mentally counting to three before asking, "So, after that? You walked back from the forest to the car, right?"

"Right. We walked back, but my car was gone. I ran down to the lake, but all I could see were tire tracks in the grass and a few bubbles on the water."

"So, you—"

"Some old guy was walking his mutt, and I told him about my car, and he took off. We, Candy and me, we sat on the grass and waited until those cops showed up." He looked over to the RCMP constables working the scene. Some continued to tape off the area while others kept onlookers and news reporters at bay. Todd's focus shifted to the lake. Zoey followed his gaze.

The two divers surfaced, swam to shore, emerged from the water, and flopped onto the firm sand. After peeling his mask off, one diver signaled to the crane operator—a thumbs up. The operator chomped hard on the cold cigar, hoisted himself into the crane's cab, and pushed a lever forward. As the giant pulley cranked the heavy chain skyward, the tow truck belched diesel smoke. All eyes and cameras remained riveted as the red Trans Am, hanging nose down, rose from the chilly waters of Lake Babine.

Water poured from the Pontiac's windows and open doors. Candy screamed. Leaping from the back of the ambulance, she stumbled down the slope to the shore, shouting, "Bradley! Bradley!"

Chapter Eleven

Crossing the cafe to the phone booth, Majorca passed Dee Dee, who carried two large trays of food—burgers, bowls of steaming poutine, and glasses of frothy shakes.

"Hey, hon, you girls gonna want ice cream with your pie? Don't be shy now, it's on me."

"Thanks, Dee Dee. Ice cream sounds yummy," Majorca lied. Her stomach twisted and pinched. Nothing sounded yummy. The very idea of food flushed a wave of nausea through her body. Faking a smile, she rushed to the back of the cafe, where the pay phone hung between the men's and ladies' washrooms. Majorca waited until a woman came out, then popped into the ladies' room and locked the door. Leaning against the sink, she slipped off one loafer and jammed her thumb under the dime wedged into the coin slot. Some kids put shiny new pennies in their shoes, but Majorca's mother had encouraged her to keep enough change in the slots to call home in an emergency.

"Never leave home without a way to get back," her mother had advised. Majorca swallowed. This was the first time she'd needed a dime from her shoe.

After using the loo and a quick wash, Majorca stepped into the hallway, dropped the dime into the pay phone, and dialed. As the phone rang, she surveyed the cafe.

Diners crowded into booths and perused menus. Others paid bills and carried doggy bags out the door. In the kitchen, the cook slipped plates of hot food under a red warming light, hit a bell, and tugged new orders from the wheel. The Blue Bird Cafe and Grill—a happy place.

"Fairhaven residence."

"Hi, mum, it's me."

"Honey, where are you? We're almost ready for dinner."

"I'm sorry, I should have called sooner, but Rhonda and I got carried away studying, and if it's okay with you and daddy, I want to spend the night over here. We're gonna study all night—we have two exams tomorrow. History and English Lit."

"I... hold on a minute. Neil, you have to wash up now. You're going to get grease all over my white tablecloth."

Majorca smiled. She could see her father in his gray work pants and plaid flannel shirt, sitting in his favorite chair behind a TV tray table covered with hundreds of screws and springs and small tubes of grease. Every evening, as far back as she could remember, her father had tinkered with car parts on that small table. The grease never went further than the tray, but her mother fussed all the same. For a moment, Majorca felt a tug at her heart. Like Rhonda's room, her home would always be warm, dry, clean. Safe.

"Honey, did you hear me?"

"Sorry, mum. The phone crackled. What?"

"I said it's alright if you stay at the Patterson's, but please don't study all night. You girls need to sleep. Rest is as important as hitting the books."

"Yes. Of course." Majorca looked across the cafe and glanced up at the silent television. A news camera panned the shore of Lake Babine. Two men in diving gear stood next to a crane. The camera swung up for a shot of the crane's extended arm and to a giant hook dangling from a thick chain. Then the cameraman cut to a reporter who spoke into a microphone, his voice muted, his expression somber. A row of RCMP cars lined the scene, their lights flashing.

"I gotta go. Mrs. Patterson is waving us to the table."

"You remember what I said about getting some rest."

"I will. And, um, mum?"

"Honey?"

"I love you."

"I love you too, sweetie. You have fun with Rhonda and say hi to Mrs. Patterson for me."

Majorca stood holding the receiver, listening to the dull buzz on the line, the clatter of dishes from the kitchen, and the twangy voice of Willie Nelson singing something about crying in the rain.

Chapter Twelve

Pushing and pulling on levers, the operator maneuvered the crane's arm until it swung the Pontiac in a slow arc from the lake to a grassy patch up the slope from the shore. Waving their arms and gesturing to the operator, two men below directed the lowering of the car to the ground. The men were younger and leaner than the crane operator. Their t-shirt logos less faded, their jobs far more dangerous. They scrambled around the car, catching and pulling on lines as the cigar-chomping man lowered the vehicle to the earth. While the young men released the car from cables and hooks, Zoey looked up the hill to the cluster of people straining at the police tape. She turned to Danny. "This is gonna get a lot worse before it gets better. I can feel it in my bones."

"Agreed," Danny said. "And we need to make sure those citizens, especially those reporters and cameramen, don't get close enough to see—"

Zoey interrupted. "Can you grab a couple of the guys and push the crowd back?"

"Sure thing. I'm guessing those folks will clear out once the car is loaded onto the tow truck. By then, they'll probably figure the show's over."

Zoey chewed her lower lip for a moment and furrowed her brow. "Maybe. I hope you're right. But it's important we keep this part out of the news until we find out what actually happened."

"Don't worry. I'll clear the crowd." Danny started toward the row of police vehicles, then stopped and turned back to Zoey. "So, what's going to happen to those kids? They're both eighteen, right?"

Zoey shook her head. "I can't even guess until we get the full story. For now, though, the girl is in the ambulance heading to Mercy, and Hendricks is taking the boy to the station. Both sets of parents are on the way."

"What about the cousin? Has anyone called her?"

"Not yet." Zoey wiped her sleeve across her forehead. "First, I have to, you know... and then..."

Her voice trailed off as a black vehicle rolled down the slope and stopped beside an ambulance. A gray-haired man in a lab coat stepped from the car and walked toward the Trans Am. He carried a black satchel.

"That's him," Zoey said.

Danny reached over and tapped her shoulder. "You going to be okay?"

Zoey pursed her lips and nodded. Leaving Danny, she headed toward the man with the satchel.

Two paramedics hunched into the car while a third waited beside a raised gurney. Zoey and the coroner stood together, facing Todd's car with their backs to the onlookers.

"Damn vultures," the man muttered. "Always rubbernecking, trying to see someone else's misery."

"No worries. They won't see much," Zoey said. "Our guys are good at crowd control." She tried to sound firm and confident, even though her words felt hollow and weak to her ears. With only a short time on the job and placement on an assignment that hadn't existed before she came on board, she'd had almost no interaction with the other constables and no idea how good they were at crowd control or anything else.

"Maybe so," the coroner said. "But I'll feel better back in the peace and quiet of the lab. Nobody there who doesn't belong."

Zoey didn't reply. She focused her attention on the paramedic pulling something from the Pontiac's back seat. In his arms, he held a small bundle wrapped in a white sheet. Keeping one hand on the bundle, he gently laid it on the gurney. The other EMT left the car and approached his partner. Zoey couldn't see what he was carrying until he placed it on the gurney and stepped aside, giving her a view of a plastic car seat—pastel blue, decorated with dancing cartoon dinosaurs, sized for a toddler.

Chapter Thirteen

Majorca stood next to the booth, glowering at Crystal and the man sitting across from her.

Laughing, Crystal slapped the table with the flat of her palm. The man smiled wide and nodded his head. "You got it, sister. That was exactly my reaction the first time I saw one. Craziest damn thing I ever did see."

Majorca cleared her throat.

"Oops, sorry, doll. I'll give you your seat back. We were havin' a laugh. Me and your friend." He slid from the booth, gave Majorca a mock bow, and gestured to the open seat. He winked at Crystal before heading to the counter to pay his bill.

Majorca scooted in next to her book bag. "Who is that guy?" she whispered.

"Roy. Roy Johnson or something like that."

"Do you know him?"

Crystal shook her head, scooped up the last bit of chocolate cream pie, and licked the spoon.

"Why was he in my seat?"

"He's a salesman. He sells shit."

"Shit?"

"Medical supplies. He was tellin' me about some of the weird things he sells to hospitals and old people's homes. You wouldn't believe the stuff they stick up those old bums to get 'em goin.'"

"That's not funny, Crystal. That's gross."

"Relax." Crystal pulled her mother's lighter and a package of cigarettes from her knapsack and tapped one out. "So, how'd it go with your folks? Did they buy it?" She clicked the lighter.

Majorca pushed a piece of pie around on her plate, dragging it through the puddle of melting ice cream. "My mum did. But—"

"You gonna eat that?"

Setting her fork on the table, Majorca pushed the plate toward Crystal. "No, I'm not hungry."

"Dibs!" Crystal dropped the lighter and unlit cigarette on the table and pulled Majorca's plate closer.

"It's only because, like I already told you, I don't like lying to my parents."

"Let it go. It's no big deal—they'll probably never find out. And even if they do, they'll be so busy dealing with the car thing that it wouldn't matter. Like I told you before, you're doing the right thing. You're giving everyone a chance to chill out and calm down. Now, listen to what that guy sells to old folks' homes—it's so funny."

"I don't want to hear about medical supplies, Crystal. And I don't think there's anything funny about old folks' homes."

Crystal scooped up a tablespoon of melted ice cream and stirred it into her coffee. "Suit yourself, but I think you're way too uptight."

Dee Dee breezed up to the table, carrying a glass coffee carafe in one hand and balancing a stack of dirty dishes with the other. "You girls want anything else? A top-up on that coffee?"

Majorca didn't answer. She leaned back against the booth, crossed her arms over her chest, and pouted. Dee Dee glanced at her and then at Crystal.

Crystal smirked. "Don't worry about her, she'll live."

Dee Dee smiled at Majorca. "Listen, honey. Don't let that boy getcha down. Boys are a dime a dozen. Like buses—one comes along every half hour. Soon as you forget this one, the next one will be right along." Dee Dee pivoted toward the kitchen, then paused and returned to the table. "Say, speakin' of boys, I got a fella down in Prince George. He called, and we're gettin' together after my shift. It'll be kinda late, but if your granny doesn't care, and if you girls wanna wait,

I'll give you a ride. Vanderhoof is on the way, and I'd like the company on the drive." She winked at Crystal. "We can sing us some more of them duets."

Majorca sat up straight. "That would be great."

"I dunno." Crystal looked down, rolled the cigarette back and forth on the table, and then glanced at the television. A giant, bald genie cleaned a kitchen floor. "The thing is, my gran—"

"Come on," Majorca said. "We don't have to catch a stupid old bus, and we can stay here instead of walking the rest of the way into town. It's perfect!"

Dee Dee nodded toward the kitchen. "I gotta grab that order, but the offer stands. You girls want a ride, you hang out 'til we close."

Majorca stretched her arms across the table. "I think we should go with her. She'll give us a ride to your grandma's house. It will save us all that walking. Besides, it's pitch black out there now. I don't want to stumble around in the dark."

"Maybe, but I don't think..." Crystal looked away and stared out the window at the parking lot. The word EAT lit up in pink fluorescence, reflected on a pickup truck's windshield. Behind the word, the blue-gray light of the television flickered. Crystal's jaw dropped open.

"What?" Majorca gave Crystal's leg a light kick under the table.

Spinning around, Crystal pointed at the television screen. "Check it out!"

Majorca glanced up and gasped.

A local program flashed the words "Breaking News" across the screen as a camera panned the scene at Lake Babine. A crowd of onlookers, held back by crime tape and a row of RCMP constables, gawked and pointed as a giant crane parked at the water's edge pulled a car, its rear end up, out of the lake. Todd's car, attached by a hook and a tangle of wires, dangled over the water. As the Trans Am slowly rotated, water streamed from its open windows and doors.

Majorca slapped her hand over her mouth as she watched a woman in an RCMP uniform trying to wrap a blanket around a hysterical teenage girl. Even though the television's sound was muted, it was clear that Candy, wearing only her short skirt and white lace bra, was screaming. A nurse joined in the attempt to calm and cover her. When a police constable stepped in front of the news camera, blocking the view, the cameraman panned to a grim-faced reporter speaking into a microphone. The reporter stood beside an open ambulance as a second ambulance rolled down the hill toward the shore. Like the other emergency vehicle, its dome light flashed.

Crystal chuckled. "That's lover boy's car, isn't it? I didn't believe you when you told me, but this is too cool."

Majorca slid from the booth, pulling her book bag after her. "We gotta go. Now," she said.

"Wait a minute," Crystal started to complain, but Majorca was already halfway to the door.

"Shit." Crystal stashed the lighter and cigarette in her jacket pocket, grabbed her knapsack, and bolted across the café. "Hey! Wait for me."

She caught up with Majorca under the ring of light cast by a single streetlamp. Grabbing the blue windbreaker, she yanked Majorca backward.

Majorca shook off her hold but stopped walking.

"What the hell is your problem?" Crystal said.

"We need to get out of here. Fast." Majorca started walking away from the light.

"Wait a damn minute, you stupid—"

Majorca spun around and pointed at Crystal. "Don't you dare call me a stupid cow."

Crystal blinked. "Cow?"

"Look, we have to get out of here. Now. I mean it—right now." Majorca stamped her foot.

"I don't get it," Crystal said. "Two seconds ago, you were all hot and bothered to stay at the café until closing time and catch a ride with that waitress. Then you see lover boy's car hangin' over the lake, and you go all ape shit. What gives?"

"Crystal, don't you see? Somebody's gonna put two and two together—me and Todd. Me and Todd's car. Maybe Todd already told the police I pushed his car into the lake. Maybe they're already looking for me." Majorca's voice rose with every sentence. "We can't wait until the café closes. We have to get to the bus station, stay low, and catch the late bus. No one will look for us, for me, on a bus." She gasped for breath.

Crystal shook her head, shrugged out of her rucksack, and let it drop to the pavement. She pulled the lighter and cigarette from her pocket. "You know what? You are one weird chick. Maybe I don't want to take you to my gran's house. She's sort of old and frail like. You being all crazy and shit might freak her out." She lit the cigarette and blew a stream of smoke upward.

"What are you saying?" Majorca shucked her book bag off and dropped it next to Crystal's pack. Her voice trembled. "We...we have to go to your grandma's house because then we'll be safe. You said it yourself. We can eat, you know, those pies and bread and stuff. And get some sleep. And tomorrow, everything will be better. You said that."

"I did say that, but—"

"Crystal, this is serious. I pushed Todd's car into the lake, and now I'm in major trouble. What else can I do?"

"You, girlie, can go home. Maybe your folks yell at you or ground your skinny ass for a week or two. Or maybe they make you dust Bibles at church or some shit like that. But you can go home. I got nowhere to go except my gran's. And I don't wanna blow that because of your crazy paranoia." Crystal flicked the cigarette onto the road beyond the circle of light. It glowed orange on the pavement, then went out, leaving nothing but darkness.

"But... but I don't understand. You can go home, too. As soon as your mom gets better from the flu."

Crystal stared at Majorca. "Man, you are such a dip. I wish I never met you." She picked up her pack and walked into the shadows.

"Crystal. Wait!"

Chapter Fourteen

The Thunderbird's headlights stretched the girls' shadows long and thin down the road. Slowing, the car pulled next to Majorca. She stopped. Crystal kept walking.

"Hey, doll. I couldn't help overhearing you girls back at the café. I sure do understand your predicament. Maybe I can lend a friendly hand."

Crystal backtracked and stood next to Majorca. "What's that supposed to mean, Roy?"

"Only that you got someplace to be, but you don't wanna wait 'til that café closes. Understandable. It's a long walk to the bus station, plus I don't think you're gonna make that last bus anyway. Might a already missed it. So, I—"

"We're going to Burns Lake, Roy. Don't tell me you happen to be going to Burns Lake too." Crystal's words came out in a snarl.

"Crystal, for cripes' sake. Let the man talk."

"No," Roy said. "I'm only goin' as far as Rose Lake tonight. Got a motel lined up there. Got an appointment in the morning. But Rose Lake has another bus stop, and if we get a move on, I can get you there before the last bus. Save you pretty girls some time."

Crystal narrowed her eyes. "I dunno. Walking is good exercise."

Roy laughed. "Tell you what, I'll even stop and grab you some burgers and fries before I drop you off at the bus stop. You're gonna need more than pie for that ride."

Majorca pulled at Crystal's jacket and spun her around. With their backs to Roy, she whispered, "This is perfect. It'll get us out of sight in case the police are looking for me. And it gets you to your grandma's before it's seriously late. I think this is a good idea. Let's get a ride with this guy."

"I don't like it," Crystal said. "He was good for a laugh back at the café, but there's something creepy about him. I'm not sure I wanna talk to him the whole way."

"That's all right. I'll ride shotgun this time. You sit in the back. Come on, Crystal. This is the best way."

Shielding her eyes from the headlights, Crystal turned and walked toward the rusting car. Mumbling, she said, "but I'm still not cool with this."

Chapter Fifteen

Their chatter floated over the bench seat and drifted to the back where Crystal stretched out, using her rucksack as a pillow. Staring out the window, she watched the silhouettes of trees flickering past in the moonlight. The steady rhythm of the car relaxed her muscles, and the front seat conversation lulled her like a bedtime story.

"This boy," Roy's voice rumbled low, "he get you in a family way?"

"No. Of course not. We never did that. I'm saving myself for marriage."

"Ah, good girl."

"I thought Todd was the one. But he...he was such a jerk. He even..."

Crystal closed her eyes. She'd already heard Majorca's little sob story—nothing new or interesting there. She let their voices drift over her like background music on a radio.

"I feel for you, doll. I really do, 'cause I know what jerks guys can be."

"You do?"

"Swear on a stack a Bibles. You wouldn't know it now, but years ago, I used to be a big old jerk. Broke some hearts, I did. But no more. Nope, now I'm a good guy. A guy you can trust."

"How come you changed?"

"Well, you see... I found Jesus."

Chapter Sixteen

Zoey slipped the key into the lock and turned it slowly, trying for a silent entry. She cracked the door wide enough to slip inside, hoping to close it before Buster made a scene. But the big dog raced across the room, barking excitedly, and twirling his tail. He body-slammed her against the door.

"Down, Buster. Down!" She tried to dance around her dog, but when Buster jumped up with his hind feet still on the floor, she grabbed his paws, placed them on her shoulders, and nuzzled his cold nose.

"See, buddy, this is exactly why you didn't make it through obedience training and why you will never be a police dog." Buster slurped a wet tongue across her chin.

A light knock on the door made Zoey jump. Buster dropped to all fours and burst into another round of barking.

"It's me."

"Rebecca, I'm so sorry. He's... we're noisy neighbors. The twins?"

"No worries. They've been out for over an hour—long day at the park and pasta for dinner. They're down for the count." She bent and petted Buster's head, then looked up at Zoey. "Hard day?"

Zoey hung her hat on a peg by the door. "You have no idea," she said.

"Like I said, the twins are down, and I have a bottle of red and a corkscrew."

"I have a feeling tomorrow is gonna be rough, so maybe I should—"

"Relax tonight?"

Zoey grinned. "You know what? You're right. A glass of wine sounds perfect. Gimmie time to walk this boy around the block and catch a quick shower."

Zoey swiped space on the sofa for Buster and plopped down next to him. Rebecca made it clear on day one that dogs and kids were allowed everywhere in her home. Her unit had the look and feel of happy children and a loving but exhausted single parent. No time for picking up the toys scattered over every surface. No time to put jars of peanut butter and jelly away, no time to clean up spilled cereal. But judging by the books on the end table next to an old recliner, there was plenty of time for snuggles, nursery rhymes, and fairy tales. Lots of time for love.

Rebecca twirled into the room with two plastic wine glasses in one hand and an open bottle of cabernet in the other. "This will take the edge off for you and help me feel like an adult, at least for a while."

She filled their glasses, pushed a toy truck from the recliner, and sat. "To neighbors," she toasted.

"To neighbors." Zoey smiled, took a sip, let the wine slide down, and allowed herself to release the tension she'd been holding since...

...since the call about the car in the lake? No, before that, since the scene of the fire.

"Penny for your thoughts?" Rebecca said.

"Sorry. Processing the day."

"I know it's probably secret police stuff and all, but if you need to talk..."

Zoey looked at the young mother sitting across from her. Not counting Danny at work and Buster, Rebecca was the only friend she had in Granisle. And sometimes, talking things out helped. "Some stuff is need-to-know only, but I can share what will be in the papers tomorrow," she said.

"First, a refill." Rebecca topped their glasses. "Now, tell me."

Leaving out the part about the chopped fingers, Zoey outlined the day. When she finished, she placed her glass on the coffee table, stood, and paced the short distance from the living room to the kitchen and back. "The hardest part, of course, was telling that woman about her baby boy."

Rebecca glanced toward the bedroom. "I couldn't go on living," she said.

Zoey paced the space again, then returned to sit next to Buster. He sprawled upside down, legs spread wide, tongue lolling, snoring.

"Several things frustrate me," Zoey said. "First, I don't know if the shed fire was accidental or deliberately set. The neighbors say a teenage girl lived in the shed, but there's no evidence of her. Next, I don't know who pushed the car into the lake. The car's owner, an eighteen-year-old boy, thinks it was his ex-girlfriend. My boss suspects it was another boy, a jealous guy who caught his girlfriend cheating. He doesn't think a girl would have the strength to push a car down a hill."

Rebecca rolled her eyes.

"Also," Zoey continued, "I don't know if the girl who lived in the shed—if a girl did live in the shed—is connected to whoever pushed the car into the lake. And I don't know whether the person who pushed the car knew there was a toddler strapped in the back seat. If he or she did, that's homicide. Of course, if it was an accident... that's for the judge to decide."

"Did you talk to any of the parents?"

"No. The people who lived in the trailer in front of the shed were so wasted that we had to send them to Mercy to sober up. I'll interview them tomorrow."

"What about the other girl? The boy's ex-girlfriend? Did you interview her yet?"

Zoey snorted. "No. I wanted to. I should have. But my boss is adamant that the car incident was a boy's doing. He wants me to poke around more before hassling the ex-girlfriend or her parents."

Rebecca took a sip of wine. "I don't know much about police work, but that doesn't sound efficient. It's almost like they want you to fail."

Zoey picked up her glass, took a long swallow and said, "You know a lot more about police work than you think."

Chapter Seventeen

Dreaming, Crystal tossed on the back seat of Roy's car. Her face pressed against the stinking fabric—fabric like on a filthy old sofa.

A woman's cry.

"Stop it. You're hurting me."

Mom?

A man's growl.

"Now, I got you right where I want you."

Clive?

A girl's screech.

Her own screech?

"Stop! Get off me!"

Crystal bolted upright. Disoriented from the dream, she shook her head to remember. The salesman's car. Roy's car. Majorca.

They had stopped in a church parking lot—dark except for a single light shining down from the steeple. Crystal peered over the seat.

Majorca lay stretched out with Roy's legs pressed tight, locking hers between them. One meaty hand clutched her wrists together above her head, the other fumbled with the buttons on her blouse.

Crystal grabbed at his arm. "Leave her alone!"

Pulling from Crystal's grasp, Roy twisted around and shoved her. She smacked against the back seat, then slid sideways. Her head hit the window with a crack.

"You hold on, sister. Wait your turn, and don't you worry 'cause there's enough of this big boy to go around. Couple a times." Grinning, he leaned down and licked Majorca's cheek.

"Stop it. Stop it," Majorca wailed.

"Not 'til I get what I want." He fumbled with another button, then seized the collar and ripped the blouse in two. "Let's take a look at what you got in there." Grabbing her bra, he tugged it up over her breasts. Roy stared at Majorca, half-naked in the light from above. "Damn. That's a disappointment. Never mind, let's check out the basement."

He lifted his knee and wedged it between Majorca's legs. Still holding her hands together, he pulled her skirt up to her waist, grabbed the elastic of her panties, and yanked them down.

"No," Majorca sobbed.

"Better," Roy said. Leering, he shifted his weight, freeing one of Majorca's legs.

She kicked out and tried to knee him in the groin.

Roy let go of her wrists and slapped her face. Hard.

Blinking away the pain in her head, Crystal reared up over the car seat and took a swing at Roy's head. He bucked out of the way and backhanded her with his forearm. She slumped down.

Between the sound of Majorca's sobs, Crystal heard the unmistakable click of a belt buckle.

Majorca's twisting and jerking rocked the car. Her fists pummeling against Roy's chest made dull thumping sounds.

Laughing, Roy said, "Yeah, that's it, little girl. Wiggle around. Gimme some action down there."

Crystal grappled with the clasps on her rucksack. She dug through the pack until her fingers touched metal. She gripped the pruning shears.

"Get ready cause here we go." Roy forced Majorca's legs apart with his knees and hunched over her.

Crystal flung herself halfway over the seat and shoved the shears through Roy's shirt between his shoulder blades.

He yowled and arched upright. Releasing Majorca, he flailed at the metal in his back.

Grunting, Crystal yanked the tool from his flesh. Roy swiveled around and grabbed at her face. Crystal stabbed the shears into his neck, pulled them out, and jammed them in again. She let go of the shears and jerked out of his reach.

His arms windmilled, and his eyes widened. Blood gushed from the gashes in his throat and gurgled from his mouth. Roy reached one hand toward his throat, swayed, then fell, face-first, onto Majorca. His body muffled her scream.

Crystal grabbed her knapsack, threw herself against the back door, and fell onto the concrete. Scrambling up, she yanked the front door open.

Majorca squirmed frantically beneath Roy's weight.

Crystal reached inside and jammed her hands under Majorca's armpits. She tugged. "Can you push?"

Majorca lugged her right leg from under Roy, stomped her shoe on the steering wheel, and straightened her leg. Crystal gritted her teeth and pulled. She tugged and twisted until Majorca slipped free, and the two girls fell backward to the ground.

"Oh my God. Oh my God." Majorca struggled to her feet. She pulled her panties up, tugged her bra into place, and flung her blood-soaked blouse to the ground. Then she bolted across the parking lot toward a shadowed patch of grass beside the church.

"Wait!" Crystal seized the blouse and raced after her, pausing long enough to toss the tattered, bloody fabric into a trash bin.

She found Majorca bending forward, retching onto the dewy grass. Crystal gathered Majorca's hair into a ponytail and held it while Majorca heaved, gagged, and retched until only thin streams of clear bile dripped from her chin.

Crystal helped Majorca straighten, then dug through her pack for the sweatshirt. The shirt was three sizes too big and hung to Majorca's knees, but it stopped her shivering and covered her blood-stained bra and skirt. Majorca sank to the wet grass, head to her knees, and sobbed.

Giving her time, Crystal gazed across the parking lot at the old Ford. It could have been anyone's car parked overnight behind the local church. Anyone's car, except for the open doors, the pool of blood on the concrete next to the passenger's side, and the trail of dark drops leading to a trash bin. After a few moments, she glanced down. "Majorca, we need to move," she said.

Majorca looked up. Her face was spattered with Roy's blood and streaked with tears. "Crystal...he was...he was—"

"Let's not talk about that now. We gotta get outta here. We need to find a place to hide until we can figure out a plan. And you're gonna need to clean up." She reached down and helped Majorca to stand.

They stood together in the chilly air as the smell of blood and vomit and early summer evening settled over them. Crystal broke the silence. "Do you know where we are?"

"Rose Lake. Roy told me before he stopped the car."

"Didn't he say this place has a bus stop?"

"I bet that's a lie."

"For sure, it's a lie. But didn't he also say he had a reservation at a motel here? Come on. I've got some cash. Let's see if we can find that motel and get a room."

Walking the three blocks from the church to the main road, they passed houses filled with families living small-town life. Scents of garlic and butter wafted from kitchens, children's laughter jingled on the wind, and the blue glow of televisions flickered behind drawn curtains. They stepped around a bicycle carelessly dropped on the sidewalk.

The town's main street boasted four commercial buildings—a bakery, now closed. A hardware store, closed. A feed store closed, but its yard lit bright with halogen lights. And at the far end of town, a crooked sign mounted on the roof of a one-story cement building announced the Sleepy Time Motel.

"That's gotta be it," Crystal pointed to the forlorn structure and the single vehicle parked in front. The car, a blue and cream two-tone Chevy, sported a string of tin cans tied to the rear bumper. The words "Just Married" were whitewashed across the back window.

"You're not looking so hot," Crystal said. "You stay out here. I'll deal with this."

Majorca nodded and wrapped her arms around herself. Despite the sweatshirt, her teeth chattered.

Crystal squared her shoulders, straightened her jacket, and walked to the dimly lit door labeled Reception.

Chapter Eighteen

WINCING, MAJORCA SQUEEZED HER eyes shut and plunged her hand into the bloody water

filling the motel sink. She pulled the plug, and as the water swirled, she twisted strawberry-colored drops from her soaking skirt.

"Hey, hurry up. I gotta pee," Crystal yelled.

"Almost done." Majorca ran fresh cold water over her skirt, soaked it through again, and then, one more time, wrung it as tight as she could. Gathering her wet skirt, underwear, and socks, she left the bathroom wearing only a threadbare towel.

Crystal bounded off the double bed and bolted for the bathroom.

Majorca draped her laundry over the radiator, a straight-backed chair, a lampshade, and the doorknob. Then she pulled back the worn bedcovers and stretched between frayed, yellowed sheets. Closing her eyes, she reached up to her left cheek—it remained hot to her touch and still stung from Ted's slap. Gingerly, she traced the scrape on her right cheek—the thin wound from Candy's fingernail. Lying on the lumpy motel bed, she tried hard to relax, to breathe. But waves of nausea rolled over her, and her tears welled.

The bathroom door swung open, and steam swirled into the room. Naked, Crystal bounced onto the bed, the scent of Ivory soap on her skin. She slung her wet underpants over the knob on the nightstand, propped herself against the headboard, stretched her legs, and wiggled her toes.

"God, that felt good," she said, covering herself with the bedspread.

Gulping, Majorca blinked back tears.

"What's eating you?" Crystal nudged Majorca's arm.

Majorca dragged herself into a sitting position. She readjusted her towel, then dropped her hands to her lap and hung her head. "Nothing," she mumbled.

"For Christ's sake. Tell me. What's wrong?"

Majorca looked up at Crystal. "What's wrong? What's wrong? Where should I start? I caught my boyfriend cheating with another girl from the cheerleading squad, then I pushed his car into Lake Babine, then I met you, and you talked me into going to somebody's house I don't know. I lied to my parents, took a ride from a stranger—a stranger who…who… and then… And now, here I am in a ratty little motel room, and I don't even know where I am, and the police are probably looking for me and…"

Crystal raised her eyebrows. "And what?"

"And I'm hungry."

Crystal nodded. "I get it. You're hungry." She jumped from the bed and crossed the room to the dresser where she'd tossed her t-shirt. Standing naked, she scanned the room until she spotted her jeans.

Majorca blushed and looked away.

"Don't be such a prude. You've seen it all before." Crystal pulled on her jeans and slipped into the shirt. She fished a few coins from her pack and headed for the door.

"Where are you going?" Majorca asked.

"I don't have any food, but I have something better. I'm going to look for ice and maybe a mixer."

"A mixer?"

Majorca stared at the closed door, then looked around their stuffy little room. She'd been in a motel room once before when her parents took her to Fort St. James for the annual horse races. She remembered that room, it was twice as big as this one. And it was bright and airy with a window that overlooked a pond where two white swans floated together. That family vacation had been the best time of her life. She and her parents had watched the races, and they'd taken long walks through the lush grounds. They enjoyed double-dip ice cream cones in the afternoon, and toasted marshmallows over a campfire when it got dark. She remembered the camp ranger telling a scary ghost story, and she remembered climbing onto her father's lap, and smelling his Old Spice aftershave as he held her in a protective hug.

The sound of banging on the door wrenched her from the memory. Slipping from the bed, Majorca tiptoed to the window and peeked around the curtain.

"Open the door, dweeb."

Crystal lined up three small packages of treats from the vending machine—Cheezies, Ketchup Potato Chips, and Salty Pretzels. She added three cans of Orange Crush to the stash before disappearing into the bathroom. Popping back into the room, she tossed two plastic glasses wrapped in cellophane to Majorca. "Unwrap those, will ya?"

Crystal rummaged through her pack and pulled out a bottle of clear liquid. "This is totally gonna take the edge off," she said.

Majorca handed the unwrapped glasses to Crystal. "What is it?"

"Vodka." Crystal pulled the tab on a can, filled both glasses halfway, and added a heavy pour of liquor.

"Crystal, I don't drink. I mean, I never—"

"Don't worry. This tastes like pop, only better. You'll like it."

"But I'm not old enough to—"

"Try it." Crystal handed a glass to Majorca, then raised hers for a toast. "To gran," she said.

Majorca sniffed the orange liquid, then tapped her glass against Crystal's. "To your grandma," she said. "I hope we get to her house real soon."

By the third glass of orange pop and vodka, Majorca forgot about the day's traumas. She and Crystal giggled over stupid things they'd done or said to boys. They laughed about kids and teachers they didn't like and took turns singing their favorite hit songs. Crystal belted out "Bad, Bad Leroy Brown," while Majorca warbled "Killing Me Softly."

Crystal added more vodka to their glasses, skipping the Crush.

"To my new bestest, bester, bestis friend," Majorca slurred, holding her glass high for a toast.

"Right," Crystal said. She tapped her plastic glass against Majorca's. They drank more.

"Hey, I have a question for you," Crystal said.

"Shoot." Majorca opened their last bag of snacks, the Salty Pretzels.

"So, your name—it's kinda weird. Does it mean something cool or whatever?"

Majorca chomped on a pretzel and nodded. "Uh-huh. It does. My parents went to Spain on their honeymoon. They stayed on a little island off the Spanish coast—Majorca Island." She giggled and took another gulp of her drink. "My dad says it was very romantic. My mom says I was conceived there. They both loved the place, so they named me Majorca."

"Ha," Crystal said. "So, your parents banged on an island and gave you that name. That is weird."

"What about you? How'd you get your name?"

Crystal picked at a hangnail. "Kinda like yours, I guess. My mom's name is Wanda-Lynn, so that's how I got my middle name. But my mom was probably on something when she got knocked up, and I bet that's why she called me Crystal."

For a while, they sat quietly, drinking and listening to the creaking of the bed springs in the room next to them.

"Jesus, that's what? Round four?" Crystal slid the bag of pretzels closer.

Majorca yawned. "I'm getting tired, so maybe they are too."

"I wouldn't count on it."

"Hey, Crystal. Do you think we're in a lot of trouble?"

"Nope. You pushed that jerk's car into the lake. Big deal. He deserved it."

Majorca giggled and took another gulp of vodka. "I forgot about Todd's car." She held the plastic glass up to the lamp light. "It's like this stuff is magic."

"Here," Crystal emptied the bottle into Majorca's glass. "You finish it off."

"So, I wasn't talking about the car. Not Todd's car. I was talking about, you know, that guy. Roy. Are we in trouble for that?"

Crystal shook her head. "Naw, we didn't leave any clues. I mean, except for the pruning shears. They might have my fingerprints on them. But I only got fingerprinted twice—for kid stuff—and I was young, so they had to seal my records. So, nope. No clues."

Majorca set the plastic glass on the nightstand and sat up straight. "Oh my God, Crystal. I left two clues, huge clues. Bigger than if we wrote our names and addresses on the windows in lipstick."

"What are you talking about?"

"My book bag. I left it in the car. And Rhonda's windbreaker. Her name is on the jacket, but my name is on all my books and... all those pictures of Todd and me." She covered her face with her hands. "I'm doomed."

"Hey, Lady of Spain. Drink the rest of that magic stuff, and don't sweat it. I'll figure something out. I'm too tired now, but I'll figure something out by morning. You'll see." Crystal stood, pulled her jeans off, and slipped into her almost-dry underpants. She slid between the sheets.

Majorca leaned over and clicked the lamp off. Still wrapped in the motel towel, she slithered under the sheets, making sure to keep several inches away from Crystal. A light in the parking lot slipped through a tear in the motel's curtain, shadowing the small room with the shape of draped furniture. The honeymooners in the next room were finally silent. Somewhere in the building, a generator hummed low and steady.

"Crystal?"

"Hmmm?"

"What if Roy... you know... what if he did it to me? What would I do?"

"You'd go on living because that's the only thing you could do. You'd keep on living."

"But I'm saving myself for... you know. And if he—"

"Look, don't let some asshole ruin it for everybody. Push him into the back of your brain. Someday, you'll get revenge."

"But what if I never see him again? Now, of course, for sure, I won't. But what if..."

"Not him. But there will be somebody. Someday. And somehow, you'll get revenge."

"Crystal, I don't think I can go on. I'm so afraid he will—not him—but somebody like him will do it to me, and he'll hurt me. I can't stop thinking about it, and I'm freaking out."

"Listen to me. If you let him get to you, even if it's only in your mind, he'll be doin' that to you for the rest of your life—whether he's dead and buried or not. Like I said, push him away. Put him in a little box in the back of your brain, and someday, when you need him—when you need to be pissed enough to get revenge—you let him out. You do what you have to do to survive. But until then, forget it. Forget him. He's shit and you don't need shit."

A new sound filled the room. Heavy rain beat steadily on the motel's roof. It slicked the street, and not far away, it drowned a dark stain in a church parking lot. Crystal rolled over, faced the wall, and pulled the sheet to her chin. Majorca stared into the darkness.

"Crystal?"

"What?"

"You killed Roy."

"So?"

"Were you getting revenge?"

"I was savin' your ass. Now go to sleep."

"Crystal?"

"*Now* what?"

"Thank you."

"Go to sleep."

Chapter Nineteen

While most residents of Granisle still slept, Zoey ran along rain-washed streets with Buster happily leading the way. The exercise and peace of predawn put her in a mellow, meditative state up to the moment when the pager vibrated against her hip. Zoey kept running until she reached the sphere of light under a lamp post. She bent over, hands on her knees, long enough to catch her breath before grabbing the pager. Glancing at the screen, she did a double-take. Code 10-45 Lutheran Church on Third Street. Rose Lake.

Code 10-45? Dead Body? The image of the burning shed shimmered.

The girl? Did someone find the girl? Move her body down to Rose Lake?

Zoey radioed in. The dispatcher explained. "The sergeant says this is your case because it involves girls. At least it probably involves girls. You better get over there, like yesterday."

"Come on, Buster, we gotta go." Clipping the radio to her belt and reversing course, Zoey and Buster raced back to the apartment.

The coroner was already at the scene. Danny too. A bevy of blurry-eyed reporters, held back by two constables, stood ready with cameras and notepads.

Zoey had thrown her uniform on over the sweat from her run, and now, seeing Danny, she hoped her raincoat and the chilly, predawn mist would cover her need for a shower. She ducked under the tape and nodded to him.

Danny glanced at her and touched two fingers to the brim of his hat before pointing to the black Ford Thunderbird center stage of the scene. Glare from portable halogen lights bounced off the wet car. Guy Hendricks directed a team of officers in photographing and gathering evidence. Off to one side, on a rolling gurney, a zipped black body bag held a still form. Danny checked his notes. "What we know so far is the fellow's name is Roy Johnson. He was a medical supply salesman out of Prince George. His wallet was on the floor of the front seat."

Zoey reached up and pulled her rain hood over her head. She didn't want Danny to read her emotions. A dead body is never good. But at least this dead body wasn't a teenage girl.

Zoey stepped close enough to Danny to speak without the coroner or anyone else hearing. "The dispatcher told me Gagnon assigned this case to me. I don't understand why. And if it is my case, why is Hendricks dismantling the scene before I even arrived?"

Danny watched Hendricks and the activity around the car before answering. He kept his voice low, continued to watch Hendricks, and didn't look at Zoey. "There's something you need to know, but you didn't hear it from me, got it?"

Zoey pretended to check her notebook.

"Hendricks is dating the sergeant's daughter. Those two men are tight. You know, Sunday family dinners, golf games, the whole show. So, you might want to be careful when picking your battles."

"If Hendricks is handling the crime scene, why did the sergeant even call me out?"

"Women and kids," Danny said. "Sarge is old school. The only women he's ever worked with are office staff. But you've been placed here, and it's his job to keep you assigned. So that's what he's doing."

Zoey stared at Danny, trying to think of a response, but she couldn't.

The coroner walked to them and spoke to Zoey. "I'm about to load him. You wanna take a look before we go?"

Glad for the interruption, Zoey pursed her lips and nodded.

Danny turned to her and frowned. "Are you sure you're ready? None of them are easy, but this one is especially vile."

"Let's get on with it," Zoey said.

The coroner coughed, then looked at Zoey. "You ready?"

Why do they wonder if I'm ready?

When the corner unzipped the bag, she understood. The victim lay face-up. Blood soaked his shirt, and his neck was slashed open.

"Two stab wounds to the neck, those are the kill shots. One to the back, between the shoulder blades, guessing that was the first, and it probably only served to piss him off. I'll have more details when I get him back to the lab."

"Who found him?" Zoey asked.

"Some guy out jogging with his dog," Danny said.

Zoey pushed Buster and their morning runs from her thoughts. "Weapon?"

Danny grabbed a clear plastic bag from a portable table.

"Pruning shears?"

"Yep. Guessing by the rust on whatever isn't covered in blood, they're old."

"We can get prints..."

Danny set the bag back on the table. "We can. But we're looking at two weeks or more."

"More," the coroner said. "Prince George has the only decent forensics lab around, and they're booked solid. Best run with something else. At least for now."

"How was he positioned before he was moved?" Zoey asked.

"Front seat, face down, pants around his knees," Danny said.

"Was there evidence of—"

The corner zipped the body bag closed. "Like I said, when I get him back to the lab, I'll have more on that too. I'll let you guys know as soon as I can."

Zoey took a step back and looked up at Danny. "Pruning shears," she said. "Strange things to carry around."

"Maybe they were in the car—a weapon of convenience," Danny said.

"But," she glanced back at the vehicle, "He was a medical supply salesman. Unless there were other gardening tools in the car, I'm guessing these weren't his."

Danny pointed to a puddle of rose-colored water. "Rain washed most of the blood away, at least the blood outside of the car. But our men found this in the bin." He held out a plastic bag labeled with the scene's time, date, and location.

Zoey snapped on latex gloves and took the evidence bag from him. She pulled out a torn blouse and stared at it for a moment before dropping it into the bag and handing it back to Danny.

"There's more," he said. He gave her a second plastic bag.

Zoey turned the blood-soaked windbreaker inside out and examined the collar and hemline. An embroidered label, hand-sewn in place, read Rhonda Patterson. Under the name, a phone number.

"My mother used to sew my name in my clothes before camp," Zoey said. She dropped the windbreaker into the evidence bag, resealed it, and handed it to Danny. "Anything else?"

"This." Danny stepped to the table and pulled a plastic sheet aside. A yellow book bag, embroidered on the front with flowers and the initials TF + MF, had once been bright and pretty—girlish. Now, dark patches of blood stained the fabric. Zoey unlatched the front pocket. Danny looked over her shoulder as she shuffled through Polaroids of smiling teenagers.

"This boy with the cat and canary grin, he's the kid we met last night, the owner of that Trans Am," Zoey said. Then she pointed to a shot of a clear-skinned, blue-eyed blonde in her cheerleading outfit, gazing at Todd as he held up a baseball trophy. "And, guessing from the number of pictures of this girl and him, I'm betting she's the one he called his ex-girlfriend. The girl he was cheating on, the girl who caused a scene, and the girl who probably pushed his car into the lake."

"I wouldn't bet against that," Danny said. "What's in the main compartment?"

Zoey pulled out various colored markers, a hairbrush, one Kotex pad, a bruised apple, and three textbooks. The books belonged to Majorca Fairhaven. Zoey shook her head, replaced the items, and removed her gloves.

"We have to get this stuff to the police lab in Prince George, but I'm guessing the prints on the pruning shears will match the prints on the tree loppers used to chop the fingers off that guy in the trailer. We don't need a forensics team to tell us there were two girls in this car along with the now deceased salesman. And it doesn't take high-powered police work to figure out that one girl was trying to protect the other."

"And, given that both crimes were committed with gardening tools, we can guess the teenager living in the shed was involved," Danny said. As he pulled the plastic sheet over the book bag, Hendricks joined them.

"Look what I found." Hendricks held an open evidence bag containing a scratched chrome lighter engraved with the initials R.J. "It was on the floor, front seat, right next to his wallet. Musta fallen out when the pants came down." He tried to drop the lighter from the bag into Zoey's hand.

"Give me a second," she said. "I need to put on gloves before I handle evidence."

"I get it. New on the job, fresh out of training, following all the fancy rules. Or, maybe that's the way they do it in the big city. Maybe this is your case, but out here, we solve crimes however and whatever it takes."

Zoey glared at him, but Danny's words came back to her.

You might want to be careful when picking your battles.

Without a word, she snapped on another pair of gloves and took the bag from Hendricks. He smirked at her, turned, and walked to his squad car.

"Ignore him," Danny said. "He did that to rile you."

Zoey counted silently to three and released. She smiled at Danny. "I'm going to make sure the scene is cleared, then I have to talk to two sets of parents."

"I don't envy you that. Hey, tell you what, I'll deal with Hendricks and the rest of this. Talking to the parents is going to be a tough job."

"Danny, you're a peach. Beers on me later?"

"It's no big deal. But yes, to the beers. Um, Zoey?"

"Yes?"

"You're still new here, and you might not have heard yet, but there's something else you should know about this area. I hope it doesn't have anything to do with this case, but—"

"But what?"

"You won't see it on a map, but the locals call Highway 16 the Highway of Tears. It's because a lot of young girls, and some women, go missing on this stretch of road. Mostly Indian girls. Most of them are never found. The girl in those pictures—she's definitely not indigenous. But still..."

Chapter Twenty

Gray light filtered through the motel's ragged curtains. Crystal contemplated the bits of glitter embedded in the ceiling's popcorn texture. Beside her, Majorca snored—long, loud, deep inhales, and rattling exhales.

Lotta noise for such a little chick.

Crystal created constellations by connecting the specks of glitter with imaginary lines. A mindless activity to distract her from the ugly truth. They were, at least she was, in serious trouble.

She did something stupid, but she's only seventeen and a skinny white blonde. Good family, parents who love her. Parents who named her after their most romantic screw, for Christ's sake. She'll be peachy. But me? I'm fucked.

Majorca smacked her lips and rolled over. She curled into a fetal position, closed fist pressed against her lips, deep in sleep.

Crystal pushed the covers aside and stood. She held onto the headboard, forcing herself to focus on her knapsack, which slumped in the corner. When the swirling and nausea passed, she peed, dressed, grabbed her pack and the room key, and stepped into the cool, misty morning. Low fog and the memory of rain hung heavy. Pulling her jacket tighter, she started the walk into town.

Stopping in front of a newspaper stand, Crystal stared at the top half of the front page. A large photo showed a Trans Am parked on a grassy slope, by a lake, behind crime scene tape. On the right side of the image, two paramedics loaded a gurney into a waiting ambulance. A third EMT stood by, cradling a child's car seat in his arms. The headline read, 'Toddler Drowned in Car in Lake Babine. RCMP Investigating.'

Oh shit, oh shit, oh shit.

Crystal swallowed and glanced back toward the motel where, with luck, Majorca still slept.

Debating, she continued walking.

Beat feet outta here. They can't prove anything. Leave her. She's not my problem—not really. Shit, shit, shit.

The smell of bacon and eggs and the rumble in her stomach tugged her from her thoughts. The Roadhouse Café housed a bar with two pool tables, a small drug store, and a souvenir shop. Crystal considered spending some of her mother's remaining money on a hot breakfast, but she found herself wandering the store's aisles instead. Pausing in the cosmetics aisle, Crystal scanned a row of boxes—hair coloring for the modern woman. She selected a color and continued perusing the store. Two aisles over, she picked up a bag of Cheezies and a box of chocolate Ding Dongs.

A frazzled clerk, the only waitress working the restaurant side, rang up Crystal' purchases and then hurried back to serve her tables. Out of habit, Crystal swiped two Mars Bars, slid them into her jacket pocket, and left the store.

Traffic had picked up—miners in trucks, car-poolers, a school bus. Crystal veered off the main road and ducked into an alley. Trash bins stood in neat rows behind fences already green with honeysuckle and morning glory vines. Small rectangular back yards, mowed and edged, sported newly planted gardens—gardens that, according to seed packets mounted on sticks, would yield peas, carrots, zucchinis, and pumpkins. Parents were on their way to work, and children headed to school, leaving most of the houses empty. Except for the hum of bees and the rustle of leaves in the warm breeze, the alley was quiet. Peaceful. Still.

Only one house, in the middle of the block, buzzed with activity. Crystal stood by a garden and feigned interest in the seed packets labeling the rows. From the corner of her eye, she watched a young woman rushing two small children toward a battered Ford station wagon. The woman carried an infant in one arm and a folding shopping cart in the other. To reach the car, she had to duck under lines of laundry drying in the morning sun. She didn't stop to lock the house or close the window where a pie sat cooling on the ledge.

The woman plunked the baby down on the front passenger's seat, helped the older children climb into the back, and tossed the shopping cart in after them. She hopped in, reversed out of her drive, and sped down the alley, away from her home, away from Crystal.

Crystal waited until the dust from the Ford settled and the alley was quiet again. Then she looked at the clothes on the line. A pair of men's coveralls, a red flannel shirt, a white blouse dotted with yellow daisies, a nursing bra, and dozens of diapers flapped in the light breeze.

The shirt and blouse fit in her rucksack. She rolled the coveralls into a tight bundle and carried them under one arm.

Just a quick look around.

Toys cluttering the floor, framed wedding photos crowding an end table, a pair of men's muddy boots near the door, and clean, unfolded baby clothing piled high in a basket told the family's story. Standing in the center of the kitchen, Crystal scanned dirty dishes stacked in the sink and the remains of a hurried breakfast left on a Formica table. Four ceramic canisters in the shape of apples gathered dust on a counter. And, on top of the refrigerator, a lone coffee can. She pulled a chair across the floor, climbed up, and reached inside the can. Slipping the bills into her pocket, she scrambled down.

In the hallway, a sewing basket caught her attention. Crystal pulled scissors from under a ball of yarn, stashed them into her pack, and then slipped out the door. Pausing at the laundry line, she looked back at the house, turned, and walked to the open window. She lifted the pie from the ledge, and after draping a clean diaper over the pastry, she hurried down the alley toward the Sleepy Time Motel.

Juggling the pie and the rolled coveralls, Crystal rummaged in her pack for the room key. Before she could find it, Majorca swung the door wide. She stood in the entry, wrapped in a bedsheet, her hair tangled and frizzy, her eyes red, her face puffy.

"Where...where were you?" Her voice cracked. She gulped for breath.

"Jesus, now what?" Crystal pushed past her, set the pie on the nightstand, then sluffed out of her rucksack. She looked back at Majorca, who continued to stand in the open doorway. "I leave you alone for what? A half hour? And you get into a crying jag?" Crystal pushed the door closed. "What is it *this* time? Is it because you're hungover? Cause if it is, crying only makes it worse."

Sniffling, Majorca pointed to the television set mounted on the far wall. An ad for toilet paper rolled across the screen.

"What?"

Majorca shuffled over the carpet, dragging the sheet behind her like a wedding veil. She sat on the bed and stared up at the television. "Watch," she said.

Following a commercial for Vicks Formula 44 (*For tough coughs*) and another for Sunbeam Shavemaster Shavers (*When every minute counts*), a young reporter dressed in pressed slacks and a blazer stood in front of the same scene featured on the front page of the morning's paper. A Trans Am was parked on a grassy slope, beside a lake, behind crime scene tape. The reporter spoke into a microphone, but the sound was muted. Crystal twisted the knob.

"And that's all we have at this time, but stay tuned because we will have moment-to-moment breaking coverage of this serious story. Ed? Back to you."

Majorca clicked the TV off. "Crystal, I...I killed a little kid. He drowned. He was in the back of Todd's car. I...I didn't know. They said he was a toddler. They said his name was Bradley." Majorca's mouth twisted into a grimace, but before she could let out a wail, Crystal grabbed her shoulders and shook her.

"Get a grip. We don't have time for your hysterics."

"But what are we going to do? I killed somebody. I killed a little kid. A baby, a—"

Crystal slapped Majorca's face.

Majorca stopped cold and stared at Crystal, her mouth slack.

"Look, you little jerk, I know you're freaked out, but it was an accident. You didn't know the kid was back there. Now, if you don't get a grip, I'm gonna walk right out that door, and you're gonna face this all on your own. I don't need you. You need me. So, make up your mind." She pointed to the bathroom. "I'm gonna take a dump, and when I come back, you better either have your shit together, or I'm walkin'." She crossed to the bathroom and slammed the door behind her.

Majorca stood beside the bed in her skirt and bra, both stained with dark, rust-colored blotches. "I couldn't get the blood out," she said.

Crystal nodded. "I figured that. But don't worry, I brought you some new clothes."

Majorca's face lit up. "Really?"Crystal grinned and pulled the daisy-dotted blouse from her pack. She unrolled the coveralls and laid them on the bed.

"But, Crystal—"

"The pants are probably too long, but we can roll them up, or I can cut them off. I have scissors."

Majorca started to object, but Crystal turned away and pulled things from her knapsack. With her back to Majorca, she continued talking. "I have a plan. We're gonna hide until things calm down. Then, when things mellow out, we'll go to the police and tell them what happened. You pushed the guy's car into the lake because you were heartbroken. But you didn't know anything about that little kid. You feel horrible, and you'll probably be scarred for life. But it was an accident. Pure and simple." She turned to face Majorca.

Majorca raised her hand as if in a classroom.

Crystal nodded.

"Two questions. First, how will we know when everything has calmed down? And second, even if it was an accident, I'm still responsible, right?""First, we know things are mellow when the stupid newspaper and television reporters stop treating it like such a big deal. And second, you're how old?"

"Seventeen. Eighteen in two months."

"So, you're a minor. You won't get charged like an adult. They can't even keep your file open. You'll do community service or something, that's all." Crystal tossed the Cheezies and the Ding Dongs on the bed.

"What about you? I know you're a year older than me, and you killed that guy."

"It was self-defense. He told us he was gonna rape both of us and then kill us."

"He didn't say that."

"Who knows if he did or didn't?"

Majorca twirled a strand of blonde hair between two fingers. "But—"

"But what? It's a perfect plan. Gets us both out of trouble and gives everybody time to chill out."

"Where will we go?"

Crystal heaved a sigh. "To my gran's. What part of this is so hard for you?"

"But they probably already know who we are," Majorca said. "They're probably going to start putting our pictures in the newspaper and on television. My poor parents..."

"I'm way ahead of you." Crystal pulled the scissors and the box of hair coloring from her knapsack. "We're both gonna have really—like really—short hair. And yours will be bright red."

Majorca reached up and stroked her hair. "I'm not sure, Crystal. Todd loves my hair. He always says how pretty it is in the sunshine."

"Fuck Todd." Crystal whirled around. Her heavy black braid slapped her back. "You think I like the idea of cutting mine? The thing is, we have bigger issues than your Goldilocks right now. Besides, it's hair, it'll grow back."

Majorca picked up the box of dye. "Red Wonder. I guess I can try being a Red Wonder, at least for a while."

"Far out!" Crystal clapped her hands once. "A cut and color, and we're on our way. But first, we have pie!"

Crystal stood and appraised Majorca. "Except for the red hair, you kinda look like that chick on the Beverley Hillbillies."

Majorca adjusted a buckle on the coveralls. After Crystal's handiwork with the scissors, the pant legs ended at her knees. The flowery blouse bloomed out from under the coveralls' canvas bib, and her wet, red hair, cut to two inches all around, stuck out like toothpicks on a cheese ball. "I look more like a clown," she said.

"Damn it, I really like this shirt." Crystal pulled a Pink Floyd t-shirt over her head and tossed it onto the bed. She slipped into the stolen flannel shirt and rolled the sleeves to her elbows.

After packing her knapsack and a quick look around the room, Crystal held the door for Majorca. "Come on, Hillbilly Clown Chick, let's go. We're gonna have to walk the back streets until we find a bus stop. Could take hours, so we should—"

The thumping and squeaking of bed springs stopped her. She placed one finger over her lips, then pointed to the car parked by the motel.

Rain had smeared the words "Just Married," leaving the Chevy's rear window to resemble the results of a massive seagull bombing.

"Shush. Get in," Crystal whispered. Before tossing it into the back seat, she rummaged through her rucksack until she found the stolen scissors. She freed the tin cans from the bumper and then crouched under the steering wheel and fiddled with wires. The car grumbled to life.

Majorca jumped into the passenger's seat and pulled the door closed. "How'd you do that?"

"I'll show you sometime. But right now, we gotta get outta here. Fast."

The vehicle pitched and yawed out of the lot, but minutes later, Crystal managed to steer the newlywed's car onto the road. She stomped on the gas, and soon they flew south on Highway 16.

Majorca rolled her window down, stuck her head out, and yelled. "Yee haw!"

Crystal grinned and shook her head. "Dweeb," she said.

Chapter Twenty-One

Before Zoey reached her VW, her pager vibrated. She stopped walking and called in on her radio.

"Constable Zoey Simard. We have a report of a stolen vehicle at the Sleepy Time Motel in Rose Lake. That's down the road a bit from your crime scene. The guy who called it in said something about two girls in a room. Of course, some of the other guys are close by, too. But I thought you might want to check it out first."

Zoey thanked the dispatcher and suggested they grab lunch sometime—her treat.

The dispatcher, a woman in her late fifties, gave Zoey enough time to reach the motel and investigate before issuing the wider call.

Zoey jogged back to the scene and pulled Danny aside. "Let's let Hendricks handle this. I got a call from dispatch."

"What about talking to the families?"

"I'd like to follow up on this call first. I have a feeling we might get lucky."

A short interview with the motel manager confirmed what the dispatcher had said. More had happened at the Sleepy Time Motel than simply a stolen vehicle.

"So, my guests, newlyweds, real nice kids, came into the office this morning all upset. Seems their car was missing. Somebody cut the tin cans from the back bumper and drove off.

"What about the other guests last night?" Zoey asked.

"Those two girls I told the police lady on the phone about. Of course, when I heard about the stolen car, I went up to check their room. Number Five. They were gone, and the room...it looks pretty strange."

"Did you touch anything?" Danny said.

The man shook his head. "I pulled the door closed, offered that nice young couple a free night's stay, and called you folks."

Zoey thanked the motel manager, gave him her card, and asked him to refrain from talking with anyone else about the matter until the police had time to investigate.

"No worries there," the manager said. "Stuff like this is bad for business. Word does travel fast, but I'd be happy if nobody hears about it." He handed the key to Number Five to Danny, and shuffled back to Reception.

Snapping on latex gloves, they entered room Number Five. Danny flicked on a light and whistled. Clothing was tossed over furniture, the television, and across the unmade bed. An empty Ding Dong box, crumbled candy bar wrappers, Orange Crush cans, and empty junk food packages littered the dresser.

Zoey lifted a wrinkled skirt and peered at a yellow flower embroidered on one panel. "I'm pretty sure this is a blood stain," she said. She pointed to a dark blotch. "And I'm guessing someone tried washing it out, but obviously, wasn't successful."

Danny crossed the room and poked his head into the bathroom. "Look in here," he said.

Zoey stood at the bathroom door scanning the mess. Blonde hair clippings carpeted the floor. An empty plastic bottle, dark with the gooey remains of hair coloring, lay in the sink. The box, tossed in a trash can, showed a smiling model with cherry red hair. Zoey removed the box and pulled out a pair of dye-coated plastic gloves. A dark, snake-like coil lay at the bottom of the trash can. Zoey looked over at Danny. He stepped closer and directed his flashlight on the coil. Zoey picked up one end between two fingers and lifted it, slowly, from the can. A long black braid. She dropped the braid into an evidence bag.

"The girl from the shed?" Danny asked.

Zoey nodded. "That's my bet. I thought the two of them might be together, and this is our proof. We know, at least we're fairly certain, that Majorca Fairhaven pushed that boy's vehicle into the lake, that she was the intended victim of Mr. Roy Johnson. And we can make a strong case that the girl who protected Majorca stabbed the attacker with a tool from her mother's garden shed. What we know for sure is that they're running. And they're running scared enough to destroy their pride and joy."

"Hair? Is it that big of a deal?" Danny asked.

"Definitely. To a teenage girl, her hair is her crown. It's a form of identity, a symbol of her sensuality and sexuality. If the girl with the black hair is indigenous, that braid may have symbolized her heritage. In any case, both girls made a huge sacrifice here."

"Maybe Majorca knows about the drowned toddler," Danny said. "It's all over the news. Maybe she feels responsible even if she didn't know about the child in the back seat when she pushed that car."

Pulling her gloves off, Zoey stepped out of the bathroom. "I think you're right. We know the two girls hooked up and got a ride in Mr. Johnson's car. He tried to jump Majorca, but the other girl rescued her by killing him, and now, they've both committed murders. Or, at least, they think they have, even though a court would probably rule otherwise. I'm gonna call for a team to process the rest of this."

"And then, the parents," Danny said, his expression grim.

"Yes," Zoey said, "and then, the parents."

Chapter Twenty-Two

Zoey sat in the Fairhaven's driveway with the engine idling as she scanned the surrounding neighborhood. Canadian middle class. Pride of ownership. Lawns mowed and edged. Weed-free flower beds, planted with care. Bird baths, garden gnomes, and shrubbery, shaped and pruned. Zoey thought of the weapon used to stab the traveling salesman—pruning shears. She flashed on Hendricks' grin as he'd held up the bloody loppers used to chop tree limbs and two fingers.

The Fairhaven's house could have been on the cover of a craft magazine—white siding, green trim around the windows, a white and yellow wreath hanging on the front door, and a hand-painted sign reading Welcome to Our Home. Two green rocking chairs with a low green and white table between them invited neighborly chats over lemonade.

The only things missing are the picket fence and the Golden Retriever.

Zoey sighed and turned the key. Most of the time, she enjoyed the RCMP's policy of one cop to a car, but now, Danny's presence would have been welcomed. Even though he'd only been on the force a few months more than her, he'd already picked up valuable tricks and techniques. And, unlike the other men on the force, he shared them with her. He'd suggested that she call the school and ask if the girls were in class before speaking with the parents. A good suggestion.

According to the attendance monitor, Rhonda Patterson was in class, hard at work on a history exam. Majorca Fairhaven had not attended homeroom that morning and was absent from her first class. Zoey adjusted her hat and stepped out of the car.

A pleasant woman in her early forties, wearing a floral print housedress, answered the door. "Hello, dear. Are you collecting for the Charity Fund? Hold on a minute, I'll get my purse."

"No. No ma'am. I'm with the RCMP. Constable Zoey Simard. I'm here on official police business. May I come in?"

Ruth Fairhaven tilted her head in question but held the door for Zoey.

Like their front yard, the Fairhaven's living room reflected care and personal investment. An oval braided rug rested on the polished hardwood floor. Hand-crocheted doilies covered the backs and arms of overstuffed chairs, and a cut-glass bowl on a coffee table held assorted wrapped candies. Vases of early summer flowers decorated end tables, and a dozen framed photographs crowded the mantle over a tidy brick fireplace.

Zoey walked to the hearth and scanned the prints. A sepia-toned wedding photo in an oval frame showed a younger, thinner Mrs. Fairhaven standing next to a tall young man who appeared, to Zoey, both proud and nervous—maybe out of his comfort zone in a tailored suit and tie.

Next to the wedding photo, a black-and-white picture showed a beaming toddler sitting in a high chair, in front of a smashed cake. Her face was smeared with frosting, and her party hat read Happy #2. A colored photo, framed in ivory, highlighted a blonde, blue-eyed girl wearing a cheerleading uniform. She was laughing and flashing a two-fingered peace symbol at the photographer.

Another frame held a professional portrait of a man, Mrs. Fairhaven, and a young blonde girl, all dressed for a special occasion and posing together as a family.

Ruth Fairhaven coughed.

Zoey spun around. "I'm sorry. I was admiring your beautiful family."

"Can I get you something, Constable? Coffee? Tea?" Zoey shook her head. "I need to ask you some questions about your daughter."

"Majorca? Is she all right? Did something happen?"

"Mrs. Fairhaven, can we sit down?"

Sparing the woman the gruesome details, at least for a little longer, Zoey only said that Majorca wasn't in class and that her book bag had been found in an abandoned car two towns down the highway.

"When did you last see or hear from your daughter, Mrs. Fairhaven?"

Ruth's face paled, and she wrung her hands in her lap. "I...she called right before dinner last night. She said she was going to stay with Rhonda. Rhonda Patterson, her best friend. I thought the girls went to school this morning. What's happened to my baby?"

"Please don't panic, Mrs. Fairhaven. There's probably a simple explanation. I need a little information from you so that I can, we can, locate your daughter."

"We?"

"The RCMP, ma'am."

Ruth jumped up and headed for the kitchen. "I have to call her father."

Zoey stood. "Please, Mrs. Fairhaven, first help me by answering a few questions."

Ruth returned to her chair, her face flushed, lines of worry creasing her brow.

"Tell me about your daughter. What are her hobbies? Does she, for example, like to garden?"

"Gosh, no. Majorca is a little lady. She hates getting dirty, always has, I can't get her near the garden. She likes to sew, crochet, and embroider. Things like that."

"Boyfriend?"

Ruth Fairhaven frowned. "She likes that boy, Todd Furlow. But her father and I hope that's a passing crush."

"Why is that?"

A shadow passed over Ruth's expression, and she looked down. "We want our little girl to be happy, and Todd... he seems like the sort of boy who might break a girl's heart. That's all." She covered her face with her hands and stifled a sob.

"A couple more things, Mrs. Fairhaven."

Ruth looked up and nodded. She pulled a crumpled tissue from her dress pocket and dabbed her eyes.

"Does Majorca have other close friends besides Rhonda? Anyone, she might say, take a little trip with?"

"Majorca is a popular girl. She's a cheerleader and she gets good grades. She has lots of friends. But...a trip? To where? This is the end of the term, and she's very excited about graduation. Where would she go?"

"I'm sure everything is fine. She's probably shopping. Or maybe holed up in a café, studying. One final thing, Mrs. Fairhaven. Do you have a recent photograph of your daughter that I can borrow?"

Zoey left the house with the now unframed colored photo of the laughing, blue-eyed girl. Two blocks away, going too fast for a suburban street, a tan sedan flew past her patrol car. Zoey knew the car would pull into the Fairhaven's driveway. Majorca's father was home.

Chapter Twenty-Three

Five cars and a cement truck followed close behind the two-toned Chevrolet with the smeared back window. One of the vehicles edged to the left, crossed the yellow line, and tried to pass, but with each attempt, a logging truck, a mining lorry, or a stream of cars blocked the way. The driver laid on his horn. Majorca swiveled in the passenger's seat in time to see him flip Crystal the bird.

"Crystal, maybe we should go a little faster," she said, "We're holding up a lot of traffic."

Crystal pressed her lips together in a tight line, hunched forward, and forced the accelerator to the floorboard. The engine protested with a grinding screech.

The driver behind them took another risk. With his horn blaring, he raced around the Chevy, dodging back into the lane with barely enough time to escape a head-on collision. Crystal yanked the wheel to the right and then back to the left. More horns. More rude gestures.

"Honest, Crystal. Go faster."

"I can't."

"Why?"

"Because I'm stuck in this gear."

Majorca stared at Crystal—at the beads of sweat crossing her brow, at her hands clutching the steering wheel so tight her knuckles blanched. "Crystal, do you know how to drive?"

"I am driving."

"Not very good."

"Fuck off."

Another driver, two cars back, accelerated and blasted around the three cars in front of him. Another near collision. More horns.

Majorca gripped the dashboard and stared straight ahead. Then she pointed to a road sign. "There, a scenic overlook, at the next turn-off. You should take it."

"We haven't even gone ten kilometers yet."

Majorca raised her voice over the racing engine and the cacophony of horns. "I don't care, I have to pee. I mean, I really, *really* have to pee. Pull over. Now!"

"Jesus," Crystal muttered. She tapped the blinker. Driving the car off the highway, she headed into the turn-off and steered directly toward a wooden guard rail separating a gravel lot from the overlook's cliff. Majorca screamed.

Crystal slammed her foot on the brake. The car jumped forward, stuttered, and died.

Breathing heavy, Crystal continued to grip the steering wheel. Majorca slapped her hand over her heart and closed her eyes. They'd stopped one car length from the railing—one and a half car lengths from the cliff that plunged hundreds of feet over rocks and boulders into a dense, dark forest.

Finally, Crystal spoke, her voice strained. "Not. A. Word," she said.

Majorca wandered from behind a stand of trees, fastening the buckles on the coveralls. "If I knew we'd be roughing it, I would have packed tissue."

"I thought you were faking it. You know, about needing to pee," Crystal said. "Thought you wanted to get me off the road."

"That was the plan at first, but when I thought we were going over the cliff, I almost—"

"I told you, we're not gonna talk about that," Crystal said. She sat on a flat boulder, face to the sky, eyes closed. "Besides, we can't drive that car anymore 'cause I'm pretty sure I wrecked it."

"You didn't wreck it." Crystal sat next to her. Drawing her legs up, she rested her chin on her knees. "You stalled it. It'll be fine in a little while. If we weren't so close to the cliff, we could push it to get it started."

Crystal opened her eyes and squinted at Majorca. "How'd you know that?"

"My dad's a mechanic, and he tells me stuff." She waited a beat, then added, "But he didn't teach me how to hot wire a car."

Crystal smirked. "I learned that from watching this guy my mom knows. Clive. Stealing cars is the only thing that bastard is good for."

They sat together, letting the sun warm their skin, listening to the twitter of birds and the hum of bees dancing in nearby wildflowers. After a few minutes, Crystal nudged Majorca's arm. "So, do you, like...do you know how to drive?"

Majorca nodded. "My dad showed me. I don't do it much because, of course, Todd does all the driving. But I know how."

"Doesn't really matter. We can't take that car, even if we can get it started."

"Why not? I can drive it."

"Because by now, those lovebirds have figured out their honeymoon ride was pinched. For sure, the cops are looking for it. We have to come up with a new plan."

Majorca's brow furrowed. She chewed on her thumbnail for a moment and then snapped her fingers. "I have an idea," she said. "My cousin, Randy, lives in Burns Lake. He drives a beer truck—makes deliveries to all the bars and restaurants from Smithers to Prince George. He drives up and down this highway all the time."

"I can't believe you have a cousin who drives a beer truck. Why didn't you say that before?"

"I didn't think about him. He was in Vietnam, and he's a little, um, a little jumpy. My mum and dad don't invite him to the house much because they say he has "issues." But he's always been nice to me. We have to get to Burns Lake, and then I'm sure he'll give us a ride, probably all the way to your grandma's house."

Crystal stared at Majorca. "That's totally brilliant. What cop would suspect that a couple of juvies were hiding out in a beer truck?" She slid from the rock and started for the car.

Majorca's lower lip shot out in a pout. "Crystal, are we juvenile delinquents?"

Crystal stopped walking and turned to face Majorca. "What do you think?"

"I mean, the whole car thing—Todd's car thing—was sort of an accident, and Roy, it was, you know… self-defense. You said it yourself."

Shielding her eyes from the sun, Crystal squinted at Majorca. She let out a long sigh. "You're right," she said. "I was joking around. We're not delinquents. As far as anyone knows, we're nice, normal people."

"Are you sure, Crystal?"

"I'm sure. Now, let's go. We got a beer truck to catch." Crystal gathered her jacket and knapsack from the back seat and walked toward the road.

Majorca continued to sit on the rock.

"Come on," Crystal said. "What are you waiting for?"

"Crystal, it just hit me. We didn't even make it to Decker Lake in a car. It's still at least three kilometers from here, and Burns Lake is another eight, maybe ten kilometers after that. How are we going to get all the way to Burns Lake without the police seeing us?"

Crystal stood with her hands on her hips. She scowled at Majorca. "I have no idea. But I *do know* that if we stay here, we'll get busted for sure. I don't think we have much of a choice at this point. Do you?"

Grumbling to herself, Majorca joined her. Halfway across the highway, Crystal stopped.

"You know," she said. "You made some good sense. For the first time. We need to give the police a distraction, something to keep them busy until we reach your cousin."

"I make a lot of good sense. I'm—"

"Leave it. The thing is, I have a plan to slow the cops down."

They hid in a stand of trees on the far side of the highway and watched plumes of black smoke swirl from the Chevy's shell. Flames shot from the windows, and small explosions sent sprays of sparks toward the sky.

"I didn't know there would be so much smoke," Crystal said. "I thought it would only be, you know, fire."

"I don't feel so bad about the car," Majorca said. "But I didn't like setting that girl's wedding garter on fire."

"We needed the fuel," Crystal said. "Don't worry. The guy's a horn dog. They don't need a fancy garter to get going." She scanned the highway. "But we better move before someone reports that fire."

The morning traffic had cleared, and except for a single tractor lumbering in the distance, the road was empty. Crystal and Majorca walked alone and unseen down Highway 16.

When the sun peaked directly overhead, their pace slowed. Majorca swiped the back of her hand across her brow. "I'm so hot, Crystal. And I'm hungry and thirsty. And these coveralls are heavy and itchy. How much farther 'til we get there?"

"Geeze, what a whiner. How the hell would I know how far it is?"

"You don't have to swear. I was only asking."

"Sorry. Look, it can't be too far. There's gotta be a café in town. I've got a little cash, so we can get lunch and cool down."

"What if somebody recognizes us?"

"Don't sweat it. They're probably looking for a cute little blonde, not a creepy-looking hillbilly clown."

"Crystal!" Majorca punched Crystal's arm, not hard. "You're a jerk, you know that?"

"Takes one to know one."

Bantering back and forth, they continued their trek along the road for ten minutes until Crystal stopped and pointed to a low, one-story brick building. A battered Ford pickup, parked in front, cast shadows across a faded wooden sign welcoming weary travelers to the Lazy Daze Motor Inn. A man wearing dirty boots, jeans, a flannel shirt, and a tattered cowboy hat sat on a bench on the motel's porch. He used a rag to polish a handgun.

"Come on," Crystal said. "Let's see if he knows about a café around here."

"I don't wanna talk to a guy with a gun."

"Fine by me. You stay here in the sun."

Crystal ambled across the dirt parking lot to the motel. "Hey!" She called out and waved to the man. He looked up and nodded to her. "Hey, yourself," he said.

"No choice now," Majorca complained as she followed Crystal across the dusty lot to the motel.

Chapter Twenty-Four

FOUR POLICE VEHICLES, ONE sporting a swiveling hula girl, filled the first row of parking spots in front of Earl's Diner. Tucking Majorca's photo into a folder, Zoey grabbed her purse and locked her car. The past two days had been rough—from mind-numbing boredom, to a fire, a drugged-out man lacking two fingers, two dead bodies, a potentially missing teenage girl, a second girl who was most certainly missing, who may have been raped and was undoubtedly hurt. Zoey bit her lower lip.

Maybe I need a hula girl, too.

Danny waved to her from a table at the back of the diner. She ignored the snide looks from three other offices as she passed their table. The sergeant had been right—it would take some members of the force more time than others to get used to a female constable. As much as she wanted to win their approval and become part of the team, Zoey didn't know how to make that happen.

They'll be happy if I fail. But I don't plan to fail.

She slid into a booth opposite Danny with her back to the other officers. Once settled, she passed the folder across to him.

"You talk to the parents?" he asked.

"Two mothers so far."

"And?"

"Mrs. Fairhaven, mother of the girl in the Polaroids, had no idea her daughter was missing. The last time they spoke, her daughter, Majorca, said she was spending the night with her best friend, Rhonda. She told Mrs. Fairhaven they planned to pull an all-nighter and study for their final exams."

"Rhonda," Danny said. "Isn't that the name on the jacket we found in the car?"

Zoey nodded. "I also spoke with Rhonda's mother, Mrs. William Patterson. Turns out, Majorca *was* studying with her daughter last night, but she headed home around dinner time. It was chilly, so Rhonda loaned her friend the jacket. Majorca had promised to return it when they met up at school today. Apparently, it was Rhonda's favorite."

Danny picked up the folder. "Clearly, Rhonda won't be getting her favorite jacket back," he said.

Zoey placed her order while Danny examined the glossy photo. When the waitress left, he leaned in close and tapped the picture. "So, you were right, the book bag is hers, she's the one in the Polaroids, and she was the girl in the front seat of that car." He pushed a salt shaker back and forth between his hands. "So, to review, she starts walking home from her best friend's house wearing her friend's windbreaker. She catches her boyfriend with another girl, and she's mad, so she pushes his car into the lake, and then, somehow, she ends up in a salesman's car. And someone else was in that car."

The waitress placed a grilled cheese sandwich and an order of fries in front of Zoey. Zoey smiled at her but didn't reach for the plate. "Mrs. Fairhaven told me her daughter is a little lady. She doesn't like getting dirty. She prefers hobbies like knitting, crocheting, and embroidery. According to Ruth Fairhaven, Majorca would never consider gardening."

Danny filched a fry from Zoey's plate. "That leaves us with someone, most likely another teenage girl, who doesn't mind handling gardening tools."

Zoey pushed her plate aside. "I'm going to talk to those folks with the burned out-building. If their daughter was living in that shed, and she's still missing..."

Danny tossed a bill on the table. "I'm coming with you."

They parked their cars on the street and stood together on the sidewalk, surveying the area. Although the neighborhood was in a poorer district of

Granisle, most of the houses and yards reflected a certain amount of care and pride. The Harsch residence, however, lacked care, pride, and even cleanliness.

The yard consisted of hard-packed dirt overgrown with weeds and occasional patches of thirsty grass. Bits of loose trash and a mound of plastic bags were piled next to a faded yellow single-wide trailer. Crows picked at the bags, and garbage scattered by the birds littered the yard and street.

The trailer sat on a concrete pad in the middle of the lot. A blue plastic tarp stretched over half of the roof while a moldy canvas sheet covered the rest. Vinyl siding bowed away from the house, exposing patches of dirty pink insulation. Pieces of plywood, nailed haphazardly around two front windows, failed to keep torn screens in place. The front door, bashed open by police, hung on one hinge. Limp crime scene tape fluttered like abandoned crepe paper after a party.

Across the patchy yard, the wet and charred remnants of the garden shed remained. And several yards from the fire scene, a rusting car sat propped on cement blocks, tireless, with two broken windows and one open door. Zoey glanced at Danny. He shook his head and looked into the distance.

"Poor kid," Zoey muttered.

The bell didn't work, so Danny knocked on the door jam. No answer. He tried again, this time knocking harder.

Zoey peeked behind the shattered door. The living room was something out of a cheap horror film. Blood splatter had dried on the floor and on the arm of a ratty-looking recliner. A tray table spilled drug paraphernalia—some legal, some not. Even from her position at the front door, the smell of garbage and something more foul, overwhelmed her. Zoey backed up a step and took a breath of fresh air.

"They're home," Danny said.

"Hey, what do you pigs want? We already told them other cops we didn't start that fire." Belly fat rolled between the man's t-shirt and his sweatpants. Black hair hung greasy over his brow. He held a can of Schlitz beer in his left hand. His right hand was bandaged in thick white gauze.

Zoey stepped forward. "Mr. Harsch?"

"Naw. Ain't no mister Harsch." He glared at Zoey, then looked at Danny. "How come you bringed a secretary over here?" he asked.

Zoey cleared her throat and pulled her badge from her pocket. "Constable Zoey Simard, Sir. My partner, Constable Danny O'Brien, and I are here to ask you and the woman who lives here a few questions about a missing teenage girl. We believe she was living in your garden shed."

Clive's jaw went slack, and he reached to scratch his belly. "Fuck." He stared at the gauze wrapping his hand. "Keep forgettin' this." He turned toward the back of the trailer and yelled. "Hey, Wanda-Lynn. Cops. They wanna talk about yer brat." Clive shuffled across the room and eased into the recliner. "Wanda-Lynn," he yelled again, "more pigs."

Crystal's mother lumbered from the bedroom, scratching her bottom and yawning. She wore a cotton skirt, stretched tight over her belly, and a white blouse, misbuttoned and layered in stains. A strand of oily gray hair stuck to her cheek. She reached up, plucked it off, and tucked it behind her ear.

"Don't mind him. He's grumpy on account a he lost somethin." She pointed to the mound of gauze on Clive's hand and broke into laughter, which turned to a ragged cough.

While Danny stood back and remained silent, Zoey introduced herself again and asked, "Mrs. Harsch?"

Crystal's mother nodded. With a loud sigh, she dropped onto the sofa. Zoey glanced at Danny, who was staring at the white lump at the end of Clive's right wrist.

"Mrs. Harsch, we understand that a teenage girl was living in the shed in your backyard. Was that your daughter?"

Wanda-Lynn shrugged her shoulders. "That kid's a funny one. Real anti-social that one is."

"You do know that the shed burned to the ground last night, right?"

"Place stinks 'cause a that shit they sprayed all over it."

Zoey curled her hands into fists, slowly exhaled, and uncurled them.

Focusing on Clive, Danny stepped forward. "Sir, I know you were treated at Mercy Hospital, and it's probably all in your report, but could you tell me what happened to your hand?"

Clive snorted. "Some asshole chopped my fingers off. Two of 'em."

"How?"

Clive shrugged. "Don't know. But them other cops, they said they had the weapon. Ask 'em."

Danny nodded and stepped back.

"Mrs. Harsch," Zoey said, "What's your daughter's name?"

"Crystal. Crystal Lynn Harsch. The Lynn is after me, Wanda-Lynn, her mama." She coughed, hacked up something, and spit it into an ashtray sitting on the sofa's arm. "Clive, baby. Toss me a smoke."

Zoey let her gaze wander around the trailer. "Do you have any photos of your daughter?"

Crystal's mother struggled to strike a match. Concentrating on the task, she cocked her head toward the kitchen. "We got one on the refrigerator, been there a while."

Zoey glanced at Danny. He crossed the room to the kitchen.

"Do you know where Crystal is, Mrs. Harsch?"

Wanda-Lynn blinked and tilted her head to one side. "You know, I don't know where she went off to." She narrowed her eyes and set her jaw. "But when she comes back around, she's gonna be real, *real* sorry."

Zoey forced herself to remain professional. "And why is that, Mrs. Harsch?"

"Little bitch stole my smokes—whole carton of 'em. You know how much smokes cost these days?"

"That's from the government taxin' regular folks to death," Clive said.

Standing on the curb beside their vehicles, Zoey and Danny inhaled deep breaths. Even the smoke-tinged air from the fire was fresher than where they'd been.

"What was the kitchen like?" Zoey asked.

"If I told you, you'd have nightmares," Danny said. "Here." He handed her a wallet-sized print.

"Jesus," Zoey whispered. She stared at the child in the faded school photo. Six or seven with stringy black hair, wide brown eyes, a faded purple spot on one cheek. A bruise? A dirty white blouse at least two sizes too large hung from thin shoulders. A little girl in pain.

Chapter Twenty-Five

THE MAN PUSHED HIS cowboy hat to the back of his head and squinted. Crystal smiled wide and waved again.

Returning her smile, he showed off three top teeth and a crooked row of bottoms. With a quick salute, he stood. "Welcome to the Lazy Daze Motor Inn. Decker Lake's finest, and only motor inn. Vernon Wilbey, General Manager and Head of Security at your service."

"It certainly looks like you've got a great place here, Mr. Wilbey." Crystal gestured toward the warped screen door and broken steps leading to the porch. Any sarcasm was lost on Vernon.

"Yes ma'am, this establishment has been around since right after the war. It used to house soldiers comin' home. Gave 'em a chance to get a rest and clean up before seein' their families again. Still in the original condition." Vernon stood a little taller.

Majorca stepped next to Crystal and, shielding her eyes from the sun, she stared at Vernon and the Lazy Daze Motor Inn.

"Wow, that's cool," Crystal said. "Would you mind showing us around? We're on a little vacation, but we're thinking of maybe stopping for a rest and maybe a clean-up. Maybe grab a bite at a local café."

"My pleasure. You ladies follow me." Vernon clomped across the porch and pushed the screen door open.

"We're going to Burns Lake, to my cousin's place, so he can drive us to Vanderhoof so—"

Crystal slammed into Majorca before she could finish. "Shut up," she said.

"What are we doing?" Majorca moved close to Crystal.

Following Vernon into the reception area, Crystal whispered, "We're checking things out. Chill out."

Vernon clicked on an overhead light. "This is where I greet my guests," he said. Placing the rag and gun next to a stack of scenic postcards, he leaned on the counter and pointed to a corner where a rusting cart held a coffee maker, plastic boxes of creamer, sugar, and packets of artificial sweetener. A stack of paper plates and a tower of Styrofoam cups sat next to a toaster oven on a TV tray table. A red and green plaid tea towel covered the table. "Over there is where we serve continental breakfast. We start at seven every morning. When we have guests."

"Very fancy," Crystal said.

Vernon beamed. "I keep it all clean and ready to go 'cause ya never know when a group of visitors might need a nice place."

Majorca wandered across the room to a plastic chair beside a table littered with magazines and old newspapers. She sat and, with a sigh, closed her eyes.

"She okay?" Vernon asked.

Crystal smiled and batted her lashes at Vernon. "Don't worry about her. She's fine. But I want to know more about this establishment. How do you keep your guests safe? I mean, there's a lot of crime out there these days."

Vernon frowned. "That's true. And that's why the owners of the Lazy Daze hired me to be Head of Security." He tapped the gun. "This here is Zelda. I keep her loaded at all times. Three bullets. Keep her right here where I can grab her whenever I need to protect our guests." He pointed to the counter. "Plus, I got a roll a that silver tape in the drawer in case I have to retain any criminals."

"That's so smart," Crystal said. "I bet the police are happy you're on their side, armed and ready."

Glancing in both directions, Vernon walked around the counter and stood close to Crystal. He lowered his voice. "Here's the thing," he said. "They, the cops I mean, don't know nothin' about Zelda. The less they know, the better. I don't need some 'Big Brother' from the government tellin' me what to do. They say to store firearms unloaded. I say, what good is that? I keep this girl loaded at all times. Three bullets—ready to go."

"Cool," Crystal said. She studied the gun, then looked up at Vernon. "Why don't you load it all the way?"

Vernon glanced at the floor and rubbed the back of his neck. "Ammo is expensive, you know. And besides, I don't need more 'an one shot." He looked back at Crystal, lifted his chin, inhaled, and puffed his chest out.

"Anybody come in here and try to mess with me or my guests, one shot. All it takes."

"Wow," Crystal repeated. "So, what are the other two bullets for?"

"Oh, them," Vernon said, "they're just for backup."

Following Vernon's directions, Crystal and Majorca walked a half mile to the café located on the outskirts of Decker Lake. Majorca chose a table close to the window before heading to the washroom. Crystal counted out the last of her mother's money and the money she'd taken from the coffee can. She made two piles of dollars and coins on the table. When Majorca returned, she pointed to one of the piles. "We can both have the lunch special," she said. "And coffee, and we can split a piece of pie."

"What about the other money?"

Crystal winked at Majorca. "We're gonna get a room at the Lazy Daze Motor Inn."

"I don't see how that will get us any closer to Vanderhoof. Shouldn't we spend the money on bus tickets?"

"Have you seen a bus go by or even a bus stop?" Majorca's brows furrowed. "Crystal, I'm freaked out. Even with these clothes and haircuts, I think the police will recognize us. Maybe we should turn ourselves in and hope for the best.

"Are you out of your mind?" Crystal leaned across the table and kept her voice soft. "You dumped a car in the lake and drowned a little kid. I killed a guy and stole some clothes and stuff. We stole a car. And then, we set the car on fire.

Now, you wanna wander up to some cop and say, 'excuse me, Constable, we're criminals, and we'd appreciate a ride home.' Are you *serious*?"

"Alright then, what are we gonna do?"

"What can I get you girls?" The waitress scratched her head with the eraser end of her pencil and waited.

"Two daily specials," Crystal said. "And two cups of coffee, with crème, and one slice of pie." She glanced at Majorca and raised an eyebrow.

"I don't care," Majorca mumbled. "You decide."

"Alright then, one slice of chocolate pie."

"That's two daily specials, two coffees, and a slice of pie for each of you, right?"

"No," Crystal said. "We're gonna split the pie. We're on diets."

Grumbling about diets, the waitress headed for the kitchen.

Crystal watched her walk away and then turned back to Majorca. "Listen, I've been thinking. Maybe you're right about the police. Not about turning ourselves in—that's plain nuts. But, for sure, they're looking for us. So, we need a car, right?"

Majorca didn't answer. She picked at a hangnail and pouted.

"And if we can't get a car, we'll end up walking. And if we're walking, we need to stay off the road. First, because the cops might see us, and also, that highway is dangerous. Lots of guys like Roy on that road. So maybe we should head through the forest. But, of course, there are all kinds of scary things in the woods, too."

Looking up, Majorca asked, "Scary things like what?"

"You know, bears and coyotes and weirdo men."

Majorca's eyes widened. "Weirdo men?"

"So, we need a car, and we have to drive it as far as we can—hopefully all the way to your cousin's. But if we have to walk through the woods, we need protection."

"Protection?" Majorca stared slack-jawed at Crystal.

"Here we go, girls. Two specials and a slice of chocolate pie to share."

Crystal winked at Majorca. "Yummy," she said, "I'm starving!"

Chapter Twenty-Six

Soft blue curls framed her face. Short and round, with a ready smile, she greeted Zoey at the front door of Granisle High School.

"Hello, dear. You must be the lady constable my son told me about. Come in, come in." She held the door wide and stepped aside.

Zoey glanced at the name tag dangling from a beaded lanyard around the woman's neck. The card read Hildy Hendricks, Volunteer. Zoey grimaced. Never in a thousand years would she have thought Guy's mother would look, or sound, like this woman.

Hildy Hendricks smiled up at Zoey. "My son is a policeman, you know. Like his father and his grandfather. All the men in our family serve in the RCMP."

"And the women in your family? What do they do?" Zoey immediately regretted the question.

Mrs. Hendricks patted Zoey's arm. "Why, the girls are mothers, of course." She turned and waddled down the hall. "Follow me, dear. I'm supposed to take you to the gym. Principal Oster is watching the boys practice. He's desperate for us to win the provincial championship this year."

They stepped onto the polished wood, and Zoey breathed in a familiar scent. Most things in life change, but the smell of wax on a gymnasium floor is timeless. Crossing the gym, she listened to the dull thud of basketballs on wood, the off-key notes of the band practicing "Louie Louie", and the rhythmic slapping of cheerleaders clapping out calls to support the home team–the Granisle Griz-zlies.

The boys practiced dribbling and shooting while two men stood off to the side with their heads bent close, reading notes on a clipboard. The man holding the clipboard wore khaki slacks and a white polo shirt. A whistle dangled from a lanyard around his neck. Zoey guessed, Coach. He stood next to a worried-looking man wearing a wrinkled gray suit.

Mrs. Hendricks didn't interrupt the men. She waited until they stopped talking before speaking. "Principal Oster, this is our visitor from the RCMP."

The man looked past Mrs. Hendricks and stared up at Zoey. She stood a good six inches taller than him, and in her full uniform, with her hand resting on her police radio, she made an imposing figure. He pulled a damp handkerchief from his pocket and mopped sweat from his forehead.

The man with the whistle spoke. "Don't worry, Don. We have all summer to work on these things, and I'm sure, come fall, our boys will do us proud." He glanced toward the band. "But I'm not so sure about them." With a quick nod to Zoey, he turned, blew a sharp blast on his whistle, and walked across the gym to the backboard.

"Donald Oster, Principal," the man offered a sweaty hand.

Zoey gave her name and title but didn't shake hands with Principal Oster.

Oster dropped his hand and again reached into his pocket for the damp cloth. "Yes, yes," he said. "I got the call you'd be coming." He swiped the handkerchief across his face. "The girls will be done with their practice in about twenty minutes. I told them to come to my office directly after practice. You can talk to them privately there."

"And their teachers?"

"All of them will see you if you want. But I thought I'd take you to the library first. One of the girls is on the cheerleading team, so she's quite popular. But the other girl is a bit of a loner. Our librarian, Mrs. Woodhouse, is the only member of my staff who knows much about her." His hand shook as he mopped his brow again. "Except me, of course. She spent a fair amount in my office and our detention hall."

"Why did she end up in detention?"

"You know, getting in fights, swearing. Stupid kid stuff." Oster prattled non-stop as they moved through corridors past rows of metal lockers, glass trophy cases, and bulletin boards ragged with announcements.

Zoey tuned him out, letting her memories block his babble. Her high school days hadn't been typical. While the other kids groped in the back of cars, filled out college applications, planned weddings, or hid their American friends from the draft, Zoey dreamed of wearing the bright red uniform and serving and protecting her fellow Canadians.

Even though the force didn't allow females to join, she'd followed the news and knew there would eventually be a gap in the old boys' club. Zoey wanted to be ready when that gap opened. She ran miles, lifted weights, and practiced martial arts in the local community center. On Saturday nights, she kept company with books on Canadian Law, memorizing cases and legal procedures. She'd never had a real boyfriend. While she'd gone on a couple of dates, she'd found the law far more interesting than the acne-scarred boys who wanted to hold her hand at the movies.

Something in Oscar's tone pulled Zoey from her memories. "I don't know what to tell you," he said. "We've never had anything like this. Maybe a teen pregnancy now and again and the odd fist fight behind the bleachers, but nothing like this. Those poor, poor parents. They must be sick with worry about those missing girls and that baby drowning in the lake and..." He stopped outside a tall oak door.

"Here we are." He pushed the door open and stepped into the still, quiet room housing the library. The library smelled of old books, paper, dust, and the pungent scent of dried binding glue. A hint of mildew rose from ancient carpeting. From a window on the far wall, dust motes floated down a stream of sunshine to a row of blonde oak tables, initials carved on some, ink stains on others. Each table was outfitted with a small cardboard box of stubby yellow golf pencils and bits of paper torn into four-by-four-inch squares.

A middle-aged woman wearing her hair in a bun at the nape of her neck, dressed in a black calf-length skirt, a white blouse buttoned to the neck, and a gray cardigan, greeted them. Zoey suppressed the urge to smile as the librarian was a caricature of every librarian joke ever penned.

"This is Mrs. Woodhouse, our librarian. Mrs. Woodhouse, this is Constable Simard."

The two women smiled and shook hands as Oster reached to his collar and tugged at his tie. "Well," he said, "I'll leave you two alone. I'll be back in about fifteen or twenty minutes, or I'll send Mrs. Hendricks to show you to my office. The cheerleaders will meet with you there." He glanced at Zoey, backed out of the room, and scurried away. A nervous little man.

"Mrs. Woodhouse, thank you so much for meeting with me."

"First, please call me Dorothea. Now, how can I help you?"

"I'm hoping you can tell me about the two missing girls." They sat across from each other at an oak table. Zoey slid the photo of Majorca to the librarian. Dorothea Woodhouse sighed.

"She's pretty and probably a sweet girl, but unfortunately, the cheerleaders don't spend much time in the library. You might have better luck chatting with the coach or our Home Ed teacher." She slid the photo back to Zoey.

Zoey slipped it into the folder and pulled out the small, faded photo of Crystal. "Sadly, this is the only image I have of her. I think she was about six or maybe seven when this was taken."

Dorothea studied the photo. "Those eyes. What's her name?"

"Crystal. Crystal Lynn Harsch."

The librarian handed the photo back to Zoey. "Yes, I know her. I'm probably the only adult in the school who does. Don, Principal Oster, puts her in detention fairly often, but I think it's because he doesn't know what else to do."

"What do you think lands her in detention?"

"She's quiet, and a loner, but when the other kids bully her, she's quick to anger. Still, she shouldn't be shut up in that stuffy old janitor's closet. It's wrong and cruel. And it's not doing her any good. I've often told Don to make her serve detention here, in the library. But he's a stubborn little man."

Zoey scanned the room. "So, she likes to read?"

"Yes. Anything. Everything. She never goes out with the others during recess—she stays in here. And she stays here throughout lunch. She skips classes and comes here, but I don't report her. As far as I can tell, that reading desk is her only oasis." Dorothea pointed to a single table and chair, both painted moss green, tucked into a corner. "I'm not going to fault a child for reading."

"What does Crystal look like now?"

"Tall, olive-toned skin. Dark, intense eyes, never smiles. She's got long black hair and wears it in a single braid down her back. Maybe one of her parents is indigenous, but I don't know that for sure. She always wears blue jeans and a black t-shirt—I think the logo is from some rock and roll band. And she wears a ratty old blue jean jacket, two sizes too big, and boots, the kind you see in the used military supply store downtown. The poor child is bone-thin and never brings lunch. Sometimes, I pack an extra sandwich and pretend I made a mistake. It's gone in a breath."

"Have you ever met her parents?"

"I don't think they've ever set foot in this school."

The oak door opened with a soft swish, and Mrs. Hendricks stepped into the library.

Zoey turned again to the librarian. "Anything else you can share with me?"

Dorothea stared at the green table in the corner for a moment and then looked back at Zoey. "Not that I can think of except that..."

"What?"

"It's that she checks books out regularly. And always returns them on time, usually ahead of schedule. But the last book she checked out is overdue. Not by much, mind you. Only a day. But that's unusual. Maybe it doesn't mean anything."

"Anything helps," Zoey said. "Thank you for your time."

Dorothea Woodhouse shook her head, her eyes soft with sadness. "I'm so sorry. I wish I could do more, but I think that child is a lost soul."

As Mrs. Hendriks led Zoey down the hall, the librarian called out. "Constable?"

Zoey turned.

"Please find her, Constable. Please help her."

"Yes, ma'am. I'm trying."

Chapter Twenty-Seven

Zoey took a quick break in the girls' washroom. The information the librarian had shared didn't offer any clues concerning where Crystal might have gone, but her current physical description could prove helpful. Securing her radio and belt, Zoey started for the door but stopped when she heard a soft sniffle coming from the last stall.

"Are you alright in there?"

A gulping sound.

"Seriously, do you need any help?"

The stall door opened. Zoey tensed, then relaxed. A girl with red, puffy eyes and cheeks wet with tears stepped from the stall.

"What's wrong?"

The girl wiped her face with the back of her hand, sniffled again, and looked up at Zoey.

"She was so happy. She...she... thought she was the luckiest girl in the world. And now...now..." The girl's face scrunched, and a tear rolled down her cheek.

Zoey pulled a paper towel from the dispenser. "Here," she said. "Tell me, what's your name, and who was so happy? Who was the luckiest girl in the world?"The girl swiped the towel over her face, dropped it into the basket, and leaned against the sink. "They were going to get married. Todd and Majorca. I was going to be the Maid of Honor. And she was going to live in student housing at the university in Vancouver. But now she's missing, and who knows what happened and...and..."

"And, what's your name?" Zoey asked.

"Rhonda. Rhonda Patterson. I'm her best friend." Rhonda burst into more sobs.

"Rhonda Patterson, you can't help me find your friend if you keep crying. So, no more tears, got it?"

Rhonda sniffled but stopped sobbing and reached for another paper towel.

Zoey wasn't sure how fast the rumor mill turned, so she eased into her questions. "So, Rhonda, what makes you think Todd and Majorca were going to get married? Were they engaged?"

"No. Not yet. But Majorca told me that right after graduation, Todd was going to take her to the hot springs for the weekend. He said he had a big surprise for her. She was sure he was going to pop the question and that he would trade his class ring for a big diamond ring. She was so happy when she left my house." Rhonda lowered her head. "She wanted to walk, but if my dad gave her a ride home..." Rhonda sucked back a sob.

"Do you have any idea where your friend might be now?"

"No. I mean, where would she go? Everybody in town knows she caught Todd making out with Candy. And Todd keeps saying Majorca pushed his car into the lake. She must be so embarrassed."

"One more thing. You said you're her best friend, right?"

Rhonda nodded. "Best friends since we were little."

"Does she have any other close friends? Someone she might hang out with but not tell you?"

"She has lots of friends. She's super popular. But we tell each other every-thing, so even if she was going to go shopping with somebody else, which she wouldn't, she'd tell me."

Zoey removed a card from her pocket and handed it to Rhonda. "Here. If Majorca gets in touch with you, I want you to call me right away. Can you do that?"

Rhonda stared at the card. "Will you...will you find her?

Zoey touched Rhonda's shoulder. "I'm going to do everything in my power to find her and to bring her home safe. I promise."

The principal's office was thick with giggles and the cloying scents of Shalimar, Heaven Scent, and Chantilly. The giggling stopped when Zoey and Mrs. Hendricks stepped into the room. Don Oster coughed, then cleared his throat.

"Girls, this is Constable Zoey Simard. She has questions for you, and I want you to answer all of them. Help her with whatever she needs." He cleared his throat again and ran one finger under his collar. He spoke to Zoey. "I'll be in the hallway if you need me."

Zoey stood silent for a moment as she sized up the group of girls. Four blondes, two brunettes. All slim with clear skin, bright eyes, and lips pouting with pink or peach gloss. They each wore white tennis shoes, white socks, a short yellow skirt, and a white blouse. They stared at her. "Ladies, thank you for agreeing to help me."

"We didn't have a choice." A stage whisper from the group. Giggles.

Zoey ignored the comment. "As I'm sure you know, there are two girls from your school who seem to be missing. I'm looking for them. So, anything you can share about either of them will be a big help."

A petite blonde closest to Zoey stepped forward. "What do you want to know?"

Zoey smiled at her. "First, your principal tells me there are eight girls on the squad. I only count six. We're looking for Majorca Fairhaven, so she accounts for one, but I'm wondering where the other girl is today. Did she skip practice?"

A tall brunette spoke up. "I heard that her mother called in and said Candy has her period." "Don't believe that for a second," another short blonde said. "I heard she was going pretty hot and heavy with Todd. Guessing she won't be having a period for another nine months." The girls snickered and whispered to each other.

Zoey jotted a line in her notebook. "Now, ladies. Does anyone have any ideas where your friend Majorca Fairhaven might be?"

The mood turned somber. A couple of girls shook their heads, others stared at the floor, one girl chewed at a hangnail.

Zoey gave them a moment, then went on. "All right. Do any of you know Crystal Lynn Harsch?"

The tall girl sniffed. "Nobody knows her. She's a weirdo."

"What do you mean, weirdo?"

"She's part Indian. And smelly," the short blonde said. "And she always wears the same black shirt."

"She doesn't have any friends," a second blonde added. "And my cousin says she lives in a little shack behind her mom's house. That's why she's so dirty."

Another girl piped in. "I heard she has sex with old men. For money."

"Where'd you hear that?" Zoey asked.

"Don't know," the girl mumbled. "I heard it somewhere."

Again, Zoey wrote in her notebook, mostly so she wouldn't have to look at the smug teens. "So, any reason Majorca would hang out with Crystal?""Are you kidding me?" The girl in the back piped up. "Majorca is cool and she really cares about her looks. There's no way she'd have anything to do with that slob."

Zoey slapped her note book shut and tucked it away. She turned to Mrs. Hendricks. "I think I've learned all I can here," she said. "Thanks for giving me the tour. I can find my own way out."

In her patrol car, Zoey stared at the small, faded school photo of Crystal. "You poor kid," she said. Her radio buzzed.

"You done at the high school?" Danny asked.

"Yes. Not very helpful but I got a more current description of Crystal. How'd it go with the boy?"

"His parents are keeping him out of school on the advice of their attorney. And, he's not talking following more advice from said attorney. So, pretty much all we have to go on is what he told us at the lake."

"Not a lot," Zoey said."Nope. Hey, you wanna grab a pizza and a beer at the Shack?"

"Thanks, Danny. But I'm gonna pick up some groceries on the way home, and then give my dog a break from the neighbor's kids. He's probably at the end of his canine patience about now."

"We'll pick this up in the morning. Bound to be a break by then."

Zoey signed off and took one more look at the sad little girl in the photo. "I sure hope so," she whispered.

Chapter Twenty-Eight

MAJORCA PACED THE NARROW room—the room Vernon Wilbey had given them at a discount after Crystal had flirted with him.

Crystal stretched out on the bed, arms behind her head. "Chill out," she said. "You should rest 'cause you're gonna drive that piece of shit truck and you need to be alert."

"I don't like this, Crystal. That man, Mr. Vernon Wilbey, he's a nice guy. A little strange, but a nice guy. I bet if we ask him, he'll drive us to my cousin's place."

Crystal yawned. "About that. We're not going to your cousin's place."

"What? I thought that was our plan. Get my cousin to drive us to your grandma's house in the beer truck."

"That *was* our plan until you blabbed to old Vernon, where we're heading. Sooner or later, the police are gonna ask everybody on this road if they saw us. Plus, our boy Vernon is gonna be a big shot and tell the cops we're on our way to pick up a ride to Vanderhoof. Crystal yawned again. "I swear, I can't take you anywhere."

Majorca stopped pacing and bit her lip. Worry lines crossed her forehead. "But what if the police see us?"

"They aren't gonna be looking for a beater truck and a couple of ragged-looking misfits. I told you before, they're looking for a boppy cheerleader."

Majorca plopped down on the only chair in the room. "I don't know, Crystal. This whole thing is getting too crazy. And I really don't want to hurt that man."

"For Christ's sake, Majorca. This is the last time I'm gonna say it. We're not gonna hurt him. We're only gonna tie him up, borrow his truck, and drive to my grandma's house. We can leave the truck a few blocks away, park it in front of somebody's driveway so they call the cops to complain. The cops will come and return the truck to Vernon. We'll be fine. Vernon will be fine. It's a great plan. Now, relax."

Crystal crouched behind the truck as stars winked across the late evening sky. "Go," she whispered.

Majorca knocked on the motel's door. No answer. She pushed the door open and poked her head inside. Vernon sprawled on his desk chair, head back, mouth open, snoring. Backing out, Majorca scurried across the lot to Crystal.

"He's sleeping," she said.

Crystal grinned. "Perfect. You tape him up and I'll get the keys to the truck."

The sound of ripping duct tape woke Vernon. "Hey, umph, hey." He jolted upright, rubbed his eyes, and started to stand.

"Sit back down, Mr. Vernon Wilbey," Crystal said. She stood across from him, holding his gun with both hands and pointing it directly at his chest.

"Crystal!" Majorca froze. A length of silver tape dangled from her hand. "What are you doing?"

"I'm keeping your skinny ass out of jail. Now tape Mr. Wilbey to his chair. Use lots of tape. Use the whole roll. And put a piece over his mouth so he can't yell for help. We need a good head start."

"Now, Miss. That ain't no toy. And it's loaded," Vernon said. "You already said that. Three bullets."

"Put it down, Miss, fore someone gets hurt." Again, Vernon started to stand.

Crystal cocked the gun. "Sit down, Mr. Wilbey. Majorca, hurry up."

Vernon Wilbey's old Ford belched smoke and leapt forward as Majorca let the clutch out.

"You sure you know how to drive?" Crystal said.

"Shut up. Just shut up." Majorca pushed the gear shift into reverse and backed out of the lot. The truck lurched as she jammed into first gear and headed onto the highway.

"Look at this." Crystal pulled a map from the glove compartment. This might come in handy. And this, too. She extracted a flashlight.

"What else does he have in there? As long as we're stealing, we might as well do it right." Majorca spat her words from gritted teeth.

"Chill out," Crystal said. "Not anything else we can use. A couple of condoms and looks like they've been in here a long, long time. Losing scratch tickets. A pencil."

Stuffing the map and flashlight into her pack, she squinted through the Ford's cracked windshield. "How come it's so dark?"

"I think one of the headlights is burned out. But that's not all. We are riding on fumes. There's zero gas in this thing."

"Great. Just great. Vernon, my man, you need to get your shit together."

"Crystal, listen to yourself. And look at us. We're the ones who need to get our shit together." Majorca stomped on the accelerator.

Chapter Twenty-Nine

Pausing outside Rebecca's door, Zoey listened to the twins' laughter and Buster's barking. In the background, Rebecca sang along to pop music on the radio. Zoey shifted the weight of the two grocery bags she carried and tapped on the door.

"Right on time!" Rebecca held the door open wide enough to smile at Zoey but closed enough to keep the twins and Buster from bolting down the hall. "Go drop those off and come on over. It's a little chaotic, but the food's almost ready."

"No, these are for you. My way of saying thanks for watching Buster all day. I know he can be a handful."

"You didn't have to do that. But thanks." Rebecca glanced back at the living room and pushed the door wide. "Hurry, the coast is clear."

While Rebecca put the twins to bed, Zoey washed the dishes. She'd set the final plate in the cupboard and reached for the bottle of wine she'd brought when her pager vibrated. Poking her head into the bedroom, she whispered, "Rebecca, I need to make a call. Open the wine, okay?"

In her apartment, Zoey pressed the phone to her ear and listened as Danny described the call from the Lazy Daze Motor Inn. "I think we got a lucky break. I was finishing up a report when the call came through. A fellow down in Decker Lake bought a twelve-pack of Labatts and was stopping by his friend's place to drink. His buddy is the manager of the motor inn there. When he got to the inn, he found his buddy duct-taped to a chair. The manager says two vicious teenage girls accosted him, and he wants to complain to the constable in charge."

"Hendricks know about this?"

"Nope, I took the call."

"Pick you up in ten."

Before leaving, Zoey stopped back at Rebecca's and gave her the photos of Crystal and Majorca. "Would it be possible for you to do pencil sketches of these girls? And maybe project what the younger one would look like if she were eighteen? Also, if you can, give them both short haircuts. I know this is short notice, but it would be a big help."

Rebecca studied the photos and nodded. "Pretty sure I can. The twins are down, and you're leaving the wine, right?"

Vernon Wilbey and his buddy, Howard Limpston, were down three beers each when Zoey pulled into the lot of the Lazy Daze Motor Inn.

"You cops sure took your time," Howard slurred. He slumped in a plastic chair and nodded off.

"It's not a problem," Vernon said, "I needed a little time to collect myself after that brutal attack. I thank the good Lord they only tied me up and stole my truck. It could a been much worse."

"What kind of truck?" Zoey said.

"Old beater Ford pickup. She runs good, but she's got some issues."

"Issues?"

"One headlight burned out, windshield cracked, no tread on the tires, and most likely, not much gas."

"Did they say where they're headed?" Danny asked.

Vernon scrunched his forehead. "They might be going to Burns Lake or maybe Vanderhoof. I think I remember something about that, but I have to do a little thinking on that one. More important, you guys gotta catch 'em because they're dangerous."

Zoey jotted notes as Vernon Wilbey regaled how he'd put up a real struggle, and how he'd valiantly attempted to protect the motel. A few minutes into Vernon's story, Zoey interrupted.

"So, Mr. Wilbey," she said, "Let me get this straight. You're a trained security guard. Head of Security at the Lazy Daze Motor Inn. And yet, two teenage girls overpowered you, taped you to your chair, and stole your truck? Do I have that right?"

Danny stood behind her, struggling to maintain a stern composure.

Deflated, Vernon stared at his shoes. Then he glanced up and shouted. "I coulda done better, but them gals was armed. Armed and dangerous."

"Armed with what, Mr. Wilbey?"

Again, Vernon looked at his shoes. This time he mumbled. "Seems they got ahold a Zelda."

"Zelda?"

After warning him to refrain from talking with the press and to keep everything about Zelda under wraps, Zoey gave Vernon her card and promised to contact him if/when they located his truck. She and Danny shook his hand and left.

Five minutes into the drive back to Granisle, Danny glanced over at Zoey. "How long do you think he'll wait until he calls the news?"

Zoey sighed. "Maybe after another beer?"

"You know, the press is going to be all over this, and it's not going to be long before every Canadian wannabe cop or cowboy is on the hunt for those girls. Especially if old Vernon mentions his gun."

"I've thought of that."

"And you know, it's not going to be good for any girl or woman out on this road, even if they're trying to catch a ride to work."

When Zoey didn't answer, Danny shifted in his seat. "Look, this is stressful, and we can't do anything else tonight. You wanna grab a beer at the Shack?"

"Thanks, Danny, but my neighbor is helping me with some sketches of the girls. I'm going to the press—circulate their identities. Maybe that will help."

Danny waited a beat before speaking. "Something to consider before you do that. It's the right thing to do, yes. But Sergeant Gagnon hates publicity unless it's about him and unless it's good. Be careful, Zo."

Chapter Thirty

Ten minutes past Burns Lake, the old truck sighed and rolled to a stop.

"Majorca, what the hell are you doing? Keep going."

"It's out of gas."

"What?"

"I told you we were riding on fumes, and we're at the end of the fumes."

"Fuck, fuck, fuck."

"Really, Crystal—"

"Shut up. We need the ride." Crystal bit a hangnail. Blood pooled at the edge of her thumb.

Majorca reached over and touched Crystal's shoulder. "Look, we can't be very far from Tintagel, and there has to be a gas station there. Maybe a quarter kilometer, probably less. We can push this piece of shit that far."

A wide grin spread across Crystal's face. "Wow. Listen to you. Getting all feisty. You're startin' to grow a pair." She grabbed the door handle and jumped from the truck. "Let's roll."

Wayne Martin, the night attendant at Maple Leaf Gas and Go, rested against the counter and stared at the television mounted over the boxed cereal and canned pet food aisle. He chewed on a sausage stick filched from a box in the back room—his boss would never notice one, or maybe two, missing sticks.

A reporter in slacks and a blazer thrust a microphone at a man in a cowboy hat standing in front of the Lazy Daze Motor Inn.

"You know, we give a good rest to any weary traveler but them two, they was vicious and dangerous."

"Mr. Wilbey, what do you mean by dangerous?"

The man in the hat puffed out his chest and leaned closer to the reporter. "I'm not supposed to be sayin' anything, but the public has a right to know. Those girls? I'm pretty sure they was on their way to Vanderhoof and them two are armed. A course," he added, "they probably won't get too far on account a my truck is low on gas, the windshield is about to go, and it has some, um, other issues."

Holding two fingers against a device in his ear, the reporter turned to the camera. "We have breaking news about the possible identities of the two dangerous fugitives. Kevin? Over to you."

"Armed and dangerous," Vernon yelled as the scene switched to Ruth and Neil Fairhaven standing together in front of their home. Bright television lights turned them pale. Ruth wept while her husband pleaded into the camera. "Majorca, honey. Please come home. No matter what happened, we're here for you. Your mother and I love you."

Pencil sketches of Crystal and Majorca flashed across the screen. The sketches taken from their photos were fairly accurate. Even the drawing showing Crystal's age progression and their short haircuts looked realistic.

Again, the coverage switched. This time, the camera focused on Wanda-Lynn Harsch and Clive Reid. Clive leaned against a weather-beaten trailer wearing a stained t-shirt. He clutched a can of Budweiser in his left hand while trying to scratch his head with his bandaged right hand. He leered at the young female reporter holding a mic to Wanda-Lynn.

"Mrs. Harsch, the police believe your daughter may be involved in this crime spree. Do you have any comments?"

"Damn straight," Wanda-Lynn said. She scratched at a scab on her arm. "She better git her sorry ass back home and bring me my smokes."

"You know how much smokes cost these days?" Clive interrupted. "That's from the government taxin' regular folks to death."

"I didn't raise her up that way," Wanda-Lynn added.

The camera panned back to the reporter. "We'll continue our up-to-the-minute reporting on this developing story," she said. "But remember, folks. These fugitives are armed and dangerous. They're driving a Ford pickup, and they may have altered their appearances. If you see them, do not engage. Call the authorities immediately."

Wayne was so caught up in the news story he didn't hear Crystal entering the store. And, he didn't realize she was standing behind him, on the other side of the counter, until he heard the click when she cocked Vernon's gun.

Wayne spun around and gaped at the teenage girl leveling a handgun at his chest. His gaze flicked from her to the girl with short, spiky red hair standing by a display of powered donuts. She held a box of donuts in one hand and a family-sized bag of chips in the other. Wayne tilted his head, squinted, and peered out the gas station window.

"Say, miss. What kinda truck you driving? That a Ford?" He backed up and, without turning, reached for the phone hanging on the wall.

"You really don't want to do that," Crystal said. She raised the gun and pointed it at his head. "Majorca, please tie this gentleman up."

Majorca froze. She didn't move.

"Majorca, I said, tie him up. Now!"

Majorca piled the donuts and bag of chips on the counter. "We didn't bring the tape," she said.

Keeping the gun trained on Wayne, Crystal walked behind the counter, grabbed the long, coiled cord on the wall phone, and gave it a hard yank. The phone's receiver clattered to the floor.

"We don't need tape," she said. Using the gun, she gestured toward a support beam in the center of the store and motioned to Wayne. "You. Walk real slow over to that pole and lean against it with your hands behind your back."

Wayne's eyes darted from Crystal to the door.

"Don't even think about it. You do what I tell you, and you'll be alive in the morning. Try something funny, and you'll be swimming in your own blood."

Wayne's eyes grew wide and round. Majorca giggled.

"Tie him tight, Majorca."

Majorca wound the phone cord around Wayne's hands and then around his chest.

Wayne glared at Crystal. "You won't get away with this, you ugly half-breed," he said. He took a deep breath, filled his lungs and puffed his chest out. Majorca punched Wayne in the stomach. He let the air out with a poof.

"Nice one!" Crystal grinned at Majorca.

Majorca gave the phone cord a hard tug and then wrapped it around Wayne again, tying the two ends together behind his back. "Now it's really tight," she said.

Keeping the gun pointed at Wayne, Crystal backed around the counter to the cash register. She hit a key, pulled stacks of bills from the drawer, and pushed them into her pockets.

"Like I said, you guys aren't gonna get away with this," Wayne said. "Somebody's gonna come for gas and I'm gonna tell em' about the half-breed and the flat-chested hillbilly who robbed the store, and then took off for Vanderhoof and then the cops will be all over you."

"You really talk too much," Crystal said. She shoved the gun into the waistband of her jeans and walked across the store to a display of bandanas. She took two off a hook and strolled over to Wayne. "Open wide," she said.

Wayne kept his mouth shut tight. Crystal followed Majorca's move and punched him in the gut—hard. When his mouth fell open, she stuffed one of the bandanas in and tied the second one around his mouth knotting it at the back of his neck. "There we go," she said. She patted Wayne on the top of his head. "So, for your information, Mr. Big Shot, we aren't even stopping at Vanderhoof. We're going straight to Prince George. We're meeting our boyfriends there. Bikers. Real tough bikers. So, Mr. Big Shot, there goes your story." Checking the knots on the phone cord one more time, she gestured to the counter. "Grab the stash, Majorca," she said. "Let's hit the road."

Wayne made gurgling sounds in the back of his throat.

Majorca grabbed the donuts and the chips and dashed out of the shop. Crystal walked to a panel behind the counter and switched off the Maple Leaf Gas and Go's outside lights, including the large florescent sign reading GAS. At the front door, she lifted a ring of keys from a hook and flicked off the inside lights. Now, the gas station, both inside and out, was wrapped in shadows.

"Night, night," she said. She shut the door and locked it.

Again, Wayne made a gurgling sound in the back of his throat.

Chapter Thirty-One

A HALF MILE DOWN the road, Crystal tossed the gas station keys out the window and turned the radio on. She twisted the knob until a station came in clear enough to hear a newscast.

"We have breaking news about the fugitives. Two girls, one with short black hair and the other with spiky red hair, are driving an early model Ford pickup with one headlight. Witnesses say they are heading to Vanderhoof. These girls are armed and are considered very dangerous. The RCMP asks citizens to report any sighting of the girls, and they have issued a warning—do not under any circumstances engage with them. Carrie, how's our traffic looking?"

Crystal snapped the radio off. "Shit, shit, shit."

"We can't stay on the highway," Majorca said. "They're gonna see this truck and pull us over."

Using Vernon's flashlight, Crystal studied the map. "I know," she said. "We're fucked. But look," she pointed to the circle of light on the map. "Until they find old Wayne, they think we're heading to Vanderhoof. That's at least an hour away, and it's a city. So, they'll burn a lot of time looking for us in the wrong place."

"Maybe...but wait, we *are* going to Vanderhoof. To your grandma's house."

Crystal looked away. "She doesn't live there. She lives in Fort St. James. I told you that when we met, because I didn't know you so—"

"You told that to Dee Dee Wine, too. But you told Roy we were going to Burns Lake. And you told Wayne we're going to Prince George."

"So, I lied. Big deal."

"Crystal, did you lie about other stuff? I mean, did you lie *to me* about other stuff?

"Buzz off, will you? Pay attention—this is important. The cops will be flying down this road to Vanderhoof, and they'll be looking around there for days. Endako is only a little way down the highway. We should pull off over there and find someplace to hide the truck."

"Then what?" Majorca wiped one hand on her pants leaving a trail of sweat on the coveralls.

"How the hell do I know? All I know is that they won't even think about Endako 'cause it's only a little dot on the map. Let's get off the highway, and then we can make a plan."

The *Welcome to Endako* sign was small, unlit, and partially obscured by overgrown weeds. Majorca drove past it.

"Stop!" Crystal smacked the dashboard. "We missed the town."

Turning the truck around on the dark highway wasn't easy. The steering was too stiff for a graceful three-point turn. When Majorca backed up, one rear tire slipped off the highway into the soft soil on the shoulder.

"Shit, we're in the ditch," Crystal said.

Majorca pressed her lips together. Gripping the steering wheel with her left hand, she downshifted with her right, ground the gears, and spun the tires. The old truck pitched off the mud, swerved, and shimmied back onto the highway.

"Yayyy!" Crystal whooped. "That was so bad-assed!"

Majorca exhaled. "Shut up, Crystal. Shut up and help me find the turn-off."

Endako's three narrow streets paralleled the highway and were crossed by three others running perpendicular to them. Majorca followed the main street through the sleeping town.

Trailers and clapboard homes squeezed onto postage-sized lots separated by chain link fences. Toys, swing sets, and abandoned car parts littered the yards. Pit bulls and German shepherds trotted to the ends of their chains and watched the truck roll by, but none of them barked. Endako's main street supported a smattering of shops—a hardware store, a five-and-dime with painted windows advertising ice cream sundaes, and a pawn shop with windows protected by iron bars. Except for one street lamp, the town was dark and still.

"What's the deal with this place?" Crystal asked.

"I remember my dad delivered a car engine here once," Majorca said. "He took me along for the ride. This is where the miners live. My dad said that the town was booming because of the copper and stuff from the mines, but it doesn't look very booming to me. If we park the truck on one of these streets, people will notice it the minute they get going in the morning." She turned down another street, drove to the end, made a U-turn and headed back toward where they'd started.

Crystal squinted through the cracked windshield and pointed to a wide driveway. "Head in there."

Majorca turned off the street and pulled into a parking lot behind a small church. The lot separated the structure from a stretch of forest. There were no lights around the building, and no movement. Only deep shadows.

"Let's stay here overnight," Crystal said. "What day is it? "

"Friday." Majorca eased the truck close to the church, put it in park, and turned the key. The old Ford coughed then stilled. She rolled her window down.

They sat quietly, letting the night settle around the truck. At first, there was silence, but then the sounds of the forest filled the night. A chirping, a faint hum, and the call of a night bird singing a soft, mournful song.

"Why did you ask what day it is?" Majorca asked.

"I'm thinking. Maybe nobody will come back around here before Sunday. That should give us time to figure out what to do."

"Should we stay here, in the truck tonight?"

"You got a better plan?"

"No, but I have to pee," Majorca said.

"So, go pee in the bushes."

Majorca peered into the night. "It's pretty dark out there."

"You chicken shit." Crystal gave Majorca a light smack on her arm. "Turn the headlight on. I gotta pee too, so I'll go with you."

As the hours passed, the night air grew cooler. Majorca slipped into the sweatshirt Crystal pulled from her pack.

"I'm starving," Crystal said.

"No problem. We have food." Majorca reached over the back seat where she'd tossed the box of powdered donuts and the bag of chips. A half bag of chips and four donuts later, they were full of salt, and lard, and dough, and riding a sugar high.

"We should try to get some sleep," Crystal said. She climbed out of the front seat and into the back and stretched out. Majorca settled across the front.

Except for the chirp of crickets and a soft brush of breeze through the trees, the night was quiet.

"Crystal?"

"Hmm?"

"That was pretty funny. What you said to that guy in the gas station."

"What did I say?'

Majorca giggled and then faked a deep male voice. "Try something funny, and you'll be swimming in your own blood."

"I don't sound like that," Crystal said.

"No, I was kidding. But it *was* funny."

"Glad you're happy. Now shut up, I'm trying to crash."

Again, for several minutes, only forest sounds drifted into the truck's open windows.

"Crystal?"

"Are you gonna start talkin' again?"

"I feel bad about my parents. They're really worried."

"So, in the morning, go out on the road and hitch a ride back to mommy and daddy."

"I don't think I can do that now. I don't think I can ever do that."

"Of course you can."

"No. We did a lot of bad stuff, Crystal. Stuff we can go to jail for. If I go back now, my parents will have to hire a lawyer, and that will cost tons of money.

My parents don't have a lot of money. They might have to sell the house or, or maybe...even..." Majorca's voice caught.

"Jesus. Are you gonna start crying?"

"No. I have the hiccups."

They lay without talking until Crystal bent forward, rolled a window up, then stretched back on the seat, using her pack for a pillow. An owl called from a tree close to the church.

"Crystal?"

"What *now*?"

"Was it weird for you?"

"Was what weird for me?""Pointing that gun at those guys. And, you know, making me tie them up."

Crystal sat up and scootched across the seat to lean against the door.

"So, was it weird for you?"

"You mean tying him up?"

"No, punching his gut."

"Sort of. But I was pissed at him for calling you names. And besides, I was so excited and nervous, it kinda... sorta, happened."

"It gets easier," Crystal said.

"What gets easier?""Hurting people. It gets easier."

"How can you say that? I mean, don't you care about anybody?"

Crystal reached for her knapsack and rummaged around until she found a pack of cigarettes and her mother's lighter. She lit up, sucked in a drag, and blew out a stream of smoke. "Did you hear my mom on the television?"

"Yes."

"Did it sound like *she* cares about anybody?"

"But, you're not like your mom, Crystal. Even though I haven't met her yet, I know, for sure, you're more like your grandma."

"Majorca?"

"What?""Shut the fuck up."

Chapter Thirty-Two

THE DREAM TERRIFIED HER. Even though Zoey knew she was dreaming, she wasn't able to pull herself into waking. She and the two girls were walking in a wooded parkland on a warm, summer day. Crystal with her long black braid, Majorca with her pale blonde curls, and Zoey in her full-dress uniform, her red jacket bright in the sunlight, brass buttons shining. They were laughing. Crystal pointed to an ice cream truck. The girls sat on a bench and waited while Zoey walked to the truck and ordered three strawberry cones. With her hands loaded with treats she turned toward the girls. But the bench was empty and the girls were running across the park. A man in a cheap suit wearing a stethoscope around his neck ran after them brandishing a medical scalpel and a pair of garden shears. Zoey dropped the cones—strawberry ice cream spattered her dress uniform. She tried to run, but her regulation shoes were glued to the ground. The girls screamed for help, but Zoey was stuck in place.

She jolted awake. Sweat soaked her hair, her pajamas, and her sheets. Buster stood on his hind paws, his forepaws on the mattress. He tilted his head and stared at her.

She reached out and patted the old dog on his head. "It's okay, Buster. Only a bad dream. I should know better than to eat a grilled cheese sandwich at midnight." Shaking off the dream, she headed for the kitchen and coffee but a radio call stopped her.

"The sergeant wants you and O'Brien here at the station in thirty. You probably don't want to be late." The caller chuckled before signing off.

"Asshole," Zoey muttered. "Don't you have crime to fight, Hendricks? Or maybe a golf game to play?"

Sergeant Gagnon held his hands behind his back and paced the space between his desk and a glass cabinet of awards—some for police work, most for golf tournaments. Zoey stood at attention and watched the man who held her career in his hands. Beside her, Danny stood ramrod straight, his eyes focused on a plaque commemorating the 35th Anniversary of the RCMP. With a quick glance, Zoey noticed that although Danny's uniform was clean and pressed, his socks didn't match. Like hers, his had been a rushed morning—the call unexpected.

"Simard. O'Brien."

"Yes, Sir." They spoke in unison.

The sergeant continued to pace. "What we have here is a full-blown media circus. The good citizens of Granisle—no, make that the good citizens from Granisle all the way to Prince George, are going into tailspins over what the news media have been telling them. The public thinks they are in danger because of a major crime spree perpetrated by bloodthirsty juvenile delinquents. Armed and dangerous. Probably out to rape and murder. Probably out to steal household pets." He stopped pacing and glared at Zoey.

"This should have been squelched and buried on the back page when they pulled that car out of Babine. But no, the press had to get shots of that dead guy's car. Bad enough, but then there's that idiot security guard going on and on about the vicious criminals who are armed and dangerous. And every front page from here to Vancouver has a shot of that burned car." Gagnon started pacing again. "This isn't the kind of publicity we need. And by the way," he spun around to face Zoey. "Why are those little girls still running around the country? They're kids, stupid kids. How hard can it be to find two silly teenage girls?" His face was red and puffy, and a drop of spit hung on his lower lip. He switched his attention to Danny.

"O'Brien. Do you have any idea how many man-hours we wasted following up on hysterical reports from freaked-out parents and scared homeowners?"

"No, Sir," Danny remained rigid, staring straight ahead.

"Too damned many. That's how many. We've had reports of stalkers, peeping Toms, scary noises, and we even had a report of stolen pie. A pie for Christ's sake! And we have to respond to every one of these bogus reports, or the public will say we aren't responsive to their concerns." Gagnon spun around, clomped behind his desk, and plunked down in his chair. He took a moment to collect his breath. Then he pointed one finger, first at Danny, then at Zoey.

"The two of you have one job and one job only. Get those little girls in custody. Immediately. After that, we'll do damage control with the press. Understand?"

"Yes, Sir." Again, in unison.

"One more thing," Gagnon said, "we get one more run of bad press out of this, and you are both off the case. O'Brien, you'll be directing traffic and Simard, you'll be in the office filing reports in alphabetical order. Again, do you both understand?"

As Zoey and Danny walked through the station's office, Hendricks held up a manilla folder and gestured to one of his buddies. "I sure hate filing these reports. I sure would rather be doing real police work." His buddy and two others smirked.

Danny and Zoey ignored them.

"Constable Simard?" The dispatcher left her desk and hurried to catch Zoey. Pulling Zoey off to one side, the dispatcher kept her voice low. "When you were in with the brass, we got a call from a lady who says she met those girls, and she'd like to have a little talk with you if you have time." She handed Zoey a pink phone message slip.

Zoey glanced down at the name and address, thanked the dispatcher, and hurried to catch up with Danny.

On the front steps of the station, Danny sucked in a long breath of cool air. "Awful way to start the day," he said.

"Got that right. But now, I'm going to meet with a citizen who might have information about the girls. Are you hungry?"

Chapter Thirty-Three

Sunlight spiked through the windshield waking Majorca from a restless sleep. She groaned, pushed herself to sit, and looked in the back seat. Empty.

"Crystal?" Panic and the urge to pee fought for her attention. The urge won out. Majorca kicked at the door and slid from the seat. Squeezing her muscles, she hobbled toward the trees.

Crystal emerged from the edge of the forest. "About time. I thought you were gonna sleep all day. Thought I'd have to leave you here."

Ignoring her, Crystal fumbled with the buckles on the coveralls and crashed into the thick brush. Relief came fast, followed by anger. Swatting at a stinging insect, she stumbled out of the forest and stomped across the lot to the truck.

"Crystal, you're such a jerk. I thought something happened to you." Majorca climbed into the driver's seat.

"Whatever." Crystal spread the map between them and traced a line with her finger. "Look at this. There's a road that parallels the highway. I think it's a logging road or maybe a road for the mining trucks. Doesn't matter. We follow it toward Vanderhoof, but we turn off at Highway 27 and head north. There's a provincial park close to Fort St. James. We ditch the truck in the park and walk the rest of the way to my grans. Easy."

Majorca stared at her. "You really think you have it all worked out, don't you?"

"What's wrong with my plan? The cops will be looking for us on the main highway. I bet they won't even think of a logging road."

"It's just that you decide everything. You never ask me what I think we should do."

Crystal glared at Majorca. "So, genius. What's your plan?"

Majorca glared back at her. For a moment, neither moved. Neither blinked. Then, Majorca huffed, looked away, and focused on the steering wheel. "Whatever." Reaching forward, she turned the key. Click, click, click, click, click. She squinted at the dashboard and tried again. Click, click, click, click, click. "Dammit."

"What's wrong with it?" Crystal asked.

"The battery is dead."

"Are you sure? I mean, maybe it's a loose wire or something. We should check."

Majorca turned to Crystal and narrowed her eyes. "You know something? You might be great at waving a gun around, and telling me what to do, but you don't know shit about cars. I grew up listening to my dad talk about spark plugs and transmissions, and motors. When I was little, I used to sit on his toolbox and watch him work."

"Would never have thought a girly girl like you would be into greasy engines."

"I'm not. But I know what a dead battery sounds like, and *we* have a dead battery. Dead. Dead. Dead."

"Why?"

Majorca stared out the side window. "Probably because we left that headlight on all night."

"Shit."

"So, what's your plan now?"

Crystal scanned the parking lot, the forest's boundary, and the back of the church. Her brow furrowed. "I guess we walk," she said.

Majorca shook her head. "Too risky. Loggers and miners work on the weekends so there will be traffic on that road. And we'll stick out. Two freaky-looking girls walking along a dirt road to nowhere. I say we find a place to hide during the day and head out after dark."

"And where do you think we should hide? This truck isn't exactly comfortable, and besides, if anyone sees it, we're hosed."

"Nope. We spend the day in the church. There must be a way in, and it's Saturday. Like you said, there's a good chance that nobody will be here until tomorrow."

"The church?"

"Yes, it's the perfect place to hide."

"Is it safe? You know, in a church?""Yes, you idiot. Why do you think they call it a sanctuary?"

Constructed of pine and painted glossy white, the church featured blue trim around narrow stained-glass windows. A brass bell hung in the steeple. A neatly mowed front yard displayed flower beds thick with daisies and roses. Marigolds and trimmed shrubbery edged a brick walkway leading to the unlocked front door. Majorca poked her head in, glanced around, and stepped back. "Empty," she said. "Come on."

Chapter Thirty-Four

THE FIRST WAVE OF breakfast diners had passed, giving Danny and Zoey their pick of seating. Zoey chose a booth at the back of the restaurant, near the swinging doors that led to the kitchen.

While Danny perused the menu, Zoey glanced around the café. The Blue Bird Café and Grill was a typical greasy spoon, decorated with photos of local sports teams, ads for Coca-Cola, a fishing trophy, and an always-on, always-muted black-and-white television hanging over a counter lined with red swivel stools. Each table sported a small glass vase of plastic flowers, a napkin holder, salt and pepper shakers, and condiments—ketchup, mustard, vinegar, and maple syrup. On the opposite wall, a jukebox flashed fluorescent lights while Patsy Cline whined about being crazy.

"Big Moose Breakfast for me." Danny slapped his menu onto the table. "And coffee, lots and lots of coffee."

"Same here on the coffee," Zoey said, "but I'm not very hungry."

"Hey, don't let Gagnon's lecture get you down. And don't pay any attention to Hendricks. He's a full-blown jerk. Quite honestly, I don't understand what the sergeant's daughter sees in him."

"It's not that, Danny. It's that Gagnon was right. We need to find those girls, but not because of the publicity he's so worried about. We need to find them before they get seriously hurt. Or worse."

"We will—"

"So, you made it." A slender woman, wearing a light blue dress and a white apron, interrupted him. Her bleached blonde hair was piled high, and her pink plastic earrings matched her shiny pink lipstick. She held an order pad and a pencil in her left hand. She held her right hand out to Zoey.

"Dee Dee Wine. You must be the constable in charge of finding those two missing girls."

Shaking Dee Dee's hand, Zoey nodded toward Danny. "And Constable O'Brien. We're both on the case."

Dee Dee smiled wide and winked as she shook Danny's hand. His cheeks flushed.

"So, your message said you might have some information that could help us?" Zoey asked.

"I hope so," Dee Dee said. "But first, what can I get you two?"

Dee Dee delivered Danny's breakfast and three coffees and then took a seat next to Zoey. "I'm takin' my break a little early so we can talk. I feel so bad about those girls."

"What can you tell us?" Zoey asked.

With a big sigh, Dee Dee launched into her story. "I was headin' in for my night shift and I picked 'em up on Highway 16. Girls shouldn't be out there, hitchhiking on that road, it's too dangerous."

Danny swallowed a mouthful of hashbrowns and asked, "When was that?

"A few days back. Thursday. I know it was Thursday because I usually do the night shift on Wednesday, but I traded with the other gal. She had a baby shower to go to."

Zoey tapped her foot under the table. Baby showers had nothing to do with missing girls.

Get to the point.

"So, I picked 'em up and had a good old visit with the dark-skinned girl. She was a hoot. We talked about boys and sang a bunch of songs along with the radio."

"What about the other girl?" Zoey asked.

"She was depressed. Curled up in the back of my car and pouted. The whole ride. She mighta been crying too."

"Do you know why?"

"Boy trouble."

"So, then what happened?"

"I brought 'em here and fed 'em coffee and pie. And I told 'em I would give 'em a ride all the way to where they were going. Crystal, she's the darker girl, said they were headed to her granny's house. She told me her mother had the flu, so they were going to stay with her granny and study for final exams there."

"Where is her grandmother's house?" Danny leaned forward, a piece of ham speared on his fork.

"See, that's what I wanted to tell you," Dee Dee said. She took a sip of coffee, set the cup on the table, and folded her hands in her lap. She looked down.

Danny reached over and touched her arm. "Anything might help us."

"The thing is, first she told me her granny's house was in Vanderhoof and they were going to take a bus there. But later, she said her gran lived in Tintagel. It was like she was making things up. Actually, I kind of thought a bunch of the stuff she said was, you know, girl talk. And don't ask me why, but I got the feeling those girls were running away. Kids do that, you know."

Zoey nodded.

"Like I said, I offered them a ride after my shift, and I thought they were gonna take me up on it. But all of a sudden, they were gone. And a creepy guy who comes in here from time to time was talking to them, and suddenly, he was gone too. And that's why I'm so worried about those girls. Something didn't feel right."

"Was the creepy guy a salesman? A medical supply salesman?" Zoey asked.

"He's a salesman, for sure. But I don't know what he sells. The thing is, if I'd insisted, or maybe offered them a full meal, they might not be in all the trouble I'm hearin' about on the news. I feel terrible."

They thanked Dee Dee Wine and promised to do everything possible to find Crystal and Majorca. Danny paid the bill, and they left the Blue Bird Café and Grill.

Standing by her vehicle, Zoey scowled. "That was completely useless."

"No, we learned something," Danny said. "We learned that the girls are not being truthful when they tell people where they're going. So, we can assume that when they told that guy at the motel they were heading to Vanderhoof, they were giving bogus information."

"How does that help us?"

"A data point right now, nothing more. But it might come in handy later."

"Should we report this?" Zoey squinted into the sun as she looked up at Danny.

Danny gazed off into the distance and spoke in a measured tone. "Well now, I suppose we *should...*"

Chapter Thirty-Five

Sticking close to the door, Crystal rocked from one foot to the other. She clung to the straps of her knapsack and scanned the windows—multi-colored pieces of glass, outlined in black. There were three tall, narrow windows on each side of the building, each depicting a scene with a young man wearing shoulder-length blonde hair and dressed in a flowing white gown. In one window pane, he sat on a rock surrounded by children. Crystal guessed he was telling them stories.

In another window, the young man scowled as he upended a table in a crowded marketplace while gold coins scattered on the ground at his feet. Crystal stared at streams of colored light spilling through the windows—scarlet, cobalt-blue, and emerald. The colors puddled on long wooden pews, on hymnals tucked into slatted fiddles behind each pew, and onto the polished hardwood floor. The air was cool, and the only sounds were the soft taps of Majorca's shoes as she walked up the center aisle. Crystal held her breath.

Majorca climbed two steps to the altar and disappeared into a room behind a large wooden podium.

But Crystal didn't move. She gaped at the altar—a solid slab of white marble with a white silk cloth draping over its surface. Strange symbols, embroidered in gold thread, decorated the cloth, and golden fringe dangled from each end. Two brass crosses mounted on marble globes sat on either side of the altar, and between them, a giant book lay open. A dark purple ribbon marked the pages.

Suspended over the altar, directly over the open book, an emaciated, weeping man hung from a huge wooden cross. A bloody circle of thorns snarled in his tangled blonde hair. His arms spread wide. Rusty nails protruded from his palms and feet. Blood seeped from a gash in his side. "Jesus," Crystal whispered.

Majorca bound back down the aisle. "Nobody in the pastor's office and the meeting room is clear. Let's go check the kitchen and see if..." She stopped and gaped at Crystal. "What's your problem? You look like you saw a ghost."

Crystal swallowed. She forced herself to glance away from the floating cross and the bleeding man. "Kitchen?"

"You know, where they make the coffee and stuff. There might be some leftovers from a potluck dinner or maybe some cookies. But even if we don't find any food, I know they'll have coffee."

She started back up the aisle. Crystal stood rooted in place. Majorca looked back at her.

"What's eating you? One minute you're waving a gun around, and the next you act like you're scared to death. What's going on?"

"I... I don't think we should be in a church."

Majorca put her hands on her hips and shook her head. "It's a building. My family goes to services every Sunday, my mum quilts in our church on Wednesdays, and my dad volunteers at the AA meetings. It's no big deal."

Crystal's pupils pooled wide, and a thin sheet of perspiration spread over her upper lip.

"I can't believe it," Majorca said. "You've never been in a church, have you?"

"We never had time." Crystal took a step backward toward the door.

"Amazing," Majorca said. She started to lob an insult, but something in Crystal's expression stopped her. Sidling up to Crystal, Majorca touched her arm. She spoke soft and low. "It's a little weird at first, all the crosses, the bleeding Jesus, and stuff. But you'll get used to it, and we need to hide today. No one will think to look for us in a church. We can leave as soon as it gets dark, but for right now, don't be scared because this really is a safe place."

Crystal slapped Majorca's hand away. "I'm not scared," she said. "This place gives me the creeps, that's all. But we can—"

The sound of clanging metal stopped her. Country music wafted from a room on the right side of the altar. Someone whistled along with a radio. Crystal froze. Goose flesh rippled over her skin.

Majorca turned slowly and faced the altar. "It's coming from the kitchen."

Chapter Thirty-Six

A RIVER OF FUEL flowed through the thick hose running from a silver truck to the holding tanks under the pumps at Maple Leaf Gas and Go. The fuel truck operator stood by, clipboard in hand, watching numbers click by on a dial. Five RCMP vehicles occupied the spaces reserved for the convenience store shoppers.

Inside the Maple Leaf Gas and Go, six uniformed constables crowded the store—one stood at the store's microwave waiting for a block of processed cheese to melt over an order of prepackaged poutine. The others gathered in front of the boxed donut display where Wayne Martin held court. The store smelled of microwaved poutine, auto air fresheners, and Wayne's perspiration.

"The delivery guy saw me through the window when he came to fill the pumps this morning. He called the day manager to come over with his keys and let me go. They tied me up over there." Wayne pointed to the support beam. "They used the phone cord and wound it tight so I couldn't employ any of the escape tactics—you know, military tactics, to get out. If they'd used plain rope, I would have been out in minutes." Wayne stopped, maybe waiting for one of the constables to ask about his escape tactics. When no one did, he continued. "After they tied me to the pole, they gagged me with a bandana. We sell 'em." He pointed to the display. "And then they took turns punching me in the gut. But I tell you, I can hold my own in a fight. Middleweight in high school." Wayne puffed his chest out.

When none of the officers asked about his fighting prowess, Wayne, again, continued, "They might look like girls, but they threw some mean punches."

Zoey glanced at Danny, caught his eye, and winked. Then, she took a step toward Wayne. "So, Mr. Martin, why were they punching you?"

"They wanted the combo to the safe."

"And did you—"

"Of course not. I'm the official night manager here. I don't just sell gas. I protect this establishment."

"So, did they gag you before or after they wanted the combo to the safe?" Danny asked.

Wayne flushed. "They beat me real hard at first, but I was givin' 'em an earful. You know, insults and such. So, they gagged me."

"They steal anything?" Hendricks stepped forward.

"Cash from the register, some donuts, and stuff. And a full box of sausage sticks from the back room. The boss is gonna be mad about that."

The microwave dinged, and Wayne jumped. "Still traumatized," he muttered.

"Mr. Martin," Zoey said, "can you give us a description of the people who tied you up, punched you, and robbed the store?"

"You betcha. I was watching the news when they came in. I knew it was them right off, but they looked different from their pictures on the television. The half-breed, she had real short hair and was wearing a flannel shirt. It looked like a man's shirt, way too big for her. Probably stole it. And she was ugly, you know, mean-lookin'."

"And the other one?" Danny asked.

"She kinda looked like a hillbilly, like in a cartoon. Real short red hair." Wayne focused on an ad for frozen pizza hanging over the freezer unit, then he turned back to Danny. "She might be cute except for a wicked-looking scratch on her cheek. She must be a scrapper."

"Did they say anything about where they were headed?" Hendricks asked.

Nodding rapidly, Wayne blurted out, "Yes, they did, and I got information the news reporters missed. It's probably worth a reward, right?"

"What information?"

"The news guys say they're heading to Vanderhoof," Wayne said, "But them girls only said that to throw you guys off. They're headed to Prince George. They're meeting their boyfriends there."

"Boyfriends?" Zoey said.

"Yep," Wayne bobbed his head. "Big, nasty bikers. Them girls are in a biker gang." A look of triumph lit Wayne's face. "That's worth a reward, right?"Danny and Zoey exchanged another glance and walked out into the fresh air. Soon after, Hendricks and the others joined them.

"Think he's reliable?" one of Hendrick's crew asked.

Hendricks pulled a cigarette from his coat pocket, lit it, and took a long drag. Exhaling, he narrowed his eyes. "That guy is a nobody with a blowhard attitude, but he gave us some valuable information. I'm pulling a team together, and we'll set up a dragnet covering the entire city of Prince George. We'll turn over every rock. Look anywhere and everywhere teenagers might think they can hide. I'm bringing those girls in and ending all this bullshit."

Zoey stepped toward Hendricks. "This involves girls, young girls. It's my case," she said. "And I—"

"Stop it right there," Hendricks said. "You had some fun playing cop, but you wasted a lot of time and, from my perspective, a lot of department resources, too. Working Prince George is way too much for a rookie. Especially for a female rookie."

"The sergeant said—"

"The sergeant wants this wrapped up. I'm gonna do that. Go back and get some experience at the desk. And Simard? I like my coffee hot with three sugars." Dropping the cigarette to the ground, Hendricks walked to his vehicle. Snickering, his buddies followed.

Zoey stood in place and watched Hendricks peel out of the lot and speed onto the highway. When only the two of them remained, Danny turned to her. "Zoey. It's a club, and Hendricks is a charter member."

Ten minutes from her apartment, the radio squawked. "Simard. O'Brien. Serge wants to see you. Like yesterday."

Thirty minutes later, Zoey and Danny left the department with new work assignments.

"We knew it was coming," Danny said.

"At least you're still on the streets, even if you only direct traffic in the school zone. Thanks to Hendricks, I'll be stuck inside, nursing paper cuts." When they reached her car, Zoey looked up at Danny. "He's not going to find them, you know."

Danny's expression turned grim. "I don't like the guy," he said. "He's the kind of bastard I'd give a right pounding to back in Ireland. And someday, he'll get his. But for now, I hope you're wrong. For the sake of those girls, we have to hope that he finds them because it's a cruel world out there."

Chapter Thirty-Seven

THE SOUND OF WATER splashing into a metal bucket drowned out the radio for a couple of minutes, but the high, sharp whistle echoed through the building.

"Who do you think it is?" Crystal whispered.

"I bet it's the janitor. At our church, the cleaning ladies work on Fridays 'cause we have bingo games on Saturdays, but maybe they don't have anything here on Saturdays."

"How'd he get into the church?" Crystal said.

"There's always a back door."

"Let's get out of here before he sees us." Crystal started toward the front with Majorca close behind, but they stopped when they heard a loud clank.

"Say, what are you two doing here?" He stood in front of the altar, one gnarled hand gripping a mop poised over a bucket of soapy water, the other running through his sparse gray hair.

"We're, um, we came here to practice for the play this Sunday," Majorca said.

The elderly man tilted his head and squeezed his eyes shut. A moment later, he opened them and squinted at her. "I don't recall hearing anything about a play," he said.

"No worries, mister. We can practice someplace else." Crystal edged toward the door.

"No," Majorca said. "We need to practice here, in the church, or we might mess up our parts on Sunday." She looked at the man and blinked. "Didn't you read the bulletin? The high school seniors are putting on a play this Sunday. A play about Jesus healing the sick."

Again, the old man closed his eyes, and when he opened them, he sloshed the mop into the bucket. Clouds of foam splashed out. Resting the mop handle against the altar, he walked down the steps to the aisle.

"No, I don't recall anything about a play. My wife types up the bulletin every week, and she reads it to me before she takes it to the printer. I'd remember if there was a play."

"Come on," Crystal said.

Majorca hesitated, then moved toward the door.

"Now, don't you worry, girls," the man said. He stopped walking at the head of the first pew and grabbed it for balance. "This is the Lord's house, and no matter your trouble or pain, you're welcome here."

"What are you saying, old man?" Crystal said.

"What I'm sayin' is that if you need a place to rest your weary soul or your wounded body, the Lord's house is always open. You wouldn't be the first to seek peace in this place. You girls need to stretch out and take a load off for a while? I'll mop up these floors, and then I'll leave you to your visit with the Heavenly Father. And if you need something to eat, there are sandwiches in the refrigerator. The ladies made 'em for after service tomorrow, but there's plenty. Help yourselves."

The man stood still and bowed his head.

"Is he praying?" Crystal whispered.

Majorca nodded and grinned. "Told you, sanctuary."

In the moment's peace, a soft country and western song, something about love, drifted through the building. Crystal exhaled.

"We interrupt this broadcast with an important notice for the public. The runaways we've been covering are on the move again. They are believed to have altered their appearances and to be heading toward Vanderhoof. The RCMP asks the public to report any sightings of these girls immediately, but reminds the public not to engage with them. We repeat, do not engage with them."

The sweet notes of the country and western song returned, then faded, and another tune, this one more upbeat, began. The old man opened his eyes and regarded Crystal and Majorca. "You girls are the ones they're after, aren't you?"

Crystal started walking up the aisle, holding her hands out as if pleading. "Look, we didn't mean to hurt anybody, it was all a mistake. We messed up. Don't worry, we'll get outta here. We'll leave you alone."

The man took two steps back, rotated toward the altar, and hobbled up the steps. Grabbing its wooden handle, he pulled the soapy, wet mop from the bucket and held it like a spear. "Don't you come near me. I've gotta call the police. I'm sorry you girls got yourselves in some trouble. But I've gotta call the police."

"No!" Majorca dashed up the aisle. "Don't call the police!"

The man gripped the mop and jabbed the air. Water and soap splashed onto the polished floor.

Majorca ran at the mop and grabbed the stringy, soapy bundle. Sliding forward on the wet floor, she drove the mop handle into the man's stomach. He lost his balance and careened backward. His right arm flailed out, caught the edge of the silk cloth, and pulled it sideways, dragging a globe and brass cross to the ground. As the cross hit the floor, the old man's head smashed against the edge of the altar. Blood spurted onto the pages of the Bible, leaving a wide red streak. The man slid to the floor and slumped over.

Majorca screamed. She leapt toward the altar but slipped again and landed on her left kneecap. She let out a sharp cry.

Crystal sprinted up the aisle. She reached for Majorca. "Here, grab my hand," she said. "We gotta get out of here."

Stumbling to her feet, Majorca sobbed. "No! We have to help him."

"We can't help him," Crystal said. She squeezed Majorca's arm. "We have to go. Now!"

Majorca yanked from Crystal's grasp and scrambled toward the altar. "No, no. You don't understand. We have to help him. We have to call an ambulance."

Crystal skated around Majorca and slapped her across her face. Majorca stopped. And blinked.

"We can't help him," Crystal said. "We have to get out of here."

"But...but..." Majorca trembled.

Crystal grabbed Majorca's shoulders and shook her. Then she spun her around to face the altar. "Look. Look at him. There's nothing we can do."

At the foot of the altar, the old man remained still, his head lying in a pool of blood.

Chapter Thirty-Eight

They left through the kitchen. Crystal stopped at the refrigerator long enough to grab a can of pop and two sandwiches wrapped in wax paper. Majorca paused long enough to dry heave outside the back door.

"Come on, we gotta go." Crystal dashed from the church lot onto the road. Wiping her mouth with her sleeve and stumbling, Majorca followed her. They sprinted through the streets of Endako until they located the logging road. The road was paved and wide for six blocks, and then it narrowed and turned to rutted dirt.

Two large dogs, a collie and a husky, joined the race, but after several minutes, maybe bored with the game or attending to a call, the dogs fell off and trotted back toward town. Crystal and Majorca continued onward.

Their pace slowed as the road's incline increased and the ruts deepened. Running became jogging, and jogging turned to a trudge. The forest beckoned with a cool, dense reprieve from the relentless sun.

"Slow down, Crystal. I'm hot and I have to pee."

"Again? You already did that."

"That was ages ago. Besides, I'm starving and my knee hurts. I wanna take a break."

Crystal scrutinized the scene. The logging road continued to climb steeper with every half-kilometer. They'd left the town at least two hours earlier, and now, a long, dusty road trailed behind them and a long, dusty road stretched in front. Walls of dark green foliage shadowed both sides.

"We can't stop here," she said. "Anyone coming up this road will spot us in a heartbeat."

"Then what *can* we do?"

"If we're gonna stop, we gotta hide in the trees."

Shielding her eyes, Majorca scanned the dense brush. "I don't even see how we can get in there," she said.

"So we keep walking until we find an opening."

"But, Crystal. I've gotta pee."

"I'm gonna keep going, but you pee right here, in the middle of the road. And if a truck comes, it will run you over and flatten your bare butt." Crystal continued trudging up the road.

Majorca groused as she followed. "You know, sometimes you really are hor-rible. A total jerk."

"Whatever," Crystal said.

The sun had ticked past high noon when Crystal spotted an opening where tire tracks gouged deep wounds into the softer soil at the road's shoulder. Several yards from the shoulder's edge, a carpet of wild strawberry tendrils, thick with tiny white flowers, hid the tracks.

"I think somebody swerved here," she said, "probably crashed into those trees." She pointed to saplings growing over the broken stumps of dead pines. "This is a good place to get off the road." Crystal tramped over low vegetation and made her way into the forest.

"What about bugs?" Majorca stood at the side of the road watching Crystal's denim jacket meld into the shadows. "I don't like—"

The thundering rumble of a logging truck, moving fast, cut her off. Majorca dashed from the road and plunged into the trees. Tripping on a root, she landed face down in wild strawberry plants. The truck roared past, churning clouds of brown dust and sending a hail of pebbles from behind its massive tires.

Majorca pushed herself up and started to stand, but screeched as a blast of sharp pain shot through her ankle. Grabbing a branch to steady herself, she brushed dirt from her coveralls and swatted at insects buzzing around her face. "Crystal, I fell, and I think I broke my ankle."

Crystal clomped back through the undergrowth. "Jesus. First, you smacked your knee, and now, it's your ankle. You are nothing but a pain in the butt." Bending down, she pressed Majorca's right foot in her hands. Majorca yelped.

"Look," Crystal said, "I don't think you broke it. Maybe you twisted it. Can you walk?"

"I...I think I can." Majorca tried a tentative step, winced, and cried out in pain. "Crystal, it really hurts, and I'm hungry. Can't we take a little break?"

"You are such a wuss. I should leave you here." Crystal started to walk away, but turned back to Majorca. "Look," she said, "I found a big log—a little ways in. If you can make it that far, it would be a good place to stop."

Sitting on the fallen log, they devoured the sandwiches and polished off the chips. "Best food we've had so far." Crystal smacked her lips.

"Those ladies make a mean ham and cheese, but now I'm thirsty," Majorca said.

Crystal handed her the cola. "Save half for me," she said. When they finished, Crystal tossed the can, the wax paper wrappings, and the crisp bag into the woods.

Majorca leaned back on her elbows and tilted her face toward the sky. Sunlight, peeking through the foliage, dappled her skin. "I think we should go back and see how that old man is doing. I'm worried about him."

Crystal hesitated, then shook her head. "No, we're not going back. First off, that old guy is fine. He's probably got one mean headache, but he's fine. Maybe he's at home having a beer right now. And second, if we go back, we'll still have to dodge logging trucks and cops. We're a lot safer in the forest than we were on the road. I don't wanna go back."

"But Crystal, it'll get dark in a few hours. What will we do then?"

"I have a plan," Crystal said.

Majorca groaned.

"No, for real. Check it out." She pulled the map from her pack and spread it on the log. "Here. This is Endako. And here is Fort St. James. I figure we're right about here." She tapped a spot on the map.

"What makes you think that's—"

"Doesn't matter. The thing is, we're pretty close. If we walk straight across the woods, we'll come out here, on Highway 27." Again, she tapped the map. "I figure we can make it to the Highway in two, maybe three hours."

Majorca scrunched her brow into deep furrows and scratched at a bug bite. "I don't think you're right, Crystal. I think it's going to take a lot longer than three hours, and if it does, it will be dark before we get there."

"Maybe, but we have Vernon's flashlight. If we get to the road at night, we can walk without being spotted. This plan is actually much better than our first one."

Majorca bit her lower lip, then swatted at a mosquito. "I guess..."

Crystal slid from the log, folded and tucked the map into her pack, and slipped the straps over her shoulder. "Right then, it's a plan. Now, go pee, 'cause I know you gotta."

Chapter Thirty-Nine

A LONG RUN THROUGH the neighborhoods of Granisle, with Buster, almost always served to lighten Zoey's mood. But not this evening.

"I don't feel like running, Buster. I don't even feel like going outside. I want to crawl under a blanket and hide."

The elderly dog trotted over to the sofa, eased down, and rested his head on Zoey's knee. He looked up at her, his eyes searching.

"I know, buddy." Zoey scratched behind Buster's ears. "You need to go out. But maybe we'll take a walk around the block. Let you do your business, then come back home."

Buster stood and twirled his tail. Zoey smiled at him. "You're happy no matter what we're doing, aren't you? I wish I could feel the same." She clipped his leash to his collar, grabbed her jacket and keys, and together, they headed out into the drizzly evening.

Despite the cold mist and her plan to cut the walk short, Zoey and Buster didn't return to the apartment until Zoey's teeth chattered and both of them were drenched. After shucking her jacket and rehanging Buster's leash, she dried him off with a worn towel. She mixed kibble and canned food, filled his bowl, and ordered a pizza before heading to the bathroom for a long, hot shower.

Warm, dry, dressed in sweats, a thick cardigan, and fluffy slippers, Zoey shuffled to the front of the building and tipped the delivery guy. She almost made it back to her apartment when Rebecca slipped into the hallway. Quietly closing her door, she held one finger to her lips.

"Took forever to get them down," she said. "We spent the day at their grand-parents, which always means hours of silly games and way, way, way too many sweets. They were bouncing off the walls until about twenty minutes ago."

"At least they're happy." Zoey edged toward her door, the pizza warming her hand and filling the hall with its aroma.

Rebecca nodded to the box. "I see you have plans, but I was wondering if I could beg a favor?"

Not now. I need alone time. I need to pout and pace and maybe cry.

"Yes, of course," Zoey said. "What do you need?"

"This day frazzled every one of my nerves, so I want to pop down to the store and grab a bottle of wine and a TV dinner. I was hoping you'd sit in my apartment while I'm gone. I'll only be a few minutes, but I can't leave the twins alone."

Zoey nodded. And then, in spite of all her hopes of eating an entire pizza and drinking beer until she crashed on the sofa, she invited Rebecca to share.

"Look, I know you prefer wine, but I have a six-pack of Molson and this hot pizza, and Buster had a long walk, he has a full belly, and he's upside down on the bed, snoring. He's a happy camper, and I'm done with my dog mommy duties for a while. Why don't you take the pizza to your place, and I'll go grab the beer?"

Zoey was well into her second beer before Rebecca even broke the foam on her first.

"So," Rebecca nodded toward Zoey's empty bottle. "I'm guessing my time with the in-laws and two sugared-up kids was light work compared to whatever you went through today. You want to talk about it?" She sat in the recliner while Zoey lounged on the sofa.

Zoey shook her head and wolfed down a second slice of pizza. But by the time she'd popped the cap on her third Molson, she changed her mind.

"I got fired today," she said.

"What?" Rebecca returned a half-eaten slice to the box.

"Not fired, exactly. But Gagnon took me off the case with the missing girls. I'm starting a new position on Monday. Filing and fetching coffee for the good old boys."

"Wait a minute." Rebecca leaned toward Zoey. "I thought you and that Irish guy were the only ones working the case. And I thought you were assigned to everything dealing with women and children."

Zoey nodded. "I was. We were. But have you watched the news in the last two days?"

Rebecca snorted. "I haven't even had time to think."

"Well, if you did have time to watch the news, you'd know about the crime spree those girls are riding. Besides pushing that car into the lake, they killed a guy, tied up a couple of men, stole a car, set it on fire, and then stole a truck. And that's what we know about, so far."

"Killed a guy?"

"I am one hundred percent sure it was in self-defense. Everything points to attempted rape, with one girl defending the other."

"Good Lord, that's awful. Those poor girls. But, Zoey, why didn't they report what happened? I can't imagine a court of law condemning a young girl for protecting another girl from rape."

"I've wondered about that too," Zoey said, "but maybe they don't know how the law works. And then there's the issue of the car in the lake. Maybe they know about that drowned toddler, and they think, at least one of them will be held responsible. And, of course, there are the chopped fingers."

"The what?"Zoey reached for another slice of pizza. "You probably don't want to know about that."

Rebecca shuddered. "I could never do police work."

Zoey swallowed a bite and washed it down with a long gulp. She held the bottle up to the lamp and watched as tiny bubbles swirled while she spoke. "What I think, but can't prove, is that those two committed minor crimes—probably fueled by teenage hormones—but things blew up and got out of hand, so, stupidly, they decided to run. I also think, but again can't prove, that all the events along the way were accidental or at least unplanned. What I know, for sure, is that those girls are smart, because they're one step ahead of us. And what I can feel in my bones is that they are frightened, too frightened to seek help. So, they keep running."

"All that makes sense to me," Rebecca said. "So, what's the problem? Why did your boss take you off the case?"

Zoey sighed. "He has me tangled up with the publicity around the girls. He doesn't like negative press. He thinks it hurts the public's perception of the Mounties. Mostly, he's worried about the public's perception of him."

"I bet he's gunning for a new position, climbing the ladder," Rebecca said, "and negative publicity wouldn't be good for that." She picked up her half-slice, looked at it, then returned it to the box. "But Zoey, of everyone on that force, you're the only one who can understand, or get close to understanding, what's going on with those girls. They should be giving you full rein on this."

Zoey looked at Rebecca with a soft, wan smile. "There's something else, but saying anything about it would only hurt every other girl and woman who dreams of serving."

"What?"

"The guys in the RCMP, at least the ones in this part of the country, aren't comfortable having a woman in the field. It's something my female classmates and I talked about. But only behind closed doors. We all knew it was going to be hard—being the first ones." Zoey set her bottle on the coffee table.

Rebecca stood and walked around the table. Scooting a toy aside, she sat down and looped her arm around Zoey. They sat still for a few moments until Zoey reached up and patted Rebecca's hand. "Thanks," she said.

Rebecca stood and walked back to the recliner. "What now?"

"Now I go home, snuggle with my dog, and go to sleep."

"And tomorrow?"

"Catch up on errands. Maybe take Buster for a ride into the country some-where. Give him a proper run. Iron my uniform, so I look sharp at my new job on Monday." She stood. "I'll leave the pizza with you and the twins. But I'll take the rest of the beer."

Sitting against her headboard, one hand resting on Buster's head, the other holding a half-bottle of lukewarm Molson, Zoey replayed the past few days.

She had no doubts that the other officers in the department were skilled and competent constables. But Rebecca had made a good point. "Here's the thing, Buster." Zoey rubbed his ears. Buster rolled over on his back, belly up, tongue out. "Men and women think differently. Those guys are looking for kids having a lark, or budding juvenile delinquents. They don't understand the emotions those girls must be feeling. I know, in my mind and my heart, that their pain and fear are driving every decision those girls make."

Zoey set the bottle on her bedside table and clicked off her lamp. Snuggling down next to Buster, she whispered, "I'm not going to give up on them. No matter what it costs me."

Chapter Forty

Spiky branches, thick brush, and Majorca's injured ankle hindered their progress, but although the going was slow, the forest was cool and shady and offered a pardon from the dust and heat of the road. Spots of sunlight peeking through the leafy canopy, along with the loamy fragrance of damp earth and the musky scent of mushrooms, created an atmosphere of tranquility. The hike would have been perfect if it hadn't been for the constant buzzing and biting of insects. Swatting and cursing the flying pests, they trudged through the bush, stopping occasionally for Crystal to check the map and to assure Majorca they were heading in the right direction.

Twilight came faster than either had imagined. The forest morphed from bright green lit by flickers of sunlight to shadowed grays and dark gloom. Even in the flashlight's glow, they tripped on roots and half-buried rocks. Crystal swore under her breath each time she stumbled. The third time her boot caught against a rock, she dropped the flashlight and went sprawling into a bush covered with thorns.

"Fuck this shit!" Her voice rang through the trees.

"Here," Majorca extended a hand to help, but Crystal slapped it away. "Leave me the fuck alone."

Majorca found the flashlight behind a rock, but the glass and the bulb were both broken. She handed the useless torch to Crystal, who swore and pitched it deep into the trees.

Crystal stopped walking after another half hour of stumbling along in the dark. Majorca bumped into her.

"Sorry."

"Listen, this isn't working. We gotta stay put for the night and start up again in the morning."

"Stay in the woods? All night? But—"

"We don't have much of a choice, now do we? You're already a gimp, and if we keep going like this, one of us is gonna break a leg. We need to find a place to crash for the night."

Crystal sat cross-legged on a carpet of moss. Majorca stretched her legs out straight, favoring her sore ankle. They leaned against a fallen tree. Blending in the soft breeze, the tang of pine, spruce, and fir produced a calming perfume.

"This is nice," Crystal said.

"Now, yes. But I have a feeling we'll get cold later on."

Crystal closed her eyes. "Don't worry. I read a book about these kids who survived in the wilderness for two weeks. All we have to do is stay close together and let our body heat do the work." Yawning, she looped her arm around Majorca's shoulders. "See? Warmer already."

Majorca snuggled closer to Crystal and released a long sigh. "Crystal?"

"What?"

"Tell me more about your grandma."

"Like what?"

"I dunno, like, what do you do when you visit her? Besides eat."

"Um, so this is kind of corny. Sorta stupid. But she likes to sit in her rocking chair and peel apples with a paring knife. She can peel a whole apple with only one long, curly slice. Sometimes I sit on the floor and put my head on her knee and watch those apple skins curl and drop into a dish on her lap. Stupid, right?"

"It's not stupid. It's like you're safe and peaceful watching apple peels curl. It's like your grandma is telling you she loves you without saying a word."

Crystal swiped at a single tear. "Don't be such a dip," she said.

They sat listening to crickets and the sing-song sound of katydids. A soft breeze ruffled the branches above them. A peaceful moment until Majorca stifled a sob.

Crystal withdrew her arm. "Seriously? You're gonna cry and ruin a perfectly good night in the woods? Unbelievable."

Majorca snuffled back a sob. "Crystal, it's that everything is so messed up. I wish...I wish I could go back to Rhonda's house and start all over. I wish I had never walked down by the lake. None of this would have happened if I didn't see Todd's car. Classes would be over. Dad always barbeques the first week of June, rain or shine, so I'd be at home having burgers and potato salad."

"Are you losing your mind?" Crystal said. "If you didn't see Todd's car, we never would have met. So, in a way, it was a good thing, right?"

Majorca burst into tears. "I forgot. I dragged you into all of this. If we didn't meet, you'd be at your grandma's by now. Eating roast chicken, and pie, and watching her peel apples. And you wouldn't be in any trouble."

Crystal readjusted her position against the tree and stretched. "You don't know that," she said. "I get in lots of trouble, all by myself."

"You...you do?" Majorca hiccupped. "Do you stab guys, and steal cars, and duct-tape people to chairs? Do you start cars on fire all by yourself?"

"No, maybe not that kind of trouble, but I do stuff."

"Like what?"

"Like one time, my mom found this sofa on the side of the road. It was gross. One of the cushions was missing, and the springs poked through. It was covered in dog fur and stains that smelled like baby shit. But my mom wanted it, so she made me help her drag it back to our trailer. Some kids from school saw us and they made fun of me. They said I was gonna glue my dirty ass to that dirty sofa and be a fat loser. Like my mom."

Majorca turned to face Crystal. "That's horrible."

Crystal grinned. "No worries, I got back at them. Big time."

"How?"

"I stole a giant tube of Super Glue from shop class, and when they went to lunch, I glued their books inside their packs, and then I glued their packs to their desks." Crystal smirked.

Covering her face with her hands, Majorca looked away. Her shoulders shook.

"Are you crying again?"

Majorca gasped for breath. "No, I...I..." A giggle at first, then a chuckle, and then a full-on guffaw. If the forest creatures were listening, they heard the high-pitched laughter of two teenage girls echoing through the night.

Chapter Forty-One

Intense eyes observing her woke Majorca. She rolled over and looked up. "Hey." She elbowed Crystal.

Crystal groaned and pushed her face deeper into the crook of her arm.

"Crystal!" The word came out in a hiss.

"Go away."

"You have to wake up. A vulture is watching us. He's waiting for us to die so he can eat us." Majorca shook Crystal's shoulder.

"Shit." Crystal rolled onto her back, blinked, and looked at the branch above them where a sleek ebony bird perched—its head cocked to one side, its glistening black eyes staring at them. "It's a fucking crow, you moron." She closed her eyes and rolled back onto her side.

"No, it's not. It's too big to be a crow."

"Then it's a raven."

"Crystal, I'm serious."

Crystal sighed and pushed herself to sit. Yawning, she stretched, then stood.

"Look, girly, who here has native blood? Knowing the difference between crows, and ravens, and vultures is in my DNA."

She left Majorca, still lying flat on the bed of moss, and disappeared into the forest. When she returned, Majorca was sitting on the fallen tree, engaged in a staring contest with the bird.

"For Christ's sake." Crystal found a rock and, with a wind-up that would impress the big leagues, she lobbed the rock skyward. The bird flew off, squawking its displeasure. The rock clattered through tree branches and dropped not far from the log.

"Thank you," Majorca said.

Crystal grunted, grabbed her knapsack, and plopped down.

"Be right back." Limping, Majorca headed for the trees.

While a flock of birds sang to the morning, Crystal focused on the contents of her bag—Zelda with her three bullets, the stolen scissors, Vernon's map, the overdue library book, her rolled certificate, the two tampons with their paper wrappers now torn, the fast-food bag containing Clive's fingers, the string, her mother's cigarettes and lighter, and the donut box. One donut remained. Most of the sugar had either flaked off into the box or had dissolved into the doughy ring.

"Pathetic," she said. She tore the pastry in two, ate one half, returned the other half to the box, and set it on the moss.

Majorca crashed through the underbrush, dragging her sore foot. "Crystal."

"What now? Some little bird bite your bare ass while you were peeing?"

"Be serious. This is horrible. I got my period."

"So?"

"So, what am I supposed to do? I always carry a pad in my book bag, but—"

"No worries. I can help." Again, Crystal rummaged through the contents of her knapsack and pulled out one of the tattered tampons. "I brought two. They should get you through until we get to Fort St. James. We can stop at a store when we get there, 'cause I'm pretty sure my gran doesn't have a supply of these." Chuckling at her own joke, she held the tube out to Majorca.

Majorca stared at the tampon but didn't move.

"Well?"

"I can't use that thing."

"You what?"

"My mother says tampons ruin your virginity. She says she never had anything, you know, stuck up there until her wedding night."

Crystal stared, slack-jawed at Majorca.

"Unbelievable," she said.

"I have to make a pad. Do you have any napkins or tissues in your pack?"

Crystal dropped her knapsack to the ground and, propping on her elbows, she leaned back against the log's rough bark. "Nope. Sorry. Fresh out of hankies. Two tampons. Best I can do."

Biting her lower lip, Majorca paced. "What am I going to do? My underpants are already soaked, and pretty soon, these coveralls will be covered in blood. I have to make a pad." She stopped pacing and stood facing Crystal.

With the girls quiet, bird songs and the low hum of flies filled the air.

Crystal sighed. She sat up, retrieved her pack, and pulled the scissors out. Shucking her denim jacket, she unbuttoned the flannel shirt. Pulling the shirt off, she hopped onto the log in her jeans and stretchy black bra.

"What are you doing?" Majorca said.

"Making you a pad."

Crystal cut the shirt's right sleeve off at the shoulder. Next, she cut the threads holding the buttons to the cuffs and handed the sleeve to Majorca.

"There. Fold it up and stick it in your underwear. It should hold for a while." She held the shirt up. "I don't know what good a one-sleeved shirt is, so I might as well make another one." She attacked the left sleeve.

Folding one sleeve into a square, Majorca hobbled back into the trees. When she returned, Crystal was stuffing her denim jacket into her knapsack. She'd tied the tails of the flannel shirt at her waist. Vernon's gun stuck out from the waistband of her jeans. She turned to Majorca. "Did it work?"

Majorca nodded. "It did, but—"

"But what?"

"The thing is, my period is, you know, pretty heavy. I don't know how long the, um... pad will hold. "

Crystal crossed her legs and lowered to the soft ground. She patted the moss. "Come here, a minute. There's something I gotta tell you."

Majorca sat.

"The thing is," Crystal said, "you really need to learn how to use the tampon because—"

"Because what?" "Because you stink."

Majorca jumped up. Looking down at Crystal, she balled her fists. "I do not stink."

"Yes. You do. And if I can smell you, every wild animal in this forest can smell you. We need to make a little detour. We'll go swimming in Fraser Lake. It's on the other side of those trees. You need to wash out your underwear and use one of those tampons."

"My body smells natural, and I already told you, tampons—"

"No, they don't. And you don't smell natural, you smell gross. We need to—"

"To hell with you, Crystal Lynn Harsh. I don't care what you say, I'm not cramming anything up there. You think you're so smart, but you've never even been in a church, and...and you always stink! The kids at school talk about how you stink. It's like you don't even have a shower at home. They say you live in a shed, and they say your mother works at the truck stop doing gross things to truckers. I don't need you or your stupid tampons. Screw you!" Majorca spun around and crashed into the thick brush.

Crystal stared at the spot where Majorca had disappeared. Pulling her knapsack close, she wrapped her arms around it and whispered, "Fuck her."

Chapter Forty-Two

CRYSTAL SAT CLUTCHING THE entirety of her worldly possessions to her chest for several minutes. Then, with a long sigh, she opened the pack and pulled out her certificate. Carefully unrolling the tube, she smoothed the document on the soft patch of moss. A fold creased the paper, and the bottom edge was frayed where the certificate had rubbed against the pack's oiled canvas. Tracing the curling letters of her name with one finger, she read the words she'd read a thousand times. ALL GRADES #1 READER OF THE YEAR 1972. She fought back tears.

She's right. I lived in a shed. I couldn't shower. And my mother is a whore.

She stared at the paper.

I'll end up like her. I'll be a mean, smelly old whore.

Crystal snatched up the certificate and wadded it into a tight ball. "Fuck you," she said. "Fuck everything."

She pitched the crumpled paper under the fallen log, then collapsed to the ground, her head in her arms. Her shoulders shook as she sobbed.

A scream sliced the morning. Crystal's head snapped up. Jumping to her feet, she knuckled tears from her eyes.

"What the…"

A second scream and the crashing of branches and brush.

"Majorca!" Reaching around her waist, she touched the gun and then bolted into the brush. Branches slashed her face and arms as she raced toward the sound. Seconds later, she bumped into Majorca.

Majorca stood frozen in place, her eyes wide, her mouth gaping. Across a clearing, not too far from them, a bear stood on its hind feet with its black fur shining in the patchy sunlight, its forepaws outstretched, and its crème-colored snout raised, as it sniffed the air. The great creature turned its head and faced the girls.

A moment of silence.

Crystal pulled the trigger.

Branches cracked overhead. A shower of leaves rained onto the clearing. Howling, the bear dropped to all fours. It crashed into the forest and disappeared into the deep shadows.

A moment passed, then Crystal whooped. "Did you *see* that?"

"Crystal, did you...did you shoot it?"

Her grin wide, eyes bright, Crystal shook her head. "Nah, I shot into the air."

Shaking and sobbing, Majorca threw her arms around Crystal. "I thought I was going to die."

Crystal returned the gun to the back waistband of her jeans and pushed Majorca away. "Do you believe me now? About needing to, you know, clean up a little?"

Majorca swiped tears from her face and nodded. "You're right. But um..."

"What?"

"I don't know how to use a tampon."

Crystal grinned. "Don't stress. I'll show you."

While Crystal waited, Majorca folded the second flannel sleeve and went behind a clump of trees.

"Don't go too far this time," Crystal said. "We only have two bullets left."

They reached Fraser Lake with the sun directly overhead. Sweat soaked their shirts, and Majorca's pale skin had turned pink with a hint of sunburn.

"What's that stuff?" she asked. She pointed to a layer of pale green material floating on the lake's surface close to the shore.

"Bug eggs. Maybe black flies or mosquitoes."

Majorca shuddered. "I spent all my summers swimming in Babine Lake, but I never saw stuff like that." Shielding her eyes from the sun, she scanned the water. "How can we wash our clothes? We need to be on the shore."

Crystal pulled the cash from her pocket and stashed it in the front compartment of her knapsack. She unlaced her boots, pushed the gun into one of them, and hid the pair, along with her pack and denim jacket, behind a cluster of rocks. Wearing her socks, jeans, and the sleeveless flannel shirt, she waded into the lake. She used a stick to push the green slime away until she reached deep water. Then she tossed the stick and swam, side stroke, to the center of the small lake.

Dropping under the surface, Crystal shook her head and let the cool water soak her hair. She went up for a breath, down again, up for another breath, and down. On her third resurface, she came face-to-face with Majorca, who stayed in place, treading water. She wore only her bra and panties.

Crystal spat a stream of water. "Nice, huh?" She rolled to her back and floated.

"You shouldn't swallow that water. It might have germs in it."

"At least I'll be clean. And my clothes will be too."

When gooseflesh rippled across their skin, they swam to shore. Crystal peeled off her socks, jeans, and shirt, and laid them across a rock in the sun. Majorca spread her coveralls on the sandy shore and patted one end.

"We can sit on these."

Crystal shook her head. "First, you need a little biology lesson."

Squatting in front of Majorca, Crystal explained how the cardboard tube worked, and she mimed the action of inserting a tampon. Around them, birds tittered, and butterflies flapped tissue wings in the light breeze. The scent of warm pine needles mixed with the cool, fresh scent of the lake.

"Got it?" Crystal asked.

Majorca grimaced but nodded and took the cardboard tube from Crystal. Then she slipped into the woods.

"Bury that tube!" Crystal yelled.

Stretched out, half on Majorca's coveralls, half on the sun-warmed sand, Crystal stared at the sky with its one fluffy cloud. She tried to see images in the cloud—a lamb, a dragon, the smiling face of an elderly woman with her head crowned in soft curls. But as hard as Crystal pretended, the cloud remained a single cotton ball flung against the powder blue sky above.

"I did it." Majorca plopped down on the coveralls.

"You feel okay?"

"I feel funny, but not too bad. And Crystal, thanks."

Crystal rolled to her side and propped up on one elbow. She looked at Majorca, who leaned back, with her face to the sky. Todd's class ring glinted in the sunlight. Crystal jumped up. "That reminds me of something."

Majorca opened one eye and watched as Crystal felt around in the front pocket of her jacket.

"Here it is," she said. "Now, I need the string." She pulled her knapsack from its hiding place and sloshed through the contents until she found the length of tangled twine. She walked back to Majorca's coveralls and plopped down.

Majorca sat up, shielding her eyes from the sun. "What's that?"

Crystal handed her the gold locket. "It's my gran's, but she gave it to me. I'm gonna put it on this string and wear it like you do lover boy's ring."

Turning it over in her hands, Majorca peered at the locket. The back side was shiny with only a few minor scratches marring the surface. A spray of small flowers was etched onto the front side. "Are these forget-me-nots?" She pointed to the etching.

"Dunno." Crystal worked to untangle a knot in the twine.

Majorca pushed her thumbnail into the thin gap between the sides and opened the locket.

One side held a wisp of light brown hair, and the other clasped a sepia-toned photo of an elderly woman. Loose white curls framed her pale, round face, and her eyes crinkled with her smile.

"Is this your grandma?"

"Got it!" Crystal pulled the knot out and straightened the twine. She glanced at Majorca. "Yep, that's her." She held out her hand for the locket.

Majorca took a final look at the smiling lady and gently closed the locket, but she didn't hand it to Crystal. "This is too special to hang on a stupid piece of string."

"String is what I have," Crystal said. "Now hand it over."

Majorca stood and walked to the edge of the lake.

"What are you doing?" Crystal scrambled up and followed her.

Standing at the water's edge, only a few feet from a patch of slimy green eggs, Majorca turned to Crystal. "Unhook my chain, will you?"

"What?"

"Unhook it."

Majorca slid the chunky class ring from the chain. "Here," she said. She handed the gold chain and the locket to Crystal. "Your grandma's locket will look great on this."

Crystal gaped at her. "Are you serious? You're really gonna put lover boy's ring on a piece of string?"

Majorca stood facing Crystal. Neither spoke or moved for a beat until Majorca silently pivoted toward the lake and pitched Todd's class ring across the water. It landed with a plunk and sank. Majorca turned back to Crystal, a broad grin on her face.

"What the—" Crystal started.

"Todd is shit. And I don't need shit."

They lay on the coveralls and snoozed until the sun dipped behind the trees, and the temperature dropped. A high-pitched whine buzzed Majorca's face. She slapped at a mosquito on her arm. And then, she slapped at another and another.

"Crystal. Wake up. We have to get away from the lake."

Crystal woke with a start. "Why?"

"Because I'm sun-burned and they're eating me alive." She waved her arms through the horde around her head and grabbed her blouse.

"Dammit, I should have turned these over. They're still damp," Crystal tugged at her jeans.

"Hurry. They'll dry on you if you still have any skin left."

They scrambled to dress while slapping at the swarm of biting insects. Biting, stinging insects, relentless in their quest for blood.

Chapter Forty-Three

HER EARLY MORNING RUN with Buster hadn't helped to clear her mind. Even the first cup of coffee tasted bitter. The three empty bottles on her kitchen counter explained Zoey's headache, but they didn't account for her dour mood. Pacing her apartment, still in her running clothes, Zoey tried to make a mental list of things she could do on her day off—the day before she started in her new position of delivering coffee to the sergeant and filing police reports. Reports written by constables allowed to work in the field.

"What do you think, Buster?" Should I clean the apartment? Iron my uniform? Go grocery shopping?" As she paced, Buster's large brown eyes followed her back and forth, back and forth. Finally, Zoey stopped. "This is ridiculous. I can't go shopping for broccoli and sliced bread knowing there are two frightened, maybe hurt, young girls out there on the run. I have to do something." She stood in the living room, thinking and biting a hangnail. The phone's jangling startled her from her thoughts.

"Look, I know it's Sunday morning, but I want to share something. Mind if I come by your place in about ten?"

Zoey hung up the phone and dashed into the bathroom for a hasty shower. She'd pulled on a pair of cut-offs and a clean white t-shirt when Buster's barking let her know that Danny had arrived.

"Want me to make coffee?"

"No. I shouldn't even be here, telling you this, but I joined the force to protect the ones who couldn't defend themselves. Not to play politics." He sat on the edge of Zoey's sofa and scratched Buster's ears.

"What's going on, Danny?"

"Yesterday evening a call came in from Tintagel. Seems a woman was delivering flowers to the church in Endako—that's a little town not too far down the road. She discovered an elderly maintenance man, sprawled out in a pool of blood on the altar. Deceased. There was water all over the floor, and a soapy mop close by, so it might have been an accident. Don't know yet. But, here's the kicker. That old Ford pickup? The one the girls stole? It was parked behind the church. Dead battery."

Zoey leaned forward. "You think the girls—"

"No telling yet. According to the police report, nothing was missing, although the pastor thought someone might have rifled through the refrigerator. A Tupperware box of wrapped sandwiches was left open. Hendricks figures the girls were hiding behind the church and maybe or maybe not, had a confrontation with the old man, but either way, they couldn't drive the truck, so they took off with their thumbs out. Based on what that guy at the gas station reported, Hendricks is positive the girls are hitchhiking to Prince George. But I don't think so, not after what we learned from that waitress. And, if I read you right, yesterday, I'm betting you don't think so either."

Watching him pet her dog, Zoey avoided Danny's gaze.

"So," Danny continued, "I'm guessing that you're going to do something really stupid, like try to find those girls on your own. And, if Gagnon finds out, it won't be good." He waited a moment and then asked, "Zoey, am I right?"

Zoey looked up and met Danny's eyes. "Hendricks is wrong. I can't prove it, but I can feel it in my bones. The girls probably saw something on the television in that gas station, or at least, by now, they've heard something on the radio. They know we're looking for them."

"You think they're hitchhiking?"

Zoey shook her head. "No, they're scared, Danny. But they're not stupid."

"Well then, what?"

Zoey stood and walked to the kitchen, where she rummaged around in a drawer. "Here," she said. She pulled out a map of British Columbia and returned to the living room, where she spread it out on her coffee table.

Danny gently eased Buster aside and leaned forward.

"Here's Endako," Zoey tapped a small dot on the map. "If you were here, and you were running from the police, and you knew hitchhiking was not only dangerous but would probably get you discovered, what would you do?"

Danny studied the map. "I'd try to figure out where the police were going, and I'd go someplace else. So, if you're right, and the girls did hear something on the radio, they'd know we're looking for them either in Vanderhoof or Prince George. So—"

"So, they've got to be crossing through the forest on foot from Endako to Highway 27." Zoey tapped the map again. "Stuart and Fort St. James are on that route. They're both tourist towns. And further up, there are a couple of ski resorts. Easy places for two high school girls to find work and disappear."

Danny looked up at the ceiling, then back down to Zoey. "I wouldn't be too sure about that. I've been hunting in the woods here, and they are nasty. Bears, snakes, flies that bite, and spiders with enough poison to drop a grown man. Those woods are no place for a couple of girls."

"You're not wrong about that, Danny. But I'm guessing those girls feel trapped and desperate. I'm guessing they'll take whatever risks they think will get them to safety."

Danny sighed, then stood. "I was reassigned to Hendricks' band of merry men, and we're leaving in about an hour. We're off to Prince George to comb the back alleys." He looked at Zoey. "I have a feeling I know what you're up to. All I can say is, be careful."

Chapter Forty-Four

Zoey waited for Danny to back out of her parking lot before spinning around. "Come on, Buster, we're going on an adventure!" Catching her excitement, Buster twirled in circles, barking and hopping.

After tossing his leash, a bowl, a bottle of water, and her wallet into a day pack, Zoey slipped into a pair of tennis shoes. Grabbing the map, she led Buster out to her car. Zoey glanced up at the fluffy white clouds as she held the car door open for her dog. "It's a long way, buddy," she said. "But we have perfect weather for a Sunday drive."

They stopped once for ice cream—a messy treat, but Zoey's optimism about finding the girls managed to override any concerns about the state of her car. She sang along with the radio and kept the windows open. Her hair, usually restrained in a tight bun, tossed free in the breeze.

In Tintagel, she pulled over and rechecked the map. Twenty minutes later, she spotted the *Welcome to Endako* sign all but obscured by roadside weeds. The church was easy to find—a pretty white building with blue trim and tidy grounds. She let Buster out of the car and followed a walkway to the front door, where a middle-aged woman was laying a wreath on a mound of flowers.

"Hello?" Zoey called out.

The woman straightened and turned to her.

Standing next to the woman, Zoey peered at the small memorial. Flowers surrounded a laminated photo of a smiling, elderly man wearing a khaki bucket hat and a khaki vest over a flannel shirt. Brightly colored fishing flies adorned the hat. A fishing pole and hand net crossed in front of the photo, and next to them, someone had tucked in a pint bottle of Canadian Club whiskey.

The woman examined the photo and made a soft tsking sound. "He was a good man," she said. "Kept the church spotless and kept half the town in trout. We're going to miss him."

"I'm sorry for your loss," Zoey said. She glanced around the street. No cars except her VW. "Was there a service here today?"

"No. I heard he slipped and fell while he was mopping the floor. I guess there was a lot of blood, so the pastor moved Sunday services over to the Lions Club building." She sighed. "I'd better be getting home. My grandbabies are coming over for Sunday dinner."

"How old are they?" Zoey asked.

"Nine and twelve." The woman smiled wide and pulled a small leather folder from her dress pocket. She flipped through photos until she found the one she was looking for. She handed it to Zoey. "Boys," she said. "Always into mischief and adventure. They drive my daughter half-crazy."

"They're darling." Zoey smiled. "Do they ever have adventures in the woods around here?"

"They've wandered into the forest a few times. But the woods in these parts are thick. Not many places you can even get in. And if you do venture into the bush, the flies and mosquitoes will drive you out real fast."

"I think I've heard that," Zoey said. "But, let's say, for grins, a kid, maybe even a teenager, wanted to have a little adventure in the woods, where would they get in? I mean, around here?"

The woman tapped one finger to her lips and looked off to one side before answering. "Lemme think," she said. "I guess they could follow the logging road. There's a place up a ways where a truck went off the side. Years ago. The fellow was blind drunk. My husband said the guy cleared a path right into the bush. So, maybe some kid could get in there." The woman took the folder from Zoey and dropped it back into her pocket. "But like I said, nobody in their right mind would stay in those woods for very long. They'd be eaten alive."

When the woman left, Zoey called to Buster. Once he resettled in the back seat, she drove through the town until she found a street where the pavement ended and a rutted dirt road began. "Buster, I think we found the logging road." Buster thumped his tail on the seat.

The uneven surface made traveling difficult, but Zoey maneuvered around the ruts while scanning the dense green walls on both sides of the road. The forest appeared inaccessible.

The temperature was falling when she spotted the section of forest flattened by the drunk driver. Pulling her car as close as possible to the road's edge, she parked, grabbed her day pack, and held the door for Buster. The old dog leapt over wild strawberry plants and crashed into the woods. Zoey followed at a slower pace, watching her steps to avoid tripping over hidden rocks or roots. Her tennis shoes slid on the sleek pine needles covering the forest floor, and although she pushed vegetation away from her face, branches scratched her bare legs below her cutoffs. As the forest shadows lengthened and the air cooled, gooseflesh prickled Zoey's arms. Worst of all, the woman at the church had been right about the mosquitoes. The further Zoey went into the forest, the thicker the swarms. When the buzzing sounded like a roar, and her skin was red from slapping herself, Zoey called to her dog. "Buster. Come. We have to get out of here." As she waited for Buster, she scanned the ground. Something caught her eye. She walked to a fallen log and bent down to retrieve a crumpled wad of wax paper, the kind used to wrap sandwiches. She found a cola can and a crumpled chip bag a foot away from the wax paper. A shiver ran through her. "They're here," she whispered to herself, "or at least they were here."

Although the desire to keep looking for the girls was heightened by her find, the mosquitoes, the chill, and the rapidly approaching darkness made continuing a fool's errand. Vowing to return in the morning, better prepared, she hurried back to the car, now less worried about tripping than about being—as the woman had suggested—eaten alive. At the edge of the road, she pulled Buster's leash from her day pack. Tying the bright orange leash to a branch, she marked the opening for her return trip.

It was late when they finally arrived in Granisle. As Buster gobbled his kibble, Zoey smeared antihistamine on her bites. She spoke to Crystal and Majorca as if they could hear her. "If I'm this bad after a short time, you two must look like raw hamburger. But don't worry, help is on the way. I'm coming. I promise."

Chapter Forty-Five

Away from the water, the onslaught of buzzing bloodsuckers became less a battle for life and more an annoyance. The sound of palms slapping skin joined the snapping of twigs and the crunch of dried leaves as Crystal and Majorca moved deeper and deeper into the forest. The temperature dropped, and the light dimmed.

"Crystal, I don't think we're going to reach Highway 27 before it gets dark."

"Maybe. Let's check."

Crouched on the ground, they scanned the map.

"I think we're here." Crystal pointed to the center of a green triangle. "See, we were at the lake and I think we came north."

Majorca tilted her head and squinted at the spot where Crystal pointed. She glanced up. "You don't know where we are, do you?"

Crystal picked up the map, folded it, and slid it into the front pocket of her knapsack. Then she pushed herself to standing. "Maybe I don't. So what?"

Majorca stood. She searched Crystal's face. In the deepening twilight, the shadows turned Crystal's eyes to hollow caverns. Her damp clothing smelled musky, and her shoulders stooped.

"Never mind, it's no big deal. But we have to find someplace to spend the night before we can't see anything. That's all."

Without a word, Crystal turned from Majorca and continued walking.

An ominous shadow stretched across the forest floor. Crystal pointed to a structure high in the center of three large trees. A rope ladder hung from the building—its lowest rung slipped over the stub of a branch two meters above the ground. "A hunter's blind," she said. "Think you can climb up with your ankle like that?"

Majorca considered the small hut high in the trees. "I don't know," she said. "Maybe if you go first, you can pull me up."

Crystal wedged her feet between two of the trees and, pressing against the rough bark of the third, she climbed until she reached the ladder. She released it from the branch and let it dangle to the ground. Gingerly, she gripped the ladder and swung one foot onto a rung. The ladder swayed with her weight and slammed her against a tree.

"Shit!"

"Are you okay?""No. I'm not. I smashed my face on this fucking tree."

"Here. I'll hold it and keep it in place." Majorca grabbed the ladder and pulled it straight using her body weight for leverage.

Crystal continued climbing until she reached the blind. Gripping the edge of the opening, she pulled herself up and flopped into the structure.

"What's it like?" Majorca called up to her.

"It's really dark."

Crystal slipped out of her pack and found the lighter. The tiny flame cast shadows around the blind. Built of branches lashed together with binding wire, the blind was big enough for two men with guns, ammo, and a beer cooler. Two small open windows and the open door let in the cooling evening air, but without the lighter's flame, the space was black as polished obsidian. The tree branches made the floor uneven, but the hunters' blind felt secure enough to hold Crystal's weight. "Hey, I think this is a good place to spend the night. It's super dark, but we'll be warmer than sleeping on the ground. Can you climb the ladder?"

"I think so, if it doesn't swing me into a tree." Majorca climbed with slow, deliberate movements until she was within a half-meter of the opening. "Ready? Pull me up," she said.

Crystal lay flat on her belly and stretched her arms toward Majorca. Grabbing the straps on the coveralls, she gave a tug. Majorca pushed off a rung and landed on the blinds' floor next to Crystal. Head to feet. For a moment, they lay on their stomachs, still and quiet.

Crystal pushed up and sat cross-legged with her back against a rough wall. Majorca sat opposite her, both legs stretched out. "You weren't kidding, it's dark in here," she said.

"I don't wanna waste the lighter, but take a look around. If we don't fall asleep and roll out the door, I think we'll be safe here." Crystal clicked the lighter and panned the space. Although the walls were constructed of dead branches, a few boughs wore new growth—tiny twigs sprouting green. Dry leaves and chunks of moss filled the open spaces between the branches.

"What's that?" Majorca pointed to a brown bundle stuffed into a gap in the wall.

Crystal scooted across the floor to the package and tapped on it. "It's a paper bag."

"Open it."

"You hold the lighter."

In the small circle of light, Crystal opened the bag, keeping it at arm's length. She dumped out a single item. A crumpled packet of aluminum foil fell to the blind's floor. Crunching the bag into a ball, Crystal pitched it into a corner, then peeled the foil packet open.

"I think it's jerky," she said. She pulled the twisted brown stick from the foil and gave it a sniff. "Yes, I'm positive, it's beef jerky."

"Do you think it's still, you know, good?"

Crystal took the lighter from Majorca and swiped the flame over the stick.

"What are you doing?"

"Are you hungry?

"Starving, but—"

"Me too. And I'm pretty sure beef jerky lasts a gazillion years. I'm burning off mold or germs or anything funky like that. So, you might say, I'm cooking dinner."

They stopped eating when their jaws were too sore to chew. Impossible to cut, even with the scissors, they'd passed the twisted stick back and forth, gnawing on opposite ends, until they managed to consume half of the dried meat. Crystal wrapped the remaining jerky in the foil and tucked it into her pack.

Despite being high above the damp forest floor, the temperature was cool. Crystal shivered and clapped her hands on her arms.

"Are you cold?" Majorca said.

"Sort of."

"Did your jeans get dry?"

"Mostly."

"You know what you said about body heat. If we spoon, we'll be warmer."

"What are you, queer?"

"Crystal..."

"Just kidding."

Majorca stretched diagonally across the floor and curled her arm under her head. Crystal stretched out behind her. Moments later, the blended warmth of their bodies slowed Crystal's tremors. They lay still, breathing softly.

Tree branches scratched the outside walls as a cold breeze blew through the woods. Tiny creatures moved through the dried leaves, moss, and branches of the blind, hunting for prey. Something large snuffed and rumbled past the trees housing the blind. Majorca pushed her body back, pressing tighter against Crystal.

"Crystal, are you still awake?"

"So?"

"I've been thinking."

Crystal groaned.

"Seriously," Majorca said, "we killed a few people, maybe only two, but at least two, and if we didn't kill him, we hurt that old man, for sure, and we sort of hurt that guy we tied up—"

"That guy was a jerk."

"Maybe—but listen, even if we stay at your grandma's for say—"

"Forever?"

"Be serious.

"So we stay there for a while?"

"Even if we stay at your grandma's house for a while, eventually, we have to go home, and the police will catch us. I mean, what will happen to us then?"

"Majorca, I wish you'd try to think things through before you bug me."

"I *am* trying to think things through."

"Doesn't sound like it and I seriously hope this is the last time we have to go through this. That jerk, Roy, tried to rape you. And he threatened to rape me and kill both of us. Self-defense, pure and simple."

"What about that old man?""He slipped and hit his head. The floor was wet, so that wasn't our fault. Besides, maybe—"

"And...and, we stole that car, and we set it on fire, and we stole Vernon's truck, and I'm pretty sure you stole some stuff, but don't tell me if you did, I mean, we committed some serious crimes..." She paused to catch her breath.

Crystal adjusted her position and pushed herself to a half crouch. She stared down at the dark form curled on the floor. Pricks of moonlight stabbing through the blind's leafy roof, dotted Majorca's pale skin.

"Think of it this way, if you're gonna get all paranoid about hurting some douche bag guys—in self-defense—then how are you gonna explain drowning that little kid?"

"Crystal!"

"I'm saying that everything, except pushing that car into the lake, was necessary. We did what we had to do to survive." Crystal lay back down and snuggled tight against Majorca.

Majorca scrunched her brow. "Even if that's true, what will happen to us?"

"You're only seventeen, right?"

"True, but—"

"So, like I said before, your parents will probably have to pay a fine, and of course, they'll have to hire a lawyer. That will cost a bundle. But they love you, so—"

"Will I go to jail?"

"No way. You might have to go to juvey for a month, but you'll probably only have to do community service or something."

"Then what?"

"Then you'll find a nice boy from another town and you'll get married and have babies. And all of this will go away."

Majorca shifted. She slid her swollen ankle to one side.

"What about you, Crystal? You're eighteen. What will happen to you?"

Crystal yawned, stretched out, and again pressed against Majorca. "I'll go to jail for sure. Maybe, if I'm lucky, they'll buy the self-defense thing, and I'll get a short sentence. Then again, we both know how lucky I am."

Majorca nosed deep into the crook of her arm, muffling her voice. "So, then what? I mean for you? After jail."

"I thought about that, back when we were walking. I think I'll go to that café. You know, The Bluebird Café and Grill. I'll see if I can find Dee Dee Wine. I really liked her. Maybe she could teach me how to be a waitress and help me get a job. Waitressing is a good job. You bring people food, and they give you tips. And I bet you get to eat for free where you work."

Outside the enclosure, the night creatures clicked and called to each other and crunched through the underbrush. A great bird swept by, silent but for the whoosh of air under its wings. Insects moved through the woven walls of the blind. Something dropped from the ceiling and landed on Crystal's arm. She flicked it away.

For a long time, they lay still until Majorca stirred. "Crystal?"

"What?"

"You're gonna make a great waitress."

Chapter Forty-Six

Deep in the night, a creature screamed.

Crystal woke, her eyes wide. She didn't move. She listened. Majorca's breathing was almost too soft to hear. That single scream, the only sound.

Moving slow, Crystal sat up, waited a breath, then tugged her knapsack closer. She pulled the map out and placed it on the floor. Then, the scissors, the smokes and lighter, the library book, the remaining tampon, and the gun. She left the cash secure in the front pocket of the pack. The crumpled fast-food bag was last. Pulling the bag from her pack, she held her breath and unrolled the top.

The smell was bad.

Grateful for the darkness, she reached into the bag. Clive's finger was cool and felt like an uncooked sausage left out on the counter too long. Although a single glint of moonlight slipped through a gap in the wall onto the bag, Crystal didn't look. Kneeling at a window, she flung the finger as far as she could—out into the woods. She didn't hear it land.

She left the second finger in place and rolled the bag closed. Turning, she pitched the bag through the opposite window and heard the faint crackle of paper landing on the forest floor.

She wiped her thumb and forefinger on the rough bark of the wall.

Wash 'em tomorrow in some dew or rainwater.

Stretching out next to Majorca, back-to-back, she whispered into the night, "You do what you have to do to survive."

Chapter Forty-seven

The high-pitched songs of birds chirping and tweeting in the trees around the hunter's blind woke Majorca. Shivering, she remained pressed against Crystal's back as she opened her eyes and let them adjust to the darkness inside the blind. A blade of sunlight sliced through a slit in the wall, promising a warm, sunny day. Easing away from Crystal and trying to move as quietly as possible, she crawled to the open door. Peeking over the edge, Majorca felt a moment of vertigo. The ground seemed much further away than it had the evening before when she'd first looked down from the small structure. Hesitating, she considered waiting until Crystal woke, but her bursting bladder urged her onward.

The ladder swayed with her weight, and she smacked her arm against a tree trunk. "Shit! I hate this fucking shit!" Working her way down the ladder, Majorca laughed at herself. "I'm starting to sound like Crystal. If I hang out with her much longer, I'll probably start smoking."

Two rungs before the bottom, Majorca released the rope and jumped to the ground. Her ankle twisted on impact. Groaning, she took a step. Quick, sharp pain shot up her leg. "That was so stupid. Crystal would kill me if she saw me do that."

Hobbling and slapping at mosquitoes, Majorca headed toward a fallen log, something to lean against as she peed. Unfastening the coveralls, she dropped them to the ground and scowled. Despite her swim in the lake, her underwear was filthy with blood and urine stains.

I'm a complete disaster. Totally gross and all of this is Crystal's fault. After we get cleaned up at her grandma's house, get some real food, and sleep, I'm leaving her. I never want to see her again.

Using the log for balance, she squatted. As she relieved her bladder, Majorca scanned the forest floor. Nut brown needles, still shiny with dew, mixed with heart-shaped leaves and dots of tiny, pink flowers. Something black and dark purple lay on a patch of moss. Majorca screamed. She jumped up so fast that she peed on her coveralls. Clutching her clothing, she scrambled away from the log and the thing on the forest floor.

Pausing only long enough to fasten one buckle, she grabbed the rope ladder and climbed, ignoring the pain as she smacked first into one tree and then the other.

"Crystal! Crystal! Wake up. It's horrible." Reaching the opening, she flopped inside and shook Crystal's shoulder.

"Ah...um...what?" Crystal rolled over and opened one eye to stare at Majorca.

"There's a...a..."

"A what?" With a low moan, Crystal pushed herself to a sitting position. She swayed and reached for the blind's wall to steady herself.

"Crystal, there's a finger. I saw it. It's big, and black, and purple. It had a fingernail. A black fingernail. It's horrible, and it's down there by the log."

"I'm so hot," Crystal said. She peeled her jacket off. "Why is it so hot in here?" She started to unbutton the flannel shirt.

"Crystal, you're not listening to me. I saw a finger. A man's finger."

Crystal stopped unbuttoning the shirt and wrapped her arms around herself. "I am so sore. Everything hurts. It's like the flu or something."

"Crystal, did you hear what—" Majorca stopped and stared at Crystal's forearm. "What is that?" She pointed to an angry red patch, then reached over and touched it. "It's hot."

Crystal curled her arm up for a better look and squinted at the ugly, raised patch. "Look," she said, "see those two little dark spots in the middle?"

Majorca bent closer to see.

"That's where the fucker bit me. Those are fang marks."

"What bit you?"

"Some dumbass spider. Probably poisonous, and that's why I feel like shit." With a moan, she eased back down and curled into a fetal position.

"Are you sure? Like, maybe it's not—"

"Girlie, I told you before, I have native blood. We know these things."

"How'd you get a spider bite up here?"

"Look at this place, you moron. This place is bug heaven. The walls are probably crawling with creepy little shits." Crystal curled tighter, facing away from Majorca.

Majorca sat cross-legged, pouting and staring at Crystal's back. Several minutes ticked by in silence until her stomach growled. "Crystal?"

"What?"

"Two things. No, three things."

"I don't feel good. Leave me alone."

"No, Crystal. First of all, we can't stay here. We can't live in a little tree house filled with poisonous bugs. We have to keep moving. When we get to your grandma's house, she'll give you some of that Irish Cure, and like you said, you'll go to sleep, and you'll sweat like a pig, and the next morning, you'll be fine."

Crystal rolled over slowly, sat up, and reached for her jacket. "Now, I'm freezing. This sucks." She drew away when Majorca tried to touch her shoulder.

"Fine," Majorca said. "Be that way. But I mean it. We really can't stay here. And I don't know if you were listening to me, but I saw a finger beside the log when I was down there. Maybe one of those weirdo men you told me about is living around here. And maybe he's chopping people up. I think we need to hurry and get out of here."

Crystal sighed. "We will, but first, there's something I should tell you so you don't start freaking out on me."

"What?"

"There might be weirdo men in the woods. I don't know for sure. But that finger? I chopped it off my mom's boyfriend. Actually, I chopped two fingers off him. I had them in my pack, but I figured they might start to stink, so I tossed 'em. Sorry you found one."

Majorca stared at Crystal, then blurted, "You chopped off some guy's fingers?"

Crystal shrugged. "I know, it sounds a little crazy."

"Crazy? It's more than crazy. It's...it's..."

"Maybe you had to be there." Shivering, Crystal pulled her jacket tighter.

Majorca shook her head and sat quietly for a moment. Then she asked, "How?"

"How, what?""How did you chop his fingers off?"

"It was easy. I used a gardening tool I found in my mom's shed."

"Was it the same tool you used to kill Roy?"

Crystal grinned. "No. It was a lot bigger. And sharper."

They sat together, staring out through the opening and listening to faint scratching within the walls. At last, Majorca turned toward Crystal. "Why?"

"Why what?"

"Why did you chop his fingers off?"

"Because," Crystal said, "he put them where they didn't belong."

Chapter Forty-Seven

MAJORCA CLIMBED DOWN FIRST, then held the ladder for Crystal. "Hurry up," she said. "I don't want to stand here all day."

"Buzz off. I'm in agony and I'm going as fast as I can." Crystal reached the forest floor, but she continued to hold onto the rope ladder.

"Come on, let's go," Majorca said. Scratching a bite, she drew blood. "Ew. I hate these bugs, and I'm covered in bites. Do you think your grandma has something to stop the itching?"

Crystal didn't answer. Still grasping the rope, she leaned forward and vomited—mostly bile, then she convulsed with dry heaves.

Majorca took a step toward her, but Crystal waved her back. After one more round of dry heaves, she wiped her mouth with the back of her hand and straightened. "Damn, I feel horrible," she said.

"Can you walk?"

"Probably, but I have stomach cramps and one minute I'm sweating and the next one I'm freezing." She slapped her neck. "And these fucking mosquitoes are driving me crazy." She started walking away from the hunter's blind.

Hobbling, Majorca followed her. "If it's any consolation, I've got period cramps and I was so scared by that finger, I peed on my coveralls."

"You are pathetic," Crystal said.

As before, Majorca's limping slowed their pace, and they stopped several times for Crystal to slip out of and back into her jacket. A little more than an hour after they'd left the hunter's blind, they passed a large gray boulder. Majorca shambled over to the rock. "Crystal, I have to sit down for a while, my ankle is killing me."

Crystal glanced at the rock. "Sure. Whatever." She pulled herself to a flat spot and sat shivering, her head between her knees.

Flinching, Majorca pulled her loafer off and rubbed her ankle. "I don't think I can walk in this shoe anymore. Look." She stretched her leg out.

Crystal lifted her head and eyed Majorca's foot. "That's bad," she said. "It might not be a sprain. Maybe you did break it."

"I don't think I could walk if I broke it. But either way, I'm pretty sure I can't get my shoe back on."

Crystal sat up and slipped out of her knapsack. "Gimme your shoe," she said.

As Majorca watched, Crystal used the scissors to cut through the waxed-thread stitching on the shoe's body. She cut both sides and then slit the threads halfway along the top of the shoe. When she was done, the dissected loafer slipped easily over Majorca's swollen foot.

"That was so cool," Majorca said. "I never would have thought about doing that."

"My mom doesn't have much cash, so I learned to fix stuff." Crystal pushed the scissors into her pack, then returned to sitting with her head between her knees. "I really feel like shit. I want to curl up and go to sleep."

Majorca scanned the canopy above. Sunlight no longer filtered through the leafy branches, and the air had cooled. She batted the swarm around them. "What time do you think it is?"

"No idea," Crystal mumbled.

"My dad always says the bugs go crazy before it rains. So, it's either getting late, or it's going to rain.

"Great, just great." Crystal curled tighter, muffling her voice. "Cold *and* wet."

"And, don't forget starving," Majorca said. "That jerky didn't exactly fill me up." She waited a beat, then gently laid one hand on Crystal's shoulder. "I know you don't feel good, but we have to keep moving. Do you want me to carry your knapsack?"

Crystal raised her head and looked at Majorca.

Majorca gasped. "Your eyes are all puffy and they're really, really red."

"Fucking spider." Crystal's words came out in a raspy croak. She stretched her legs and slid off the rock.

Majorca followed her. "Your pack?"

"I got it."

Their steps were slow and halting, but they moved onward through the deepening gloom. In the far distance, a low growl of thunder rumbled across the sky.

Chapter Forty-Eight

Buster's soft snoring nudged Zoey awake. She lay cocooned in the warmth of her comforter with Buster stretched full-length by her side. She pulled one hand from under the covers and stroked the old dog.

"Monday," she said. "First day of my new job. Wonder if they'll start me on typing reports or filing them. In alphabetical order, of course." With her hand resting on Buster's warm belly, she stared at the ceiling—at the cheap overhead light, standard issue for government strata housing. "Remember all that training, Buster? You ran miles with me, and you guarded the car for me while I worked out at the gym and took martial arts classes. And remember all those nights you snoozed on the floor by my chair while I read Canadian law? And now, look at us. A file clerk and her old dog." She choked back a sob. Buster smacked his lips in his sleep and sighed. Zoey watched the rise and fall of his chest and then shook her head. "I wanted to serve and protect my fellow citizens, not deliver coffee and stuff reports into manila folders." Pushing the comforter aside, she stood. "Too bad I'm going to miss my first day on the new job, but I'm not feeling well enough to work. Better call in."

After Buster's run, his breakfast, and her shower, Zoey dressed for a hike in the woods by layering bug spray, a long-sleeved shirt, long pants, hiking boots, and a warm jacket. She tossed the bug spray, a bottle of water, a flashlight, her badge, and wallet into a small day bag. While dressing, she practiced what she'd say when she called in sick. Flu was a reasonable excuse—she didn't want to expose everyone in the office to this crud. Or, a bad case of food poisoning—a reaction to something she ate at a Sunday neighborhood potluck. In the end, she decided to give her male colleagues a gift, something they could gloat over, something to add to their feelings of superiority. "Lady problems," she told the recorded line. "Female issues. I need to stay warm, drink tea, and get some rest."

After dropping Buster off at Rebecca's, she headed out. Commuter traffic was heavy on Highway 16, but fueled by a combination of anger and determination, Zoey drove aggressively and made the drive to Endako in under two hours. Marking the entrance to the forest, Buster's bright orange leash hung where she'd tied it. Once again, she parked her VW as far off the road as possible, then donned a baseball cap and tromped into the bush.

The girls hadn't tried to hide their movements, and following their trail was easier than Zoey had expected. Broken branches, overturned rocks, and trampled patches of leaves and pine needles made clear signposts along their route.

At one point, she noticed a flash of silver in a pile of leaves. It turned out to be an old flashlight, dented and rusting, with a broken lens and bulb. It could have belonged to one of the girls, or more likely, a hunter. Zoey tossed it into her day pack and moved on.

The hardest part was the trek through the dense underbrush and thickets. The buzz of mosquitoes was irritating, but the spray she'd applied earlier did its job at keeping the pests from landing and biting.

These bugs could drive a horse mad. Those two kids must be miserable.

On the two occasions when she temporarily lost their trail, she considered confessing to Gagnon and pleading for his help.

Dogs could follow their scent and track them down in no time.

But she abandoned the idea, knowing that her boss would reprimand her and demand that she end her search in the woods. No, better to go it alone.

Hoping it wouldn't be necessary to return a third time, but in case it was, Zoey marked her path with the lime green doggy-poop bags she always carried in her pockets.

In the mid-afternoon, she stumbled into a small clearing flanked on one side by a large, fallen log. The carpet of moss by the log was flattened, as if someone had lounged there. Searching the area, Zoey found an empty donut box, sugar still clinging to the cardboard. She scanned the log and found three white buttons resting on the rough bark. Looking behind the log, she spotted another button.

Why buttons?

Bending to retrieve the fourth button, Zoey paused. A crumpled piece of paper, the color of parchment, was wedged under the log. With a gentle tug, she released it and smoothed it out on the moss. It was a preprinted certificate with space for writing in achievements, recipients, and sponsors. Flicking a roller bug from the paper, Zoey stared at the page. Neat printing spelled out the award. ALL GRADES #1 READER OF THE YEAR 1972. Swirling calligraphy congratulated Crystal Lynn Harsch as the recipient of the award. On the bottom line, there were three signatures and printed titles, Donald Oster, Principal. Dorothea Woodhouse, Librarian. And, Mrs. Hudson, Grade Ten Teacher.

Why toss something so important to her?

Zoey rolled the certificate into a tube and slid it in her day pack. Zipping the pack closed, she looked to the awning above. The bright spots of sunlight were replaced with deepening shadows. The temperature had dropped several degrees, and in the distance, a thunderclap warned of an impending storm. Zoey picked up her tempo, moved faster through the dense foliage, and took longer strides until the first flash of lightning lit the forest with stark white light. Seconds later, thunder boomed through the woods, and the rain came. Fat plops at first, then heavy drops turned to icy sheets. Visibility plunged until she couldn't see limbs and branches enough to avoid them. Continuing would be futile.

Zoey turned and retraced her path to the logging road, which she knew was morphing into a river of mud.

Chapter Forty-Nine

The rain started with big, slow splats. "Here it comes," Majorca said. "We have to find a place to stay dry."

Crystal staggered and reached for branches to stay upright. "I don't care," she said. Her breath came in raspy drags. She tripped, her right leg folded, and she fell to the ground, landing on her rump. The rain came faster and heavier, soaking through their clothes.

Majorca spun around, looking for any form of shelter. Spotting a large fir with tightly packed branches, she grabbed Crystal's hand and pulled her to her feet.

Crystal swayed and started to sink again.

"Come on. We can sit under that tree." With her arm circling Crystal's waist, Majorca floundered toward the old-growth fir. She managed to pull Crystal under the tree's low-hanging umbrella and propped her against the sappy trunk. Then she scootched under the heavy branches and huddled next to Crystal. The earth around the base of the fir was cool but dry.

"It smelth god in her." Crystal slurred her words and dropped her chin to her chest.

Majorca sat up straight. She lifted Crystal's chin and searched her face. Crystal's eyelids were red and swollen, her skin was blanched, and her mouth hung slack. "We have got to get you to your grandma's house. And then, we have to call a doctor, or maybe go to the emergency room."

Crystal shook her head, but the movement was slow and slight.

When Majorca propped against the tree, a crack of lightning split the sky directly above them, turning the woods to silver. Crystal and Majorca jumped and clutched each other. Seconds later, thunder shook the forest. "We have to get out from under this tree. It's so tall, we could be fried." Majorca looped her arms under Crystal's and dragged her to the edge of the branches.

Crystal moaned. "I can't. My legs hurt. And I'm so cold."

Gritting her teeth, Majorca hauled Crystal across the small, dry space into the pouring rain and onto the slick, wet carpet of fir and pine needles. "You have to get up, Crystal. Put your arm over my shoulder, and I'll support you. We're going to find some place warm and dry. I promise."

With Majorca's help, Crystal stood. She draped her arm over Majorca's shoulder and they stumbled through the soaking underbrush. Lightning scissored the night sky, thunder crashed, and heavy, cold rain drenched them.

"Where are we going?" Crystal mumbled.

"Someplace warm and dry."

"Where?"

"I don't know, but we might be close to the highway, and there will be a bus stop."

"A bus stop?"

"You know, like the ones with a bench and a roof and advertising on the walls."

"Advertising..."

Majorca's ankle cried in agony, and her muscles ached from the cold and from carrying Crystal. Hunger and menstrual cramps knifed through her gut. But her fear was greater than her pain.

Snagging her boot on a root, Crystal almost dragged Majorca to the ground. "No more," she said. "No more."

A streak of lightning, farther away, lit the scene in soft blue. "No way," Majorca whispered. "I must be seeing things." Half-dragging Crystal, she pulled them both from the tree line to an open patch of grass, a yard of sorts. "Crystal, look!" Extracting her arm, she pointed to a small log cabin squatting in the middle of the grassy area.

"A bus stop?"

"No, goof. A cabin. Come on."

They stumbled around a stack of firewood piled close to the cabin's front door. Two steps lead to a porch. An awning over the porch offered respite from the pounding rain. Majorca helped Crystal up the steps and propped her against the cabin's rough exterior wall. "I'm going to see if anyone's here."

No one answered her pounding on the door or her knocking on the cabin's only window. She tried peering through the glass, but the cabin's interior was dark, shadowless. Grabbing the door handle, Majorca rattled it, pulled, and pushed. The door remained firm. In frustration, she screamed out, "Open up, you fucker!"

Crystal looked up at her and blinked once. With a slow, floating motion, she pointed to a flat rock on the grass by the porch. "Key," she said.

Majorca lifted the rock and stirred wet earth until the tip of a brass key poked through. She glanced at Crystal. "I don't even want to know," she said. She helped Crystal to stand, and then, keeping one arm wrapped around her to hold her steady, Majorca slid the key into the lock. An easy turn. The scent of mold and a long-forgotten campfire drifted from the cabin's inky interior.

"Mom's lighter," Crystal said.

Stepping over the cabin's threshold. Majorca held the lighter high and clicked. The flame leapt up and lit the room. Shadows loomed. An enormous beast with sharpened horns and glowing yellow eyes glared at them. Majorca screamed. She spun Crystal around and shoved her down the steps. Crystal fell, face-first, into the woodpile. Majorca leapt from the porch, slipped on the grass, and slammed down hard. "It's the Devil," she screamed. "We're going to Hell."

Groaning, Crystal rolled off the woodpile and crawled on her hands and knees across the grass to Majorca. They stared at each other. Rain streamed down their hair, their clothes, and their skin. Finally, Crystal laughed. It came out as a squawk followed by a fit of coughing. When she gained her breath, she shook her head. "White people," she said.

Chapter Fifty

HEAVY FLOODING ON THE highway made Zoey's drive time from Endako to Granisle almost double what it had been that morning. The heater in her old VW hadn't worked for months, so she remained wet and shivering until she arrived at her apartment, took Buster for a short sprint around the block, and stepped into her shower. Although the hot water hadn't helped her mood, it had served to relax the tension in her muscles.

She wrapped her hair in a towel, slipped into her flannel bathrobe, and went to the kitchen to feed Buster. She'd started to pull a cold beer from the refrigerator when the doorbell rang.

Danny stood at her door, his rain slicker dripping. He held a take-away bag from the local Chinese restaurant and a bottle of white wine. "Interest you in dinner?"

While Danny opened the wine and placed cartons of rice and steamed veggies on the coffee table, Zoey dressed in her favorite sweatpants and sweater. She fed Buster and then joined Danny in her living room.

Handing her a glass of wine, Danny made a slight toasting gesture.

"What's the occasion?" Zoey asked.

"I wanted to catch up with you," Danny said. "And I didn't want anyone to see us together."

Zoey glanced toward the window. Lightning flashed in the sky over Granisle, thunder rumbled, and rain pelted the glass. "Not much chance of that, tonight," she said. "But why does it matter?"

"Maybe we should eat first and have some wine."

They'd finished scooping food from the cardboard containers and had shared half of the bottle when Danny turned to Zoey. "I thought Gagnon pulled me off the case and eliminated our unit because of the way I—the way we—were handling things. I thought maybe I should have made different decisions, or given you more guidance. I thought he put me on patrol to teach me a lesson."

"Didn't he? Isn't that why I'm supposed to be alphabetizing folders?"

Danny sighed. "No. I was pulled off patrol before I even hit the streets. Hendricks's doing. He wants me on his team. It wasn't what we were doing to find the girls or how we were doing it. And it wasn't the press coverage following us. It was you, Zoey. Hendricks doesn't like you. And he doesn't want you on the force."

Zoey set her glass on the table. "Why? He barely knows me."

Danny contemplated her for a moment before answering. "It's because you're a woman. It doesn't make a damn bit of sense, but Hendricks doesn't believe females should serve. He wants women to stay," Danny made air quotes, "where they belong. At home, caring for their men and their babies."

"But—"

"I know. I know. My best guess? Women threaten him. Only the good Lord knows why. But the bad news is—"

"That was the *good* news?" Zoey interrupted.

"The bad news is, I think Hendricks is passing his thinking on to Gagnon. And the sarge might be thinking of a way to give you the boot."

"Ah, I see. And you don't want to be associated with me for fear—"

Flushing, Danny interrupted. "It's not right, Zoey. You're good at this. You're new and inexperienced. But you're a hard worker, and a quick learner, and most of all, you care about the people we serve. All of them. Hendricks only bloody well cares about...some of them."

"Why, Danny O'Brien. I don't think I've ever heard you swear." Zoey gave him a wan smile.

They sat without moving for a moment until Danny reached for the bottle and topped their glasses. "So, that's what I learned today. How about you?"

"What about me?"

"I know you called in sick. And I know your lady troubles," Danny made air quotes again, "would never keep you from work or anything else. Did you wear bug spray?"

Zoey sighed and took a swallow of wine. "Such a short time and already you know me so well."

Danny sat back and listened as Zoey told him about her search for Crystal and Majorca. She told him about the logging road and about marking the entrance to the forest with the bright orange leash and the path with lime green poop bags. She shared how she found the wax paper, the buttons, and the Reader of the Year certificate. "I should have been better dressed for the woods the first day out. And today, the weather chased me away. But Danny, those girls are out there, in this storm, most likely without food or warm clothing. Maybe they're drenched and freezing. How much longer do you think they can survive?"

"I told you before," Danny said, "Those woods are no place for a couple of girls."

"Exactly. So, this storm is going to pass, and I'm going to be there at first light. I'm going to find them."

Danny scrunched his face, narrowed his eyes. "I dunno know," he said. "Chances are the rain has washed all their tracks away. I can't imagine how you're going to pick up their scent."

Zoey turned from him and bit her lip. Then she swiveled back around. "A dog, a good tracking dog, could pick up their scent. A dog could find them in a quarter of the time it would take a team of humans."

"Maybe, but—"

"Doesn't the department use dogs?"

"Wait a minute," Danny held his hands up, palms to her. "Stop it right there. You know you can't request that. If you did, Gagnon would know what you're up to, and it would be immediate dismissal. No further questions asked."

"I know, but..."

Buster padded into the living room, sat in front of the sofa and put his head on Danny's knee.

"What about this old boy?" Danny scratched Buster's ears.

"He couldn't track a squirrel if it wore a tutu and danced past him." She leaned forward and looked into Danny's eyes. "But you could make the request. You don't have to let on, the dog isn't for your search. I have that certificate, and it has to have Crystal's scent all over it. I'll locate the girls and get the dog back to you before anyone knows."

Danny sat up straight, folded his hands in his lap, and stared at them.

"Look, I know I'm asking a lot." Zoey spoke fast, the words tumbling out. "It would be bad if the sarge found out. But he won't. No one will. I'll only need the dog for the morning. Endako is less than two hours from the city, so I could find the girls, get them warm and safe, drive the dog down to Prince George, and you could have it sniffing empty streets by lunchtime. Once the girls are rested, I'll tell Gagnon what I did. Take my lumps."

"Zoey, that is a first-class crazy plan. And, it might work and I want to help you. I really do. But my parents...they're so proud of me. Their son, a Constable in the RCMP. Everyone in my village back home... They..."

Zoey sat back. She took a moment before she said, "I understand. You need to distance yourself from those girls and me. Your future is on the line. Nobody, especially me, can fault you for protecting that. I'm sorry I even asked. That was beyond the pale. Forgive me."

When Danny left, Zoey took Buster out again, then changed into her pajamas and invited her old dog to share the bed. She sat in the dark, with her back against the headboard, facing the window. A single tear rolled down her cheek as she watched the raging storm slash the summer sky.

Chapter Fifty-One

CRYSTAL CONVINCED MAJORCA THAT the Devil wasn't chasing them and they weren't going to Hell. "Juvie, maybe," she said, "but not hell."

They helped each other stumble across the wet grass and climb the two steps to the porch. This time, when they entered the cabin, Majorca held the lighter up high and clicked it until its tiny flame illuminated the one-room cabin.

"Wow, he's huge." Majorca stared at the head of the horned ram mounted over the fireplace. The ram, with its curling horns and bulging glass eyes, stared at Crystal and Majorca, his devilish grin preserved forever.

Crystal shuffled across the cabin to a straight chair and a crude wooden table. She sat, crossed her arms on the table, and lowered her head to them.

Majorca explored the room. She found a kerosene lantern and shook it. Liquid sloshed. After several clumsy attempts, she managed to ignite the cotton wick. A warm, yellow light flooded the cabin. She found a canvas cot pushed against a wall. A woolen blanket, folded in a neat square, rested at one end of the cot. A second woolen blanket lay on a shelf over the cot.

"Here." She nudged Crystal's shoulder. "We need to get out of our wet clothes." She set a blanket on the table and walked to the fireplace, where she shucked off the soaked coveralls and the cotton blouse. After draping her clothes over the back of a second chair, she rifled through an aluminum tub near the hearth. The tub held kindling, yellowing newspapers, and a stash of split logs. "I never made a fire," she said. "When my family went camping, my dad always built the fires, so I don't know how. But I bet you do." She glanced at Crystal.

Crystal's wet clothes lay in a pile on the floor. She continued slumping at the table, her head on her arms, the red plaid blanket wrapping her like a shroud. Majorca shook her head and turned to the tub.

Forty-five minutes later, Crystal lifted her head, blinked, and looked around. "What's that smell?"

"Baked beans and Spam," Majorca said. Wrapped in a black and green plaid blanket and crouching by the fire, she stirred a pot tucked into embers at the edge of crackling flames. "I found the cans in a cupboard. And I found two tin bowls and spoons and forks. And, guess what? The hunters who use this cabin left a can of bug spray. No more mosquito or spider bites for us. And, there's more." Pulling the pot from the heat, she stood and walked across the room with her woolen blanket trailing behind.

Grabbing a square bottle from a counter, she spun around and faced Crystal. "Ta Da!" She held the bottle high.

Crystal squinted. "What is it?"

"Whiskey. Almost half a bottle. Tonight, Crystal Lynn Harsch, we are going to be warm and dry. And tonight, we're going to eat a hot dinner and drink whiskey. Lots and lots of whiskey."

They sat in their now dry underwear on the cot, side by side, facing the fire. With the cabin warm, the blankets hung loose over their shoulders. The sounds of wood crackling and popping mixed with the steady patter of rain on the roof and the occasional rumble of distant thunder. The fragrant scent of burning pine blended with the smell of canned port and beans and the fatty odor of Spam.

"I never liked Spam at home," Majorca said. "But that was delicious."

"Anything is delicious when you're starving," Crystal said.

"Maybe, but there's some stuff I'd never eat."

"Like what?"

"Pickled pigs' feet." Majorca wrinkled her nose. "A lady brought a jar of them to a church potluck, and they looked so gross I almost got sick."

"One time, Clive ran over a possum. Mom baked it like a chicken, tail and all. That was the best Christmas dinner I ever had." Crystal picked at the paper label on the whisky bottle. "This stuff isn't bad, once you get past the burn." She took a hit and passed the bottle to Majorca.

Majorca peered at the label. "Jack Daniels—Tennessee Whiskey, U.S.A.—Old Number 7." She lifted the bottle and let firelight shine through the amber liquid. "I wonder if this was named after the seventh president of the United States."

Crystal stared at her. "Unbelievable," she said. "Don't you ever read?"

"I read."

"What? What's the last book you read?"

"None of your business."

They passed the bottle and continued to poke fun at each other. When the flames began to drop, Majorca slid off the cot and added another split log to the fire. She stood facing the hearth, letting the blaze toast her skin, and then turned to warm her backside. She looked at the cot and at Crystal, who sat cross-legged, eyes closed, breathing slow as if in meditation. "Crystal?"

"What?" Crystal answered without opening her eyes.

"Are you feeling better? You look better."

Crystal opened one eye, glanced at Majorca, and closed it. "You look like shit," she said.

Majorca giggled and settled back on the cot. She pulled her blanket around her shoulders.

Opening her eyes and yawning, Crystal adjusted her position. She stretched her legs out toward the fire and dropped the empty bottle to the floor. "Another dead soldier."

Majorca laughed. "If we keep hanging out together, we'll turn into alcoholics."

"If it's genetic, I already am one."

"You're feeling better, I can tell." Majorca reached from under her blanket and gave Crystal a light slap.

"Seriously," Crystal said, "I feel better than I did in that rain, that's for sure. And the whiskey is a big help, it sorta numbed the ache in my gut, but my legs feel like rubber."

"Hang in there. We'll get to your grandma's house tomorrow, and she'll have some medicine to help you. Maybe some of that pink stuff that tastes like chalk."

"For a spider bite?"

"I don't know. But she'll have something."

As they watched the fire, a piece of log burned through, dropped into blood orange coals, and sent a fan of golden sparks dancing through the flames. The ram's shadow draped them like a cape. Majorca sighed. "This is nice."

Crystal nodded. "It is nice. What if we stay here? In this cabin? We can hunt for rabbits and pick berries and...and maybe we can grow stuff."

"Are you nuts? There's no way I'm staying in a cabin in the woods. Tonight, it's great—it's warm and dry, and we found some food. But I didn't see any berries when we were tromping through the trees, and I don't know anything about growing stuff. And, seriously? You expect me to kill a *bunny*? Either the whiskey or that spider poison is messing with your brain."

"I thought that maybe—"

"There's no maybe. We're walking out of these woods tomorrow. Before noon, we'll be on the road. I'll hitchhike and get us a ride all the way to your grandma's house. By this time tomorrow night, we'll be clean and dry and fat from your grandma's cooking. And after that, we'll figure out what to do. Maybe I'll call my dad. He'll come and get me, no matter what. I'll dust bibles, or feed oatmeal to old people, or whatever they want me to do. And we can drive you to that café, and Dee Dee Wine will teach you how to waitress. And we'll visit each other. Sometimes."

"But if the cops catch us, I'll spend the rest of my life in jail for killing that asshole."

Majorca picked at a scab left by a bite. She shifted around to face Crystal. "You killed Roy to save me, but we'll tell everybody I killed him. We'll tell everybody I did everything and that I made you come with me."

"You? Made me?"

"Yes. I'll take the gun and tell everybody I threatened to shoot you if you didn't come with me."

"You won't last two days in prison."

Majorca took Crystal's right hand and held it between hers. "That's true. But like I told you, my birthday is in August. I'm still a kid for two more months. Don't worry, Crystal. I'll take all the blame. You go find Dee Dee Wine and learn how to sling hash."

They sat facing each other in the flickering light of the flames and the hazy warmth of Tennessee whiskey. The fire's crackling played a melody to the rain's gentle rhythm. Shadows skipped along the log walls. In a corner, a cricket chirped. Crystal leaned forward and pressed her lips on Majorca's.

Majorca put two more logs on the fire and returned to the cot. She stretched out and snuggled up close to Crystal. They lay still and quiet for a while until Majorca spoke, her voice soft and low. "Crystal, you never told me your grandma's name."

"I call her gran. Or sometimes, granny. Go to sleep."

"But, I mean, what do other people call her? She must have a real name."

Crystal didn't answer.

Majorca nudged her. "What's your grandma's name?

"If I tell you, will you shut up and go to sleep?"

"I promise."

"It's Dorothea."

Chapter Fifty-Two

CRAMPING WOKE CRYSTAL. A churning in her gut, a tugging in her intestines. Throwing the blanket off, she bolted for the door. Fumbling with the latch, she barely made it outside to the porch, where she puked on the steps. Beans and Spam. She rushed down the stairs, slipping on her vomit. Rain washed over her bare skin, and her body quaked as Crystal squatted in the cold, wet grass and emptied diarrhea and urine.

She ripped up handfuls of grass and cleaned herself. Then, wobbly and shaking, she returned to the cabin, to the cot, and the warmth of Majorca's body.

Predawn, Crystal woke again. This time, drenched in sweat, feeling disoriented, and needing to pee. She glanced at Majorca, who slept with her fist flat against her mouth. Leaning on the table for support, Crystal dressed in her jeans, shirt, and jacket. She left her boots by the door and her knapsack on the table. Tucking the gun in her waistband, she padded to the door.

Damp air cooled her flushed cheeks and burning forehead. Crystal stood in the center of the yard, her focus foggy. In a slow-motion rotation, she gazed at the shadowy scene. Distorted through the lens of fever, the cabin seemed small and far away, while the thick underbrush and wall of trees shimmered and appeared close and inviting. Her steps were faltering and unsteady as she walked toward the forest. The dark silhouette of a stocky thorn bush caught her attention. "Mom?" she said.

Chapter Fifty-Three

Majorca stretched her arm, and it slipped over the side of the cot. Blinking awake, she patted the empty space next to her. "Crystal?"

She sat up and looked around the room. Only a few flames still danced since most of the logs had burned down to glowing embers. Long shadows haunted the cabin walls. Crystal's clothes and the gun were gone, but her rucksack remained on the table, and her boots stood by the door.

"Probably went out to pee, or smoke," Majorca grumbled. "I better go look for her."

Sliding from the cot, she walked to the table where she'd spread her blouse out to dry. The aerosol can of bug spray sat between her blouse and Crystal's knapsack. She grabbed the can, gave it a good shake, and sprayed her bare legs. Giving the spray a moment to dry, Majorca returned to the cot and to the chair in front of the hearth where she'd hung her coveralls. Still holding the can, she stood in the warmth of the embers and reached for the pants.

A tiny gray mouse dropped from under the coveralls and scurried across the floor, skittering over Majorca's foot. She screeched, jumped and dropped the can. She smacked her knee onto the edge of the cot. "Ow," she said. Rubbing her knee and catching her breath, she looked around for the dropped can. It lay nestled in a bed of deep orange coals. Majorca stared at it. The paper label curled, then shot into a burst of flames. The once-silver-colored can glowed red and pulsed as if breathing.

"Shit!" Majorca bolted to the door, flung it open, and leapt off the porch, smashing into Crystal. They both tumbled to the ground.

Crystal's face contorted in confusion. "What the fu—"

"Get up," Majorca yelled. Scrambling to her feet, she grabbed Crystal's arm and yanked. "Run!" Gripping tight, she pulled Crystal toward the trees. They stumbled and slid, but they'd made it halfway across the yard when Crystal slipped, slamming them both to the ground. Majorca flung her arm over Crystal's face as the explosion blew the door off its hinges. Seconds later, flames shooting from the cabin's roof painted the indigo dawn in a brilliant blaze of light. Tugging on Crystal's arm, Majorca crawled backward until they tucked into the cover of the forest and under trees still dripping rain.

Sitting with their backs against the trunk of an old Douglas fir, they held hands as they watched the cabin burn. Cracks like gunfire shot through the roar of the blaze, and flames stretched skyward, jagged and scaly.

"My knapsack was in there," Crystal said. "Everything. The rest of the money, my mom's lighter, and the cigarettes. And my boots. I left my boots in there." They sat watching the inferno until Crystal spoke again. "Worst of all, the library book. I'll never get to return it."

Majorca's teeth chattered. She sat forward, turned, and looked at Crystal. "I don't know anything about a library book, but I know my clothes were in there."

"We're fucking hosed," Crystal said.

Majorca slouched back against the tree. "At least there's some good news."

"What?""It stopped raining."

Chapter Fifty-Four

Majorca shook her head. "Look at us," she said. Sunburned skin peeled from her nose, her lips cracked, and the scratch on her cheek was red with infection. Crystal's sleeveless flannel shirt landed mid-thigh, covering her blood-stained panties. Bites and scabs blotched her arms and legs, her filthy bare feet bled at the heels, and her left ankle was swollen and dark purple. "We don't have to worry about any weirdo men. If a scary guy takes one peep at us, he'll run screaming for his mommy."

Crystal held onto a tree branch for support. Grass stained her bare feet, her jeans drooped loose over sharp hip bones, and her dirty denim jacket hung open over her black stretch bra. She watched Majorca scratch at a bite.

"You only make it worse when you scratch," she said. Her voice was hoarse, and her breathing shallow. Her skin was sallow except around the bloody forehead gash she'd gotten when she fell into the woodpile.

"I know, but they itch so much I'm losing my mind." Majorca attacked another bite on her arm.

Though still cool and fresh, the dawn promised a dry day—a day with sunshine.

Crystal looked at the remains of the cabin, now a pile of smoldering logs and ash. "You should go on without me," she said. "I feel like shit, and I don't wanna walk anymore. You go find the road." She released the branch, closed her eyes, and eased down to the ground. The slap surprised her. "What the—"

"Don't be a jerk." Majorca grabbed the lapels of Crystal's jacket and dragged her to standing. "See that?" Gripping the denim, she pointed beyond the smoke-choked burn pile. A muddy path led away from the smoldering remains of the cabin.

"What? What am I supposed to look at?"

"It's a trail. We couldn't see it in the dark, but those hunters drove in here, and all we have to do is follow their trail out. It will lead us to the highway."

"Are you sure?"

"Of course, I'm sure." She held onto the jacket until Crystal straightened and nodded.

"But I'm so thirsty. I need to find some water."

Majorca wrapped her arm around Crystal's shoulder and nudged her toward the path. "Don't worry, we're going to get water, and a bath, and food, and clean clothes. Real soon. We're almost there now."

The path was squishy with mud, and their feet sank with each step, but they made headway. In some places, the path widened, in others, it all but disappeared. Whenever Crystal slowed or hesitated, Majorca distracted her with the sorts of activities her parents had used to keep her occupied on long car rides.

"Bad, bad, Leroy Brown," she sang. "Baddest man in the whole damn town. Crystal, you do the next part."

Crystal's words came out low and scratchy, but she sang along. "Badder than old King Kong. Meaner than a junkyard dog."

They sang through "Rocket Man," "You're So Vain," and "You Are the Sunshine of My Life." Crystal wouldn't sing Cher's "Half-Breed," and Majorca refused to even hum, "Let's Get It On."

After working through the top ten hits, they focused on food. What they would eat first, after of course, whatever Crystal's grandmother made for them. Majorca wanted a slice of her mother's award-winning lasagna. Crystal said she'd kill for a tuna fish sandwich like the kind the librarian sometimes brought to school, and sometimes shared with her.

As the sun climbed higher, Crystal's breathing became more labored and despite Majorca's encouragement, her steps slowed. At one point, she bent down and cupped her hand into a puddle of water by the path.

Majorca slapped her hand, splashing water on Crystal's jeans.

"Why'd you do that?"

"Because that water is probably full of bug eggs or…or…bear pee. You're already sick. Do you want to make it worse?"

"Fuck you," Crystal muttered.

They continued walking until the sun moved directly overhead and the path dead-ended at a dense wall of trees. "This is the end," Crystal said. "The end of the path and the end of us." She tried to sit, but Majorca kept one arm tight around her waist.

Twisting slowly, Majorca scanned the trees on all three sides. And then she saw it. "Crystal, look! That has to be the way to the rest of the path." She pointed to a ragged, yellow ribbon dangling from a branch on the far side of a thicket.

Crystal squinted toward the strip of silk. "Where's the opening?" she asked.

"It has to be close. Come on." Half-dragging Crystal and keeping her eyes on the ribbon, Majorca stepped off the path and pushed her way through the dense foliage. The bushes spouted thorns that scraped and stabbed their skin. For several yards, the underbrush was almost too thick to penetrate, but they pushed on until they reached a narrow passageway marked by the yellow silk. The trees on both sides loomed tall and dark with their branches spreading across the passage. The going was slow, but eventually, the passage opened to a circular clearing within a ring of white mushrooms. Pale green moss, dotted with tiny white flowers, carpeted the space. Golden sunlight poured through the opening high above the clearing.

Releasing Crystal, Majorca dashed to the center of the circle and, holding her arms out wide and her face to the sky, she twirled.

Crystal shuffled across the moss and plopped down close to where Majorca spun. When Majorca stopped spinning to catch her breath, Crystal asked, "What is this?"

Majorca sat down next to her. "I don't know the real name for these kinds of clearings," she said, "but in folk tales they're called Fairie Rings."

"Fairie Rings?"

Gently brushing the surface of the moss with her palm, Majorca nodded. "Yes. My mother used to read fairy tales to me, and I remember stories about fairies coming out every full moon to dance in big rings. They dance round and round and round until they leave a circle like this one."

"Are they, the fairies...are they dangerous?" Crystal stretched out on the moss, resting her head in the crook of her arm.

"I don't think so," Majorca said. "I think they're mostly good luck. Some fairies will help you find true love, and some of them will help you find your way to heaven when you die." She stretched out beside Crystal. "At least that's what I think I remember."

Chapter Fifty-Five

She hadn't slept much, maybe not at all. The relentless rain, her raw nerves, and visions of two frightened girls hiding in a forest prevented any rest. At one point, Zoey hoped that maybe the girls had heard a rumble on the logging road, that they'd flagged down the driver, that the truck's cab would be warm and dry, that the driver would be a good, decent man, and that this time, the girls wouldn't need a garden tool.

Skipping a shower, she dressed, threw essentials into a day pack, and slipped a note under Rebecca's door asking her to take Buster out. The note promised a grown-up dinner in the best restaurant in town, her treat, complete with a babysitter for the twins.

The dawn drizzle wasn't a problem, but small lakes created by dips in the highway caused the VW to lose traction and hydroplane, forcing Zoey to reduce her speed. The sun had already begun to peek over the church steeple as she drove through Endako to the logging road, or what had been a road, the day before. Now, it resembled a lava flow. Determined, Zoey slipped into low gear and, keeping her speed at a crawl, she urged the VW up the hill.

She'd made it about halfway to the marked entrance when the old car became firmly embedded in thick mud. "Dammit," Zoey said. "Hiking boots. I wore hiking boots. Clearly, the wrong shoe selection." Slipping into a rain jacket and ball cap, she stepped into the gooey sludge and began the slog to the bright orange leash.

She'd lost over an hour by the time she crossed the trench at the side of the road and entered the forest. Her boots were heavy with mud, and her pants were soaked to her knees. Once in the woods, making headway was easier. Although slippery, pine and fir needles, along with fallen leaves, made a mat over the rain-soaked earth. The lime green baggies she'd hung to mark the way were a big help, and Zoey covered her previous trail quickly.

When the line of baggies ended, her progress slowed. Danny had been right—the rain had obliterated footprints, but what she'd discovered earlier held. The girls had not tried to cover their tracks. Again, Zoey searched for broken branches and overturned rocks. And she searched for anything that didn't belong in a forest.

She'd trudged deep into the woods when she spotted a hunter's blind built high above the forest floor between three stout trees. A rope ladder dangled from the blind to the forest floor, and despite the rain, Zoey could tell that the ground below the ladder had been disrupted.

They were here. Maybe they spent the night here and got out of the rain.

Her hiking boots made climbing the ladder difficult, and because it swung with her weight, Zoey smacked into one tree trunk, then the other. "Dammit, I'm gonna be covered in bruises." As she climbed, she thought about the girls swinging into the rough bark of the trees, and she hoped that, like her, they had the protection of long pants and jackets.

The interior of the hunters' blind was dark and smelled musky, like wet wood and moss. The small space was cool, but dry. A good place to shelter from a storm. Zoey grabbed her flashlight from her day pack and flicked it on. The blind was empty, save for one crumpled, empty paper bag.

It would be nice to find a clue—especially something hinting they'd return here. But still, maybe they were dry and safe last night.

With mixed feelings, she climbed back down the ladder, again smacking into the trees on either side. As the sun rose, the woods warmed, and steam spiraled from the forest floor. Zoey continued with her search.

She stopped to pee and to take a drink of water from the bottle in her pack. Twisting the cap closed, she sniffed the air. To this point, the cool air held the fragrance of wet leaves, moss, and damp earth. But now, a new scent tinged the light breeze. Smoke. Not the kind of chemical-laced smoke she'd inhaled at the site of the shed fire in Granisle. This smoke was clean and woodsy, reminding her of camping with the Girl Guides decades ago.

They've stopped. They've built a campfire.

Following her nose, Zoey crashed through the underbrush, picking up speed with every step.

Chapter Fifty-Six

The smell of smoke grew stronger, more pungent and acidic as Zoey clomped through the forest. The air developed a hint of gray, letting her know she was close. She broke into a careful jog, mindful of the slippery ground beneath her hiking boots. Ten minutes later, she stepped from the forest into an open, grassy space surrounding a smoldering pile that had once been a building, very likely, a hunter's cabin.

Before approaching the ruins, Zoey stood in place and scanned the scene. A door lay several feet away from an unburned woodpile. Debris littered the area. Bits of what might have been furniture were scattered across the grass, and a blackened bowl, filled with rainwater, sat off to one side. "This wasn't simply a fire," Zoey said, "there was an explosion here."

Gritting her teeth, she picked a path through the rubble and approached the smoking pile. Standing where she guessed the door would have been, she studied the remnants of the building. Very little remained.

Zoey sniffed the smoky air. She remembered a training session when the instructor had burned a cadaver so his students could recognize the smell of a scorched body. It had taken her several days to get the smell out of her clothing and out of her mind. But now, she was grateful for that class. While the smoke was intense, it did not carry the stench of burned flesh.

The pile was still too hot for much of an investigation, but Zoey grabbed a stick from the woodpile and stirred the ashes close to where she stood. She heard a thump when she hit something. Digging in, Zoey cleared the area around what appeared to be a boot. She shoved the stick into the object and dragged it from the hot ashes. Although it was severely burned, with parts melted, there was no doubt it had been a military-style boot.

And she wears boots, the kind you see in the used military supply store downtown.

She dropped the stick and walked back to the grass. Zoey stood still and slowly scanned the area. The woods were dense on all sides, but a muddy path, wide enough for a jeep or small truck, led away from the cabin. Zoey knew that if the girls were still alive, they had followed that path.

She hurried across the grass. The mud would make running impossible, but she had long legs and was strong and healthy. "I'm coming," she said. "Please wait for me."

Chapter Fifty-Seven

Sitting on the soft moss in the center of the clearing, Majorca leaned back, her arms supporting her, her legs outstretched. She tilted her face to the sky and closed her eyes. The sun, still visible in the clear space above the circle, warmed her skin. Her shirt smelled of smoke from the cabin fire, but the moss beneath her held a faint, sweet scent, and a light breeze carried a hint of almond from the ring of mushrooms. She breathed in the rain-cleaned air, and as she exhaled, she imagined letting go of all the pain and fear of the past few days.

It won't be much longer. Everything will be cool, and someday, maybe I'll tell my babies about the amazing adventure their mommy had when she was only seventeen.

Majorca thought of Crystal and opened her eyes. She looked down at the girl sleeping on the ground beside her.

Crystal had stretched out on her back, one arm behind her head, the other resting on the ground. Her breath came in ragged gasps, and her body twitched with each inhale. Her forehead furrowed, and she frowned as if experiencing a bad dream.

That spider really messed her up. She needs sleep, but we have to keep moving.

Majorca lowered to the ground and stretched out next to Crystal. Closing her eyes, she reached over and took Crystal's hand in hers.

A few more minutes.

She woke when the sun had traveled past the clearing. While the sky was still cloudless and bright, the temperature had dropped. Sitting up, she shook Crystal's shoulder. "Come on, sleepy head. We have to get going."

Crystal groaned but didn't open her eyes.

In a mocking threat, Majorca said, "I'm going into the woods to pee, and you better be up and ready to move when I get back. Or else." She stood, stretched, and walked to the wall of trees.

When Majorca returned, she found Crystal curled tight on the ground. "Crystal, I'm not kidding. It's time to move."

Crystal uncurled and slowly rolled to her side, but she didn't sit up. "I can't move. Everything hurts and—"

Majorca bent down, jammed her arms under Crystal's, and dragged her to her knees. "Get up! You have to." She let go and pointed across the clearing to another strip of yellow ribbon. "Look. That's where the path is. We're almost there, I can feel it. A little bit further."

Crystal lowered to her heels and shook her head. "You go. I'm staying here. I'm home now."

"What are you—" The faint, distant baying of a dog interrupted her. Majorca froze. "Did you hear that?" she whispered.

Crystal started to lie down.

Majorca yanked her to her knees again. "Crystal, did you hear that dog?"

Another low baying, a howl.

Crystal swayed. "I'm so tired, I want to sleep."

"It might be the police. They might be tracking us with a dog. We have to go. Now." She grabbed Crystal's hand and pulled. "Come on, get up. We're almost at your grandma's house. We're almost safe, and everything is going to be great."

"No, it's never going to be great," Crystal said. She pulled out of Majorca's grasp. "There isn't a safe place. There isn't a grandma."

Majorca stared down at Crystal, her eyes wide. "What are you saying?"

"I'm saying I don't have a granny."

"But, but...what about the pies and the roast chickens? And the Irish Cure? What about the grandma in your locket?" Majorca's voice rose higher and louder, and her body shook. She balled her hands into fists. "Crystal, what about the *fucking* apple peels?"

Crystal looked up at Majorca, her eyes glazed with fever and pain. "I made her up. I made everything up. My mom traded a blow job for the locket, and I stole it from her."

Majorca reached down, grasped the gold chain, and yanked. The chain snapped. Crystal tumbled forward.

Majorca shrieked, "Why?" She threw the chain and the locket as far as she could. It landed at the edge of the mushroom circle. Then, she dropped to her knees, grasped Crystal by the shoulders, and forced her to kneel. Face to face, she searched Crystal's eyes, and this time, she whispered, "Why?"

Crystal swallowed. Her lower lip trembled, but she returned Majorca's gaze. "I made her up because nobody ever loved me. I needed somebody to love me."

Majorca released Crystal's shoulders and sat back on her heels. She watched Crystal slowly sink onto the moss and close her eyes. Majorca leaned over Crystal and pulled the gun from her waistband.

Chapter Fifty-Eight

NOT FAR FROM THE burned cabin, the sound of a dog baying echoed through the forest. Zoey stopped for a moment.

Danny. He brought the dog.

She considered waiting, but even if Danny and the hound traveled fast, it would take time for them to reach her. Zoey didn't have much time.

She followed the path until it ended at a wall of trees. She spun around, searching. There were no other paths or clear entries into the woods. Then she saw it, a yellow ribbon tied to a branch on the far side of a thicket. Leaving the path, she walked to the edge of the tightly-packed bushes, many of them spiked with thorns. The underbrush seemed too dense to penetrate, but the ribbon beckoned.

It's the only way they could go.

Halfway through the thicket, Zoey heard a high-pitched voice. A girl's voice. Almost a scream.

"Why?"

Ignoring the thorns, Zoey doubled her speed and forced her way through the thicket until she reached the ribbon that marked a dark passageway obscured by heavy limbs. She raised her arm over her face and pushed branches out of the way.

The shot reverberated through the trees.

"Nooo!" Zoey ran. Branches lashed her face, her lungs ached, her heart raced. "Nooo!" she screamed again.

The second shot was louder.

Zoey burst through the trees and into a mossy clearing circled by a ring of small white mushrooms. She walked to the center of the circle.

If it weren't for the blood, they could have been embracing in sleep.

She forced herself to look away. Something bright caught her eye. Nestled in the moss, at the edge of the mushroom ring, a golden locket glittered.

Zoey looked to the trees surrounding the clearing. Her eyes traveled up their dark trunks, and through their green branches, to the powder blue sky above.

Acknowledgements

My sincere thanks to Joe Mynhardt and the dedicated team at Crystal Lake Publishing. I cannot imagine a kinder, more intelligent, or more supportive publisher than Joe. He encourages creativity and community, and offers a safe, friendly literary home to his family of creators.

Special thanks to Cathy and Gord Bradshaw for sharing their memories of British Columbia in the 1970s. And my deep appreciation to Sonja Blom of the Prince George Royal Canadian Mounted Police, who shared insights into both the past and present culture of the RCMP—the force has come a long way since the early 70's.

As always, I am indebted to the fantastic writers, agents, editors, and promoters who generously give of their time and expertise at the Surrey International Writers' Conference. I attend SIWA whenever possible—it really is the best little conference on earth.

Many people offered help as I worked on this novel, but one deserves a particular round of applause. Despite suffering from a broken ankle (sustained during a battle with the Prince George Roller Betties), Megan Bradshaw hosted me as I conducted research in British Columbia. While it's true she abandoned me in the middle of a dark, mosquito infested forest, left me alone to deal with a pack of wild dogs, and tried to hook me up with a sketchy backwoods man, she did drive me the entire length of the Highway of Tears and waited patiently as I interviewed locals, explored a haunted church (we assumed it was haunted), and took hundreds of photos. She introduced me to poutine and a brand of strong Canadian whiskey. I am still recovering from the poutine.

Megan is a talented writer and is currently working on a smoking hot memoir. I can't wait to read every word.

And, as always, my deepest love to my two best friends—multi-talented author and artist, Melanie Cool, and my silly Havanese, Sir Parker of Cherry.

About the Author

Jes Hart Stone writes dark psychological suspense featuring troubled, yet strong female leads. Her award-winning novels explore themes of oppression and revenge, fear, courage, hidden desires, and the struggle to assert female agency in a male-dominated world.

Stone's YouTube program, *Her Poison Pen*, helps women write dark fiction for and about women. It airs every new and full moon.

Living bi-locationally, Stone divides her time between a seaside town in the Pacific Northwest and a Pueblo Mágico in the mountains of Mexico.

Jeshartstone.com

THE END?

Not if you want to dive into more of Crystal Lake Publishing's Tales from the Darkest Depths!

Check out our amazing website and online store or download our catalog here. https://geni.us/CLPCatalog

We always have great new projects and content on the website to dive into, as well as a newsletter, behind the scenes options, social media platforms, our own dark fiction shared-world series and our very own webstore. Our webstore even has categories specifically for KU books, non-fiction, anthologies, and of course more novels and novellas.

Readers…

Thank you for reading *Then We'll Be Safe*. We hope you enjoyed this novel. If you have a moment, please review *Then We'll Be Safe* at the store where you bought it.

Help other readers by telling them why you enjoyed this book. No need to write an in-depth discussion. Even a single sentence will be greatly appreciated. Reviews go a long way to helping a book sell and is great for an author's career. It'll also help us to continue publishing quality books.

Thank you again for taking the time to journey with Crystal Lake Publishing.

You will find links to all our social media platforms on our Linktree page.
https://linktr.ee/CrystalLakePublishing

Follow us on Amazon:

Mission Statement

Since its founding in August 2012, Crystal Lake has quickly become one of the world's leading publishers of Dark Fiction and Horror books. In 2023, Crystal Lake officially transitioned into an entertainment company, joining several other divisions, genres, and imprints, including Torrid Waters, Sinister Smile Press, Crystal Lake Comics, Crystal Lake Games, Crystal Cove Press, Crystal Lake Kids, Memento Mori Ink, and The House of Shadows & Ink on YouTube.

While we strive to present only the highest quality fiction and entertainment, we also endeavor to support authors along their writing journey. We offer our time and experience in non-fiction projects, as well as author mentoring and services, at competitive prices.

With several Bram Stoker Award wins and many other wins and nominations (including the HWA's Specialty Press Award), Crystal Lake puts integrity, honor, and respect at the forefront of our publishing operations.

We strive for each book and outreach program we spearhead to not only entertain and touch or comment on issues that affect our readers, but also to strengthen and support the Dark Fiction field and its authors.

Not only do we find and publish authors we believe are destined for greatness, but we strive to work with men and women who endeavor to be decent human beings who care more for others than themselves, while still being hard-working, driven, and passionate artists and storytellers.

Crystal Lake is and will always be a beacon of what passion and dedication, combined with overwhelming teamwork and respect, can accomplish. We endeavor to know each and every one of our readers, while building personal relationships with our authors, reviewers, bloggers, podcasters, bookstores, and libraries.

We will be as trustworthy, forthright, and transparent as any business can be, while also keeping most of the headaches away from our authors, since it's our job to solve the problems so they can stay in a creative mind. Which of course also means paying our authors.

We do not just publish books, we present to you worlds within your world, doors within your mind, from talented authors who sacrifice so much for a moment of your time.

There are some amazing small presses out there, and through collaboration and open forums we will continue to support other presses in the goal of helping authors and showing the world what quality small presses are capable of accomplishing. No one wins when a small press goes down, so we will always be there to support hardworking, legitimate presses and their authors. We don't see Crystal Lake as the best press out there, but we will always strive to be the best, strive to be the most interactive and grateful, and even blessed press around. No matter what happens over time, we will also take our mission very seriously while appreciating where we are and enjoying the journey.

What do we offer our authors that they can't do for themselves through self-publishing?

We are big supporters of self-publishing (especially hybrid publishing), if done with care, patience, and planning. However, not every author has the time or inclination to do market research, advertise, and set up book launch strategies. Although a lot of authors are successful in doing it all, strong small presses will always be there for the authors who just want to do what they do best: write.

What we offer is experience, industry knowledge, contacts and trust built up over years. And due to our strong brand and trusting fanbase, every Crystal Lake book comes with weight of respect. In time our fans begin to trust our judgment and will try a new author purely based on our support of said author.

To date we've published around 300 books, and with each launch we strive to fine-tune our approach, learn from our mistakes, and increase our reach. We continue to assure our authors that we're here for them and that we'll carry the weight of the launch and deal with third parties while they focus on their strengths—be it writing, interviews, blogs, signings, etc.

We also offer several mentoring packages to authors that include knowledge and skills they can use in both traditional and self-publishing endeavors. This includes Shadows & Ink Creators on our The House of Shadows & Ink YouTube channel and our Crystal Lake Academy.

We look forward to launching many new careers.

This is what we believe in. What we stand for. This will be our legacy.

Welcome to Crystal Lake Publishing—Where Stories Come Alive!

Thank you for purchasing this book!